HENRY IN LOVE

BANTAM NEW FICTION

HENRY IN LOVE

MARIAN THURM

BANTAM BOOKS
NEW YORK • TORONTO • LONDON • SYDNEY • AUCKLAND

*Grateful acknowledgment is made for permission to re-
print lyrics from the following:*
"Bidin' My Time" copyright 1930 WB Music Corp. (Re-
newed), "That Certain Feeling" copyright 1925 WB Music
Corp. (Renewed), "But Not For Me" copyright 1930 New
World Music Corp. (Renewed), "Embraceable You" copy-
right 1930 WB Music Corp. (Renewed), (George Gershwin-
Ira Gershwin), "I've Grown Accustomed To Her Face"
copyright 1956 Chappel & Co., Inc. (Renewed), (Allan Jay
Lerner, Frederick Loewe), "Young At Heart" copyright 1954
June's Tunes, (Johnny Richards-Carolyn Leigh). All rights re-
served. Used by permission.

HENRY IN LOVE

A Bantam Book / March 1990

Published simultaneously in hardcover and trade paperback editions.

Library of Congress Cataloging-in-Publication Data

Thurm, Marian.
    Henry in love / Marian Thurm.
        p.   cm. — (Bantam new fiction)
    ISBN 0-553-34821-3
    I. Title.   II. Series.
PS3670.H83H46   1990
813'.54—dc20   89-15165
                                                              CIP

Published simultaneously in the United States and Canada

*Bantam Books are published by Bantam Books, a division of Ban-
tam Doubleday Dell Publishing Group, Inc. Its trademark, consis-
ting of the words ''Bantam Books'' and the portrayal of a rooster, is
Registered in U.S. Patent and Trademark Office and in other coun-
tries. Marca Registrada. Bantam Books, 666 Fifth Avenue, New
York, New York 10103.*

PRINTED IN THE UNITED STATES OF AMERICA

FG   0   9   8   7   6   5   4   3   2   1

In loving memory of Meryl Bennett

HENRY IN LOVE

PART ONE

CHAPTER ONE

I was soaring, sailing high above the waxed corridors of St. Peter's, the hospital where, exactly two hours earlier, at 5:56 A.M., Kate had given birth to a big bald baby who weighed in at just under nine pounds. "Never again," Kate had said fiercely as the doctor stitched her up. "I mean it, Henry." We'd held hands and cried, and admired the baby for a while until the nurse took her away into a corner of the delivery room for a bath.

We were married a year ago, when I was sixty-eight and Kate was twenty-eight. Our wedding was a strange affair—all friends and no family. Even Nina, my thirty-three-year-old daughter from my first marriage, and my only relative, wasn't there. But Kate was loaded with family; two brothers and a sister, nieces and nephews, cousins and aunts and uncles, not to mention a mother and father. Incredibly, not a single one of them showed up to wish us well. Forget 'em, I told Kate, who cried a little over the loss of her parents but managed just fine without them. She was a treasure. No one had ever loved me this way, not even my second wife, Cynthia, who I had been married to forever. Or at least eighteen or nineteen years. It was true that Cynthia divorced me, though it wasn't because she didn't love me. It was her shrink who did us in. He kept insinuating that our marriage wasn't worth saving, until one day Cynthia finally believed it. A few years later, when I was crazy in love with Kate, my own shrink had tried to talk me into giving her up. *Let her go, Henry, you have just got to let go of this young girl*. Over and over again, week after week, until finally it hit me that he was jealous. Like me, he was in his sixties; of course he was jealous. When I told this to him, he laughed a little and then the laugh turned into a cough.

"Everything I know about people, about life, tells me that you're headed for disaster," he said as soon as he got his coughing under control.

"Everything?" I said. The man's pessimism was not to be believed. "Lighten up," I told him, but he just sat there at his desk with his head in his hands, looking exceptionally gloomy, even for him. I stood up and opened my mouth to say something, anything, and then there I was singing *"Fairy tales can come true/It could happen to you . . ."*

"Ha ha ha," said Dr. Schonfeld slowly and without any expression at all. He was staring right at me with those sad, pale eyes of his. "Ha ha ha," he said again.

I was laughing now as I pushed hard against the doors at the main entrance to St. Peter's and walked outside to my car. Although it was still March, it felt better than that, like the best part of April, perhaps. A sharp yellow sun floated in a perfect sky, and the air was soft, windless. I tapped out a cha-cha on the roof of my car with both hands, bouncing around on my heels for a while. A woman carrying a dog and a pile of laundry in her arms crossed the parking lot, ignoring me. I continued with my song and dance a moment or two longer, and then I unlocked the GTI. A hot little Volkswagen, powerful engine, velour interior, FM radio. Three months old and in pristine condition. Except for the passenger seat up front, which was still, eight hours later, slightly damp to the touch. Kate's water had broken halfway to the hospital the night before, and I couldn't help sighing as I got the news. Kate knew exactly what that sigh was about.

"If I hear one word on the subject of your beloved velour, I'll tear you apart with my bare hands," she warned me.

Laughing, out of nervousness and surprise, I suppose, I took hold of her hand, which was icy and stiff and seemed very small. I opened the second button on the corduroy shirt I was wearing and slipped her hand in against my chest. When it had warmed, I kissed it and gave it back to her.

"I love you," she told me, and just then her knees began to shake.

I got us to the hospital about ten minutes later, running red lights at every opportunity. It was midnight, a cold, bright night with a lovely full moon and plenty of stars. I tried to hurry Kate inside, but she tipped her head back and studied the sky for what seemed like a long while.

"Everything's changing," she said in amazement.

Parking the GTI under the carport, I saw my neighbor, Rob, in his driveway, tossing an assortment of riding toys—Big Wheels, a motorcycle, a pink plastic tricycle—onto his lawn. "You'd think just once they could get their act together and put everything away in the garage," he said. He was a real estate lawyer and dressed in tan pants and a jacket and tie every day. Today the pants and jacket sleeves were too short, I noticed. Perhaps, at the age of thirty-six, he was still growing.

"Congratulations, Henry," I said, coming toward him with my hand outstretched.

"Congratulations, Henry," he repeated, and shook my hand.

"Boy or a girl?" I said.

"Great going, Henry," Rob said. "That's terrific. How's Kate?"

"Resting uncomfortably, as they say."

"Great." Rob smiled. "And allow me to give you a crucial bit of advice: never let yourself hear a crying baby in the middle of the night."

"Never?"

"I've got four kids, Henry. Trust me: you get up once and it's all over. Kate will start thinking she can count on you and before you know it, she'll have you marching around at three A.M. looking for Wet Wipes and teeny tiny undershirts and pacifiers and—"

"Go to work, Rob," I said, gesturing toward his old, beat-up silvery Lincoln.

"You'll love being a father, Henry," he said as he disappeared into his car.

I crossed the lawn to his house (which, like mine and all the others on the road, faced the ocean) and entered through the front door after a single knock. I headed straight for the kitchen, where I figured Tiki was probably giving the kids breakfast. Tiki Axelrod was Kate's best friend. She had a law degree from Columbia and a masters degree in history, and had worked for a think tank in Westchester before moving to Maine. Her children were not quite six, not quite four, not quite two, and almost nine months. All of them were standing around naked, except for the baby, who was wearing dungarees, a checked shirt, and soft red elf shoes with turned-up toes. Tiki herself was dressed in a gray sweatsuit and was smoking a cigarette as she searched through a cabinet for something. The instant she noticed me she let out a cry and ditched her cigarette in the sink.

"A girl!" she said, embracing me wildly, displaying all of her passion for Kate and their friendship. "Am I right or am I right?"

"That you are," I said. "And Kate's fine."

We stepped back from each other at precisely the same moment. "Was it awful?" Tiki whispered.

"It's over," I said. I shrugged my shoulders. "Now there's only happiness . . ."

Tiki sighed. "There's that, too," she said. "Of course."

Fudge, her oldest kid, had climbed on top of the washing machine and was eating from a pan of Jiffy Pop with both hands.

"Get your naked bod off my washing machine," said Tiki.

"Why?" said Fudge. "This is good popcorn."

"Get dressed," Tiki said. She grabbed him by the waist and deposited him on the kitchen floor, along with the Jiffy Pop, which his arms were circled around lovingly. "Didn't I get all you guys dressed at least once today? And where's your diaper, Kathryn?"

"Don't know," said Kathryn, who was squatting by the pan of popcorn, trying to decide which kernel to choose for herself. Her hair was in a tight shiny bun at the top of her head, and I couldn't resist giving it a pat.

Tiki smiled at me, then roared, "Get dressed!" No one responded. By now, all the kids were eating from the pan of popcorn, including the baby, who I whisked away and handed back over to his mother. "Attention, everyone," said Tiki. "I want you people to be the first to know that I'm going to start work on my résumé in a couple of minutes. My intention is to find a lucrative and intellectually satisfying job by nightfall. So after today, you guys are on your own."

"Great popcorn, Mom," said Spencer, who was soon-to-be four.

"I like to threaten them every now and then," Tiki explained to me. "It makes me feel better." She rubbed my shoulder briefly. "Let me get you some breakfast. There's Life, Total, Fiber One, Lucky Charms, Cinnamon Life, Cocoa Puffs, Nutrific . . ."

"I'll try the Good Luck Charms," I said. "Or maybe I'll just go on home and take a nap. It seems to me I haven't been to sleep since Wednesday."

"Today's only Friday," said Tiki. "*I* haven't been to sleep since June."

"Don't lie, Mom," Fudge said. "You were sleeping when I woke you up this morning."

"Possibly, but I assure you it wasn't quality sleep. What I lust after is a deep, deep, dreamless sleep, the sleep of the truly innocent, or the truly dead, I guess."

I could feel my mouth widening into an extravagant yawn. "I've really got to go," I told Tiki.

"Let me at least pack you some breakfast." With the baby draped over her shoulder, Tiki filled a Ziploc bag with handfuls of exceptionally garish cereal. "Take your Lucky Charms and scram," she ordered sweetly.

Much to my disappointment, the house was exactly as we'd left it, but I whizzed past last night's dishes spread across the kitchen counter and the newspapers and magazines opened against the coffee table, and headed straight for the bedroom, where I collapsed on our king-size mattress and waited for sleep to overtake me. No luck: my arms and legs refused to settle down, and my mind kept leaping from one image of Kate to another; Kate in unspeakable pain, white-faced with worry and surprise, turning her head away from me as I attempted to comfort her; her lovely smooth bare knees knocking together violently in the last stage of labor; her head rising from the delivery table as she let out a roar of pain and effort, and finally triumph, just at the moment the baby shot out into the ice-cold world where I'd been waiting a lifetime, it seemed, to welcome her. "Oh Kate," I said out loud now. I was a smiling fool, dancing shamelessly in my bedroom with the shades up and the sun in my eyes, doing a simple, unadorned cha-cha over and over again because it was the only dance I knew. The phone was ringing now and I danced my way to the night table to answer it.

"Yes," I said into the receiver. A breathless old man, I sat down at the edge of the bed, my heart racing.

"Henry?"

"You've got him."

"It's me, Henry."

"Me who?"

"It's Cynthia," a voice said, sounding apologetic. "I couldn't sleep," she added, as if that were to adequately explain our first phone conversation in nearly five years.

Five years, and yet in an instant I knew that not much had changed.

"It's almost nine in the morning, Cynthia. Out of bed, let's go," I said, taking charge as always.

"Is the sun out?"

"*Here* it is. I wouldn't know about New York."

"Me either," said Cynthia.

Out the bedroom window, beyond the sea wall, I watched a neighbor's kids, two big fat twelve-year-olds, flying a kite in the shape of a fish. They were fat like you didn't see much anymore these days, old-fashioned fat, with big wide behinds and puffy faces, but nice polite boys, both of them. I wondered briefly what they were doing on the beach at this hour, why they weren't in school. The ocean, as I gazed out toward it, looked safe from here, a cool dark surface without mystery, utterly predictable. But people had drowned not far from our front lawn, unlucky surfers mostly, one a year during the past few years, I'd heard. Kate and I, first-class cowards, rarely went in; even in summer, the water was numbing. And yet I could see our baby, dressed in a miniature-sized bikini, folding her toes into the wet sand, running along the water's edge and beyond, her baby-hair flying back in the wind, revealing her small, perfect face.

"Baby," I murmured out loud.

Cynthia cleared her throat directly into the phone. "I think we'll just let that pass," she said. "And incidentally, your wedding present is in the mail. A bowl from Tiffany's, not too inspiring. I spent two hours in the store and finally I just gave up. But a plain glass bowl is always welcome, I guess. You can fill it with some nice polished apples or shells from the beach or put a goddamn goldfish in it. And anyway, what do I care *what* you do with it?"

"Don't get all worked up over this," I told Cynthia. "I'm sure whatever it is, it's useful, anyway." Now it was my turn to clear my throat. "We have a baby, Cynthia," I said in my sweetest, softest voice.

"Pardon?"

"She was born today, in fact. Nine pounds five ounces," I said, adding a few extra ounces to impress her.

"No fooling!" said Cynthia in amazement. She took a moment to consider this and then let me know she thought it was wonderful. "I suppose it's kind of a miracle, isn't it, at your age and all . . ."

"Speaking of miracles, it turns out this baby of ours is actually able to do simple arithmetic, addition and subtraction of single digits, that kind of thing. A real superbaby."

"Cut it out, Henry," said Cynthia sharply, and I could see her perfectly shaped mouth turning pinched and mean. I'm *so* glad we're not married anymore, I told her silently. If I wasn't careful, the words might have come spilling out joyously at any moment.

"You academics are all alike," I said instead. "No sense of humor."

"Our first conversation in five years, Henry, and look at the way it's going. I have to say I was expecting better from you."

"What *were* you expecting?"

"A pat on the back, a little cheering up, I don't know. It didn't seem like too much to ask from an old friend."

In fact, nothing had ever been too much to ask. My indulgence, my sympathy, my patience, my strength. She had never quite understood what hard work it was being her husband. There had been love, too, or declarations of love, anyway, and God knows, I'd earned it. When you're married to a woman who runs away from home every now and then, you take nothing for granted. The notes she left behind were always inscrutable:

> Be back whenever I'm up to it. There are some crudités and a very nice spinach and sour cream dip on the second shelf in the refrigerator.

Or:

> The emptiness I feel burns like acid in the pit of my stomach. Call you Tuesday.

Or:

> If only you could massage the ache in my soul.
> But don't feel too bad about it.
>
> P.S. Try the deli counter at the A & P—the shrimp
> salad looked particularly good.

Sometimes there wasn't a note at all, just a stretch of
empty hangers dangling in the closet and a stillness as I
walked through the rooms of our apartment, a light left
burning in the kitchen, a forgotten mascara wand lying in
a shallow puddle at the side of the bathroom sink. And
once, the only time I never forgave her, she left just after
we'd made love. I'd slipped into the shower immediately
after getting out of bed, and when I came out she was
gone. I cried then for her bad timing, for the sheer mean-
ness of what she had done. Half an hour earlier her ankles
had been locked lovingly around mine and then there she
was in a taxi rushing toward Grand Central or Penn Sta-
tion or La Guardia or wherever it was she was off to. She
never left without letting her shrink know where she was
fleeing to. The man knew everything and kept it all to
himself. I always felt like stringing him up by his thumbs
after one of our conversations.

"Let's have it, Dr. Hochberg," I said. It was less than
half an hour since I'd gotten out of the shower, taken a good
look around, and wiped the tears away with a few handfuls
of cold water tossed against my face. "You know I know
Cynthia called you," I said. "So what's the good word?"

"Mr. Simpson? Okay, listen, I'm on the other phone.
Can I get back to you?"

"Absolutely not. What did Cynthia say?"

"You know that's confidential. Why do you keep
calling me when you know I can't help you?"

12

"I don't give a flying fuck about confidentiality!" I hollered at him. "This is my wife we're talking about. My *wife*! Don't you think I have a right to know what's on her mind?"

Dr. Hochberg sighed. We'd been on the phone for ninety seconds and already he was bored. Clearly, he hated wasting his time with people like me, crazies who did not understand, or refused to understand, the way the world worked. People whose expectations were shockingly unreasonable. "She left you a note," I heard him say.

"A note?" I said, grabbing the little square of paper from my bathrobe pocket and waving it in front of the phone. "Listen up," I ordered. *"Dear Henry, The turkey ought to be good for the rest of the week; I left a damp towel over it so it should certainly stay moist for another couple of days.* There's your note," I told Dr. Hochberg. "Revealing, isn't it?"

"Don't be bitter," Dr. Hochberg said, and then he hung up on me.

"Bastard," I said now, oblivious of Cynthia at the other end.

"You can't do this to me," she said. "I refuse to allow it. If you can't change your tune I'm hanging up right this minute."

"Excuse me," I said. "It was just good old Dr. Hochberg I was—"

"Remembering so fondly?" said Cynthia.

I was lying flat on my back on the bed now, raising my leg straight up in the air, and then my arm, trying to touch my toes with my fingertips. "He was a very rigid guy," I said. "Inflexible. Unyielding. Heartless." I paused. "And, of course, without a doubt, he was the one who wrecked our marriage."

"He took me to the theater," Cynthia said casually. "To see *A Chorus Line*. And *Cats*. And *Cage aux Folles*, as well, I believe. Maybe not. *Cage aux Folles* I saw with the Guarinos, actually."

Attempting to reach my toes, I lost my balance and rolled off the side of the bed and onto the floor. The phone rolled with me, but, miraculously, the connection was unbroken. "He what?" I said.

"We dated," Cynthia said. "It was a while after the divorce, a couple of years, at least."

"Dated?" I said. "What is this, high school? What do you mean you 'dated'?"

"He picked me up in a taxi, we went to the theater, had dinner afterward, and then, whatever . . ."

It was that "whatever," of course, that offended me most of all. I could just see the two of them sinking into the soft center of our old double bed, breathing hard and then harder, Dr. Hochberg's damp mouth whispering psychobabble into Cynthia's ear as he slid toward home. Afterward, I guessed, he paraded around in my old brick-colored velour bathrobe, examining Cynthia's books and orderly collection of sociology journals. He was a tiny bearded pipe-smoker, a comic figure in a bathrobe that was so large it was swimming on him. Never mind that I'd never even met the man—I knew exactly who he was.

"You two disgust me," I told Cynthia from my seat on the floor, where I was wedged in the narrow space between the bed and the window. The back of my head hurt where it had hit the oak flooring, and the tip of my spine felt sore. "The thought of all this just turns my stomach," I said.

"It was just one brief shining moment," said Cynthia. "Well, maybe three or four."

"He *wanted* our marriage to fail!" I shouted. "He had the hots for you all along."

"Oh, please," said Cynthia. "We had three or four dates and that was the end of it. And then he died, anyway."

"Little Dr. Hochberg has met his maker?" The relief I felt was overwhelming, as if he had been, until this moment, a very real threat to my happiness. "And here I thought he led such a charmed life," I said. "What happened?"

"Apparently he was riding a bicycle near his country house in Connecticut and was hit by a car," Cynthia said. "I was paging through the *Times* one day and there it was."

"Poor guy." I saw the bright trickle of blood streaking the grass at the side of the road, the bicycle tires spinning in the sunlight as Hochberg's life faded fast. But I resented him still, for the secrets he heard and savored, the private, interior life that Cynthia had shared only with him. And God knows the things she told him about *me*: that I was a slob who sometimes spit on our Persian rugs when I was enraged by something; that I was a bully who forced her into her clothes and out the door and into the world to visit friends when all she wanted was to lie in bed and read her scholarly journals; that I was a pain in the neck who talked incessantly when silence and solitude were what she was after. Almost as soon as I met Kate, these thoughts of how I'd failed Cynthia ceased to trouble me. I'd been crazy in love with Kate and our life together for five years, and since then I'd never once awakened in the middle of the night calling out Cynthia's name or heard her soft voice in my nightmares or anywhere else. And yet it seems that what we think of as history, as safely over and done with, is never truly, entirely, finished. Wounds

15

heal, but not perfectly. Every so often you feel a painful little pinch, a reminder that this is what it was all about, all those weeks or months or years ago.

"Hands off," I told Cynthia now.

"What?" she said.

"Hands off my life, Cynthia."

"I see."

"Don't call me. Don't write to me. Don't send me wedding presents."

"Actually," said Cynthia, "I never did make it downtown to Tiffany's. Not that I didn't think about it from time to time. But truthfully, my heart wasn't in it."

"It's just as well," I said, relieved. "It's really just as well."

"Henry?"

"Hmm?" I said. I put the base of the phone in my palm and carried it back to the night table, preparing for the conversation's end.

"Today's my birthday, the big 6-0, but I don't want you feeling sorry for me."

"Happy birthday," I said. "Why would I be feeling sorry for you?"

"You might, but that would be a mistake." Cynthia was silent. Then she said, "I saw a fat man on the news the other night, not an ordinary fat man, but a man so fat all he could do was stay in bed and read all day. Do you know what he said would make him happiest in all the world?" Cynthia said, her voice a little shaky now. "To walk in the snow and see his footprints."

Oh, Lord. Listening to Cynthia's quiet, well-mannered weeping, I was stunned to feel the tears that had sneaked up on me and were now slipping past my eyes and down my face. There was the fat man smiling in the snow, leaving his enormous footprints in a perfect oval across his lawn.

"They've got him on some kind of liquid diet," Cynthia said, still sniffling but already beginning to recover. "He's got nine hundred pounds to go, but he's under medical supervision and he's going to be all right. So promise me you won't worry."

"I won't worry," I promised. "How about you?"

"I won't worry either," Cynthia said. "I'll just go about my normal business and hope for the best. And expect the worst, of course."

"Get up, get dressed, make the bed, that's the crucial thing. After that, you're on your way."

"You make it sound so easy."

"Pretend I'm there with you," I said. "My hands are on your wrists and I'm pulling you out of bed. One two three and up you go. Here are your clothes—I'm throwing them to you from across the room. I'm tapping my foot, waiting for you to get dressed. And I'm exasperated, because, as usual, you're moving too damn slow."

"Sounds like old times," Cynthia said, and both of us laughed a little, because it certainly did. "Don't kid yourself," she said. "There was nothing all that terrific about them, not ever."

A silence fell between us and the sound of it unnerved me. "Well," I said, "good luck in this life and the next. And the next after that."

"Henry?"

"Whatever it is, the answer is no," I teased.

"I just wanted to know if I could give you a call at the turn of the century."

"What the hell," I said. "Let's go for it."

CHAPTER TWO

The problem with newborns, Kate discovered, was that they couldn't tell the difference between night and day. Kate found that she couldn't either, those first few weeks. She stumbled along from one hour to the next, oblivious of just about everything except the baby's cries, which commanded attention as effectively as any alarm clock she'd ever owned. After six days of indecision, she and Henry finally named her. Henry decided to call her Elizabeth, which was all right but lacked originality and suffered from a certain stiffness, Kate thought. She named her Darlan, her own version of what she had been calling the baby all along, since the day she was born. Henry hoped and prayed that Kate would come to her senses on the subject. Her response to him was: good luck to *you*, buster.

It was four A.M. and she was in bed next to him now, on her back with her arms glued to her sides. Her breasts were engorged with milk, which meant that they were as large and as firm as boulders and that they were on fire. If she raised an arm to scratch the side of her nose, the pain became unbearable. And so she lay motionless, dreaming of the half-dozen plastic bottles of aspirin that were lined up in the medicine cabinet a thousand miles away. Like a desperate man moaning for water in the desert, she whimpered "Excedrin, Anacin, Bufferin, Tylenol."

Henry stirred, yawned, cast an arm over his eyes.

"Henry," she said. She could not bring herself to tap him on the shoulder; the cost, in pain, would have been too extravagant.

"What, is the baby up again?" he said. His voice was fuzzy with sleep; staring at him hard in the darkened room, she could see that his eyes were closed.

"It's me," Kate said. "My breasts are killing me."

"Let's have a look," he said, instantly alert.

"Touch me and I'll have you arrested."

"You know," said Henry, raising himself up on one elbow, "you hear about all this domestic violence stuff on the news and you say to yourself, Who *are* these people, anyway. Is it possible they're people like you and me, you wonder. And then one day you realize, Jesus, they *are* you and me."

"You'll have to forgive me," she told him. "I tend to exaggerate a trifle when I'm in agony. Just get me a couple of extra-strength anything and I'm yours forever."

"Deal," said Henry, and headed for the bathroom. He was gone so long that Kate began to suspect he had gotten lost in the dark. Then it occurred to her that he was probably sneaking a look at the baby, standing over the bassinet and gazing at her in disbelief. He still couldn't quite get it through his head that she was his. Theirs. He couldn't quite believe that any of it was his. He was living the life of a man half his age and in the middle of the night he was up wondering how and when he was going to lose it all. You're safe with me, baby, Kate would tell him and then he would carefully slip his arms through hers. They would sleep that way for a while, until one of them unwittingly shrugged the other off in the darkness. You have got to feel comfortable with your happiness, she kept telling him. You're finally, after all those years, where you want to be! What could be better! His first two marriages had ended with a great deal of unhappiness, she knew. When they'd first met, she'd pressed for details, but mostly she remembered him saying, "People get in each other's way, lose interest in each other, love flies out the window, what can I tell you?" Her mother and father were not thrilled by this. "His track record stinks," was how her father put it. She'd broken the news to them alone, in person, in the house on Long Island where she'd grown up, but had not lived for years. Her mother and father had the advantage, playing it all out on their own turf.

"You're a smart and beautiful young girl," her mother began. Kate had heard this line many times before—invariably as a preface to bad news.

"Forget the beautiful," she said.

"Forget the smart," said her father. He had a bread knife in his hand and was slicing off large pieces of a round challah, baked for the Jewish new year, which the three of them were celebrating alone.

"Do you know why this challah is round?" her mother asked. Without waiting for a response, she said, "So that your happiness should be never-ending, going round and round and round like this." She moved her hand in a spiral around the bread, smiling out at them warily.

"For crying out loud, Kate," her father said to her. "Have you stopped to ask yourself if you're losing your mind? You're going to marry a man who can get into movie theaters at the senior citizen rate. A retired person.

How much can he offer you? This isn't exactly a long-term investment we're talking about. I keep thinking he could have a heart attack, a stroke, or worse. . . . What's his cholesterol level, anyway? Do you know if it's above three hundred?"

"Everything in life is a risk," Kate said.

Her father rolled his eyes. "I'm heartsick, honey," he said. "My hands are tied and I'm heartsick."

Her mother was busy spreading honey across the pieces of challah. "For a sweet year," she said, and dropped a slice on Kate's plate.

"I never could eat that stuff," Kate said and handed it back to her.

"You have to," she said. "It's probably bad luck if you don't."

"It's the honey I can't stand."

"I'm afraid I'll have to insist," her father said. His voice was quiet but his face looked threatening.

"Your hands are tied," Kate reminded him.

"Listen, you're going to need all the help you can get," he said. "Now take a goddamn piece with honey and force yourself to eat it."

She ate it. It was the last thing she was ever going to do that would please her father, and all of them knew it.

"A sweet year!" her mother said as they bit into the bread.

Her father sighed deeply. Not for a minute did he believe they were headed anywhere even close to happiness, and he wasn't taking any chances. He reached across the table for the half-empty jar of honey, and, with his eyes closed, polished off the rest of it, one slow spoonful at a time, as Kate and her mother looked on in horror.

"Put it on my tombstone," he said. " 'At least the man tried.' "

Even so, Kate would have taken him back in a minute. It was just over a year since they'd lost each other, and it was easy enough for Kate to fantasize a reunion: no apologies, a minimum of tears, one long late-night phone call followed by a few more and then a short visit, three or four days, perhaps. She could see her mother kissing Darlan's tiny red feet, smoothing Vaseline in the crease of her velvety neck, bathing her in the crook of her steady arm. And there were her father and Henry hanging around discussing cholesterol levels and the stock market and the joys of retirement, their voices a little stiff at first, then warming up as Henry's exuberant self took over. *Lighten up, Seymour,* he would urge. *This is family you're talking to!* All of this came to Kate effortlessly and yet she could not bring herself to make the first move. It was clear to her that she'd been wronged by her father and mother, denied their loving attention for no good reason at all. Stubborn stupidity ran in the family like hay fever, it seemed, shutting out the pleasures of love without even a hint of an apology.

"Two Extra-Strength Anacin and a side order of cole slaw," said Henry, suddenly appearing at the bed. Kate opened her mouth and he dropped the pills in. Raising a cup of water to her lips, he pushed the hair from her face tenderly. "What a great-looking baby we've got ourselves," he said. "I stood in her room with a flashlight and got a nice long look."

"Actually, I was thinking about getting her a wig. I hate bald babies." In the light cast by the bathroom fixture, just across the hall, she could see that Henry was alarmed.

"You can't be serious," he said.

"The Bride of Frankenstein look might be cute. You know, kind of a high beehive."

"Too extreme," said Henry without missing a beat. "I myself would prefer a nice shoulder-length pageboy."

"I don't know, maybe we ought to leave it up to the baby."

"She's awfully young to be making decisions like that," said Henry. "On the other hand, it's never too soon to start growing up."

"Absolutely. And it's so true what they say about youth being wasted on the young, isn't it?"

"What?" said Henry. He kneeled at the side of the bed and lay his head on Kate's stomach, which was astonishingly soft, a perfect plump pillow. "You're such a loon," he said.

"One of my many endearing qualities."

"Marry me," Henry said into her stomach.

"We already did that. About a year ago."

"Then let's have a baby."

"We did that, too," she reminded him.

"We did? Well then, what's left?"

"Death?" she said. "Divorce? How should I know?"

Henry began to tickle her and immediately she started to squirm. She was laughing and pushing Henry away, and the pain that pulsed in her breasts became overwhelming. She was weeping now but still laughing and at last Henry understood.

"I wasn't thinking," he said, and thrust his hands behind his back. "I'm sorry."

"Just take me home," she told him.

"I have news for you, kiddo," Henry said in his breezy way. "You *are* home."

"Are you sure?"

"You bet."

Looking around her, she wasn't convinced; nothing seemed familiar, not even the bedspread turned back over her feet or the comforter at her knees or the enormous old nightshirt she was wearing that she'd had since college. And there was a baby in the guest room who was wailing her heart out now, frantic for her mother.

"I'll go," said Henry. "You rest."

"Turn on the light."

They blinked at each other in the sudden brightness; Henry looked at her expectantly as the baby's cries grew stronger.

"Don't go," she told him.

"What do you mean?"

"I'm not sure, but it seems I can't face being alone," she mumbled, her hand half-covering her mouth.

"Take your hand away," Henry said, but he did it for her and brought her fingertips to his mouth for a kiss. "Listen to me," he said. "Everything is exactly as it should be." He took her face in his hands; their noses touched. "We fell in love, got married, had a baby. It's what people do," said Henry. "It's the normal course of events. And now it's four in the morning and you're tired. Exhausted. This, too, as I understand it, is perfectly normal. Lucky for you, I'm not tired at all. An old guy like me doesn't need his sleep anymore. So you go back to bed and let me take over."

"Sounds good," Kate said. "All except the part about the old guy. I hate that kind of talk. My whole body stiffens when I hear it—even my toes are clenched now."

Henry hopped down from the bed and was halfway out the door before he answered her. "Sometimes," he said, "I'm actually younger than you are, sweetie pie."

CHAPTER THREE

When Kate and I first met I was in a deep depression over my failed marriage, but Kate managed to pull me out of it in no time, dragging me all over Manhattan to movies and concerts, Serbo-Croatian cafés, Greek nightclubs, poetry readings at the Y. It was at the Y, in fact, that we met, both of us enrolled in a workshop called "Letting Go of Clutter." The course was for people who were overwhelmed by the stacks of newspapers and magazines and piles of old clothes that had accumulated in their homes, people who simply could not get their act together. The instructor, a sympathetic young therapist of sorts named Gil Rosenthal, helped us explore the reasons we had difficulty throwing anything away. We sat around an old battered-looking conference table and it was one sob story after another. When it was my turn to speak I talked about my divorce and my sentimental attachment to all the material things connected to the marriage.

"Any questions or comments?" said Gil hopefully.

Kate, who was seated opposite me, raised a finger in the air. "Wouldn't you think a divorce would be the perfect catalyst for getting rid of all your old junk? I mean, if your wife threw you out of the apartment, why didn't you just leave everything behind and start from scratch in your new life?"

"First of all," I said with great dignity, "she did not 'throw' me out of the apartment. She gave me four weeks to move and as it happens, it took me three months to find something suitable. During that time I heard not a peep out of her on the subject, I might add."

"Not a peep?" said Kate.

"She's a woman of enormous compassion, patient, kind, gen—"

"Are you done cataloguing her virtues yet?" said Kate. "How much longer are we going to have to listen to this?" All around the room people were lighting cigarettes, playing with the caps of their ballpoint pens, examining their cuticles. Kate looked me straight in the eye. "You are so full of it," she said.

"What the hell is that supposed to mean?" I said.

"You are a man in great pain and my heart goes out to you," said Kate.

"Bravo!" said Gil, and people around the table clapped quietly. "I can't tell you how impressed I am. Are you a therapist-in-training, by some chance?"

"Me?" said Kate. "I illustrate greeting cards."

Gil shook his head. "I feel so good about what just happened here, I can't tell you. What a breakthrough!"

"Really?" I said. "You mean I'm cured?"

"There's a time and a place for sarcasm," said Gil, "and believe me, this ain't it. See me after class, please."

When the class ended, Gil approached me and immediately placed his hands on my shoulders. "Anxiety and guilt, Henry, those are your key words," he said. Kate stood behind him, looking very serious.

"Listen, Gil," I said. "Magazines are piled up to the window ledge in my living room. And my closets are filled with all kinds of crap. I still have the Nehru suit I wore to Cynthia's brother's wedding in August of 1968. And the pajamas Cynthia thought I looked sexy in sometime around the early seventies."

"Oh yeah?" said Kate. "What kind of pajamas were those?"

"None of your business," I said. "They were from Brooks Brothers and that's all I'm saying."

Gil squeezed my shoulders. "Your marriage is over, buddy," he said. "The good times, the bad times."

"Get rid of all your junk and get rid of the memories," said Kate.

"Have you ever been married?" I asked Gil.

He shook his head.

"You?" I asked Kate.

"Me? Never."

"Case closed," I said. There was still the matter of Gil's hands on my shoulders. "Do you mind?" I said, and wriggled out from underneath them.

"I've been in relationships," said Gil. "Some very serious ones."

"Me, too," said Kate.

"I was married for almost twenty-five years," I said. "You can't possibly understand what that kind of thing is all about."

"Twenty-five? I thought you said nineteen during class. Don't exaggerate," said Kate.

"You're an interesting, attractive guy, Henry," Gil told me. "You've got to get rid of all this bad karma and seize life by the lapels and go out there and live it up."

Kate was nodding her head after giving me the once over. "More like *very* attractive," she said.

"Come on," I said, but of course I wanted to hear more. I tried to remember the last time a young girl had flattered me like that. Nineteen thirty-five sounded about right.

"Put it this way," said Kate, "if James Garner had an older brother, you'd be it."

"*The Rockford Files?*" I said. "Big, tall, dark-haired guy, kind of a smartass, can talk his way out of or into anything?"

Kate smiled at me for the first time. "That's the one," she said.

I stood up a little straighter and ran my fingers through my silvery hair, which I had to admit was a good head of hair even for a thirty-year-old. I noticed then that Gil was about to slip away, and I put out a hand to stop him. "Not so fast," I said.

"Listen," said Gil, "there's a couple of other people here I need to talk to, but I wanted to take the time to suggest that you enroll in the Clutter Follow-Up Group. I want to hear about your progress and setbacks, if any." He turned and began to walk away. "Catch you later," he said.

"Did he wink at me or was that my imagination?" I asked Kate.

"Clutter Follow-Up Group!" she said. "Give me a break."

We left the room and the building together and it soon became apparent that she was walking me to the subway. It was the end of a Sunday afternoon right around Halloween, a warmish cloudy day when you just knew the air quality had to be highly unacceptable.

"Stupid dirty city," I said, and kicked away an empty Pepsi can that was coming straight at me on the sidewalk. My car had recently been stolen from the parking space

I'd found right in front of my apartment building, and I still hadn't forgiven the city.

At the entrance to the subway, a woman was selling rubber noses that were pinned to a velveteen-backed board she'd set up on a folding table. "Now *you* look like a man who could use a nose," she said cheerfully.

"Why me?" I said, but I had slowed down and was already reaching for my wallet.

"I don't know," said the vendor. "You just have that look about you." She had nearly two dozen noses on display, including cat noses, anteater snouts, elephant trunks, and of course a classic pig nose, which I bought without hesitation. Kate chose the anteater snout, and I paid for that, too. We slipped them on and walked down the steep stairs to the subway. The clerk selling tokens in his booth nodded at us approvingly.

"Nice," he said. "Real nice, guys."

"Well," I said to Kate as the train pulled in, "I'm heading down to my apartment on Twelfth Street. Where are you going?"

"I thought I'd help you let go of some of your clutter," she said, and hopped onto the train.

"You don't even know my last name," I whispered fiercely into her ear. We were holding onto a floor-to-ceiling pole, along with a couple of other people. "This is New York City," I whispered. "What if I'm an ax murderer?"

"What if I'm a gold digger?"

"Then you're doomed to disappointment," I said. "Buying this co-op really cleaned me out."

The train swung back and forth for a while and then the lights flickered and died and then returned. I looked at Kate, admiring her eyes, which were large and strangely colored, kind of a dark olive green I'd never seen before.

With or without the anteater snout, she just missed being pretty—there was something a trifle squared-off and mannish about her face—but she was smart and you could see it there instantly. I loved looking at her.

Suddenly there was a pale, young guy in a cheap black suit staggering through the length of the car. "Help me," he moaned. "Won't somebody *please* help me? I have to go to a funeral in Miami Beach and I need money for the airfare." People looked up at him briefly and then went back to staring at their knees. "Won't somebody *please* help me get to Miami Beach?" the man begged. "The funeral's *tomorrow*." His voice had a whiny quality that annoyed me, but he looked terrified, and my fingers began to search my pockets for loose change. "Nobody?" the man said in disbelief. "Nobody at all?" He stood next to me now, resting for a moment before trying his luck in the next car.

"There you go," I said, and handed him a couple of quarters.

The man frowned at them, turning them over and examining them in his palm as if they might have been counterfeit. "Weren't you listening? I said *air* fare." He lifted the flap of my jacket pocket and dropped the coins in one at a time.

My face went red and I looked down at my leather sneakers. "You're welcome," I said. "Think nothing of it."

"Jerk," said Kate, as the man started up his chant again and moved away from us. She ran two fingertips slowly across my cheek and it was as electrifying as if an ice-cold hand had touched the inside of my thigh. I imagined then the two of us on our knees, bent over dusty stacks of *Esquires* and *New Yorkers*, my hand trailing bravely down the length of Kate's spine. I could see us

30

turning in slow motion toward each other and her smile that mirrored my own. Up went her arms and I lifted her sweatshirt over her head. I was in luck—no bra! And that was as far as I went. My longing was a dull, leaden ache somewhere between my ribs. It might even have shown up on an X ray—a mysterious shadowy image that no one could be sure of. Love, desire, an end to loneliness. It was what everyone was on the lookout for, what everyone was listening hardest for.

I checked on Kate, whose lovely calm face told me not to worry, to go right ahead and make a fool of myself if I had to.

"Just how old are you, anyway," I asked her, keeping my voice down so that the whole world didn't hear.

"Sixty-two," she said. "Sixty-three next week."

"A pig and an anteater," said a well-dressed woman who was holding onto our pole. "A match made in heaven."

Kate examined my clutter with great interest, starting first with the magazines, most of which she decided were worthless, and then moving on to all those yellowish newspapers, dating back a good five years.

"What are you saving *this* for?" she said, holding up a news section of the *Times*. The article I had circled in green ink was about a man who had broken his puppy's neck and then watched TV as it lay dying. The man had been sentenced to a month in jail for displaying "wanton and cruel disinterest."

"Poor Goliath," I said, shaking my head. "Eight weeks old and he never even had a chance."

"Who's Goliath?" said Kate, but she was already onto something else, tossing one newspaper after the other into the center of the room.

"The poor little mongrel," I said. "Always stop to read the fine print or you'll never learn anything."

"None of this has a thing to do with your marriage," Kate said. "So what's it doing here?"

"Cynthia and I used to read out loud to each other from the paper. Things that caught our fancy—ludicrous things, pathetic things, things you had a hard time believing. It brought us closer together somehow, sharing all the nuttiness that was out there."

"I can accept that," said Kate. "What I can't accept is that a human being could actually live in this place. Look at this!" she said, circling the room slowly, her hands held behind her back. "I mean, look at this!"

"I keep meaning to buy some furniture," I said, "but somehow it always slips my mind." I knew what she was complaining about—except for a desk made of two white metal file cabinets with a Formica board thrown across the top, a couple of folding chairs, and a pair of bookcases, the room was empty. I wasn't about to apologize for all this barrenness, though—the truth was, I wasn't particularly bothered by it. Worrying about interior decorating was the farthest thing from my mind. "Actually, it's deliberate," I told Kate. "It's the minimalist look."

Kate laughed out loud. "I don't suppose the bedroom is any better," she said. "What do you do, sleep on a pile of straw?"

"I happen to have a brand new queen-size mattress in there."

"Box springs?"

"Maybe later," I said, "when I'm feeling a little more settled-in."

Kate nodded. "Where do you eat your meals?"

I lifted myself onto the top of the desk. "Usually right

up here," I said. "I get myself a spoon and a container of vegetable cottage cheese and I'm as happy as can be."

Crossing the room noiselessly in her high tops, Kate arrived at my side and put her head in my lap. "I hate your wife," she said. "I don't even know her but the thought of everything she's taken from you makes me sick."

"Which wife is that?" I said. I stroked her hair with the back of my thumb for a while and then, without a word, I kissed the top of her head.

"The one who was so enormously compassionate," Kate said. "Patient, kind, sympathetic, you name it."

"Oh, that wife," I said. "That was actually Anne, my first wife, the one who divorced me in 1958 so I could marry Cynthia. As it turned out, we didn't get married for another two years because Cynthia kept getting these awful anxiety attacks every time I wanted to hustle her over to a justice of the peace."

"Two failed marriages," said Kate. "What have you got to say for yourself?"

"Some people have a knack for marriage," I said. "They know how to be accommodating, not to look too closely when their husband or wife isn't measuring up. The first time around, it was Anne who did all the accommodating. I was pretty young and pretty selfish and I made poor Anne miserable. I threw that marriage away as if it were nothing to me." I didn't tell Kate what a womanizer I had been in those days, how I'd shamelessly seduced anyone I could get my hands on. And this was in the fifties, when you had to work a little harder than you do today, when you had to make lavish promises and send flowers and do a lot of hand-holding afterward. The thrill of breathing in unfamiliar perfume, of feeling the unfamiliar planes of someone's body beneath my hands, of hearing a new voice whispering confidences into my ear—all of this had been so utterly exciting that I simply had not been able to give it up.

"And then I met Cynthia," I said out loud.

Kate lifted her head from my lap. She shoved me over a little and eased herself onto the desk. "The one who kicked you out and kept all the furniture," she said.

"Don't be too hard on her," I said. "The woman had a lot of problems. She couldn't even cope with the grocery shopping." I tried to remember then why it was that I had fallen in love with her but all I could come up with was that she was beautiful and also impossibly difficult and that the combination must have been irresistible to me. "I did everything I could to keep the marriage going," I said. "She was afraid of crowds, afraid of escalators, elevators, cigarette smoke blowing an ill wind in her face . . . dentists, getting behind the wheel of a car, hairdressers, the chiropractor's office . . ."

"The chiropractor's office but not the chiropractor?" said Kate. "That's the one I don't get."

"Well, she went once but she would never go back, even though she was sure the guy had helped her. So this is what we did—we drove to his office, got him to come downstairs and out into the street and reach through the window of the car and adjust her, or whatever it is they do. She wanted him to help her, but she wouldn't let him in the car. He had to stand on his tiptoes and do everything through the window."

"You loved this woman?" Kate said. She was laughing now, either at me or at the thought of the chiropractor on his tiptoes, I couldn't tell which.

"Absolutely."

"Did she love you?"

"Sometimes she thought she did. Other times, she wasn't that interested."

"I don't understand any of this," Kate said.

"It's like this," I said, taking her face lightly in my hands, "people get in each other's way, lose interest in each other, love flies out the window, what can I tell you?"

Kate thought this over for a while and then she said, "Let's see that Nehru suit you wore to your brother-in-law's wedding in 1968."

"It's in the bedroom," I said. My voice came out a little nervous and highpitched, so I tried again. "In the bedroom," I said, nice and deep this time.

"The room with the queen-size mattress but no box springs?"

"Actually, there's not a whole lot to see in there," I said, "other than a closet that is truly a nightmare."

Hearing this, Kate slid down off the desk and tugged at my hand like a child. "Great," she said. "Maybe we can go through it and throw half of its contents out."

"What about *your* clutter?" I said. "How come you're so hot to take on mine when you can't deal with your own?" But my heels were already flat on the floor and before I knew it we were on our way to the bedroom.

"I don't have any," Kate told me. "I only took the course out of curiosity."

"Now wait a minute," I said as she followed me through the doorway and into the bedroom. "What's this about curiosity? What you're telling me is that you took the course because you wanted to meet lonely guys with messy apartments. Admit it."

"To be honest," said Kate, "my closets are a wreck. Did I mention in class that my ex-boyfriend left behind an assortment of baseball bats, a couple of dead soccer balls, a heavy case full of tools, metal-tipped snow boots, about five pairs of sneakers, lumber that he was going to use for bookcases . . ."

"I wasn't really paying close attention in class," I said. "I think I may have dozed off during your recitation." She looked so offended that I had no choice but to put my arms around her. "You have to understand that I've been deeply depressed for so long I hardly pay attention to anything," I told her. "So please don't take it personally." What came next was a passionate kiss, but it was never clear to me who removed their nose first or who approached whom. When it was over, I tried to get my breathing under control. I sat down at the edge of the bed and watched in astonishment as Kate crossed her arms over her head and pulled off her sweatshirt.

"No bra!" I said joyfully.

"Glad to see you're paying attention."

"Oh, I am," I said, "believe me, I am."

Kate tied the sweatshirt around her waist and took a step or two in my direction. I was dying to touch her but something held me back, and I stayed put at the edge of the bed. I was dangling my feet in the pool, not quite brave enough to push off into the water. I told myself I wasn't ashamed of my body, though the hair on my chest and my legs had mysteriously disappeared in recent years and the flesh just above my knees sagged a little whenever I stood up. A queasiness took hold of me then, just as I could feel the first faint stirrings of excitement.

"So tell me about yourself," I said, and on its own my hand went up to stroke her breast. "Any hobbies?" The softness of her skin against my fingertips seemed unbearable but I could not take my hand away.

"Squash," said Kate evenly. "I was on the squash team at Vassar."

36

"Poughkeepsie, New York," I said, "right?"

Kate nodded. "Your Levolors are open," she said. She crossed the floor to close them and in an instant the room darkened. I could no longer make out the details of her face with any ease, and oddly, there was comfort in that. When she returned, I grabbed her wrists and pulled myself up.

"I've been out of circulation so long," I said. "Maybe that's why none of this feels quite the way it should to me."

"It will," said Kate. "Stop talking and it will." Gently, she helped me out of my clothes and then I took over. I covered her with tiny, careful kisses, as if I loved every bit of her. Already I loved the warm pale space between her breasts, the sharpness of her hips, her hard slender ankles. If I was lucky, the rest would come later, I knew. In the meantime, there was this, the two of us moving together so beautifully, so confidently, finding our way in the dark without any trouble at all.

CHAPTER FOUR

Sometime in June, three months after the fact, Kate finally decided to inform her parents of the birth of their new granddaughter. She explained to me that she could no longer tolerate feeling cut off from her family, that she simply felt an overwhelming need to gulp down her pride and send her mother and father a birth announcement. Perfectly understandable, I said. Of course, what she didn't tell me was that she'd changed the date on the announcement with a little Wite-Out and her caligraphy pen and was hoping to pass our daughter off as a newborn.

And so here were her parents sitting in our living room in the middle of the afternoon, examining their granddaughter in amazement. Having driven up from New York twenty-four hours after receiving Darlan's birth announcement in the mail, they seemed, at least to me, to be suffering from a serious case of jet lag.

"She's a beautiful baby," Bunny said slowly, running her hand down one side of Darlan's jaw, then under her chin, and back up her jawline again.

"Magnificent," said Seymour, but frowned slightly.

Darlan grabbed his index finger. He waved it from side to side but still she did not let go. "Prodigiously large," he added. "For a newborn."

Kate, cross-legged on the floor at her parents' feet, made a strangled noise that could have been anything—a snort, a groan, a laugh. "What's with you?" I said, thinking this must have been some kind of joke between my wife and her father. But there was no response from Kate.

Smiling at Seymour, I asked if he would like a drink. We'd only met once before and I couldn't remember whether he'd been drinking or not that night.

"A Scotch on the rocks might be nice," he said. "Though normally, you know, Jews aren't big drinkers." He was a slender man, not very tall, with gray eyes that matched the snappy little bowtie he was wearing. About five years younger than I was, but with half my hair, which cheered me enormously.

"Scotch on the rocks?" I said. Then, "Did someone say something about a newborn?"

"Three weeks is still a newborn, isn't it?" said Seymour.

"Without question," I said. "But this baby's three months old."

"Three *weeks*," said Bunny. She had a sweet round face that I found very appealing, thick ankles, and a big round bosom that was probably a comfort to anyone— man or child—who felt a need to rest his head upon it.

"According to the Hebrew calendar, maybe, but not according to the one in this house," I joked.

"Hurry up with that drink, Henry," Seymour said. "I'm feeling unusually agitated all of a sudden."

Scooping up the baby from Bunny's lap, Kate began pacing the room in exceptionally large strides, then abruptly headed for the front door.

"Just one moment," I said, handing Seymour his

drink. "Aren't we going to have a revealing little chat before you make your escape?"

"In some cultures," Seymour said, "a woman would sooner be a whore than a liar."

"What cultures are those?" I asked him. Positioning myself behind Kate, my hands firmly at her shoulders, I steered her back to the center of the room.

"I don't know, it's just something I read in *National Geographic*."

Bunny took a sip from her husband's drink, shuddered slightly, then smiled. "So the baby's three months old," she said. "She's healthy, she's thriving, and I'm not asking any questions. God knows, this family's had its share of misunderstandings. Frankly, I don't want to know anything more about it."

"Inquiring minds want to know," Seymour said. "Even if you don't."

"Let's have it," I urged Kate. I tightened my grip on her shoulders. "Every last sordid detail."

Shaking me loose, Kate backed up to the fireplace and rearranged Darlan in her arms.

"Louder," said her father. "I can't hear a thing."

"I wanted to see you," Kate said. "I needed to see you."

"Great beginning," said Seymour, and drained the last of his drink. "Go on."

Kate wound her way around an elaborate story involving birth announcements, the engraved ones she sent out several months ago, and the doctored one she sent to her mother and father only last week. "I just didn't want you to think that I'd waited forever to give you the news," she finished.

"I, for one, am truly touched by your thoughtful consideration," said Bunny.

"What did you think, we were born yesterday?" Seymour said. "You think I don't know a three-month-old baby when I see one?"

"I got you all the way up here, didn't I," said Kate. "If I'd given you the real facts and figures, you might have been too angry to make the trip."

"Entirely possible," Seymour said. "But maybe not." He held his empty glass out toward me, rattling the ice cubes to make sure he got my attention. "What about you, Hank? What's your part in all this?"

"I'm a total innocent," I said. "And please don't call me Hank. It lacks dignity."

"Sorry." When I handed him a new drink, he patted my wrist in a friendly manner. "You have a daughter, Henry," he said. "Even older than Kate. So what would you think if she pulled a fast one on you?"

"Nina," I said, and my mouth went dry. She was lost to me. When she was a child, I'd failed her; in all the years that followed, we'd failed each other. I knew little of her, only as much as could be fit onto a Christmas card. When I was still living at home, before the time when her mother and I divorced, I could see that I had a flair for fatherhood. I patiently checked over Nina's arithmetic and spelling homework every night, read her favorite books in a soothing voice, ran my palms across her cheeks and into her hair with the deepest sort of pleasure. One night, when she was about seven, and did not know that I was soon to leave, I lay next to her across the length of her small bed and sang love songs to her in a whispery voice, songs from *Carousel* and *The King and I* and *Gigi*. When I finished, she said, "There are some things in life I'm afraid of, and death is one of them." I was floored by the words themselves and even more by the sadness in her voice, which seemed profound. "I think I'm going to cry," she told me, but it turned out, after all, that she had been mistaken. "I hope I don't die until the twenty-first century," she said, and I promised her then that she wouldn't, kissing every one of her soft-skinned, tiny knuckles as I spoke. In a few months I was gone, and we never did pick up where we'd left off, though that was another one of my promises. Anne, my first wife, was well rid of me and she knew it. She let Nina know it, too, and that made it nearly impossible for Nina to feel anything like love for me ever again. At first, I came around occasionally at her bedtime, always our best time together, but she would never confide in me, or turn in my direction when I wanted to kiss her. I could not win her over, could not force love on my own child. What a revelation! It was over between us: stupidly, unbelievably, I had simply let it go.

"What would I think?" I answered Seymour now. "I'd think what a lucky son-of-a-bitch I was that my daughter actually loved me."

"He's really kind of a sexy guy," Bunny was saying. She batted lightly at the Beatrix Potter characters that formed the mobile hanging over Darlan's crib, setting the plastic figures into frantic motion. "He must have been quite something in his younger days."

Kate sprinkled scented corn starch between the baby's legs, then grabbed an ankle in each of her hands and pushed Darlan's feet up and down so that it looked as if she were peddling a bicycle. "He's quite something *now*," she told her mother. "Half the time I'm wondering how I can keep up with him."

"What do you mean?"

"Look at me," said Kate. "I'm just another new mother—someone who's sleepwalking from one day to the next. When Henry and I first met, I was a match for him. I was wide awake; I saw everything, everything was so vivid and distinct. Now it's like I'm looking through a haze—there's a fine dust over everything."

"*Of course* you're exhausted," her mother said. "You have a new baby and endless laundry and a house that needs to be kept up and probably you can't see a way out, can't even see who you are when you look for yourself in the mirror. But you're happy, aren't you?"

Kicking off her shoes, Kate vaulted over the bars of the crib and stretched out beside the baby. "I'm happily married," she said. She thought of a day last week, a day no different from any other: she and Henry were sauntering through one of the malls in Portland, pushing Darlan in her stroller, wandering in and out of stores, gazing idly at copper-bottomed pots, bright kitchen towels, at white wicker nursery furniture and a display of hand-painted baby bottles decorated with tiny balloons. In Babyland, she had noticed a middle-aged saleswoman, eyebrows raised in curiosity and bemusement at the sight of Kate's family. Signaling to Henry that they were, as usual, the object of a stranger's scrutiny, Kate watched as Henry approached the woman. "Take a look at this," he said, and pointed to the dark blue T-shirt he was wearing. Emblazoned across his chest in white were the words "I'm the Father." The saleswoman reddened, began to speak, then faltered. Recovering, she said, "That's an exceptionally cute baby you have there." "You bet," Henry said. His smile was enormous and lasted until he returned to Kate. Together they laughed a little at the saleswoman's embarrassment, then paraded proudly out of the store. The T-shirt was a recent gift from Kate: the joke had not yet worn thin. When it did, they would simply come up with a new approach, a new way of staring down the world. She had come to see that this was what Henry thrived on—taking on the salespeople in the mall, cashiers at the supermarket, passersby on the streets in town, anyone at all who could not believe that Henry, Kate, and Darlan were exactly as they appeared, a family bound by love in its usual arrangements. She loved his passionate boasting, his willingness to let strangers in on his happiness. *Go ahead and look at me,* he seemed to be saying. *Just look at how great I'm doing!* He had taught her to take it all in stride, to try and enjoy the attention. *We're like goddamn celebrities,* he liked to tell her. *Some day some old man is going to come right up to me and ask for my autograph.*

"If you're happily married, then you're happy," Bunny said with relief. "Never mind that you're in thrall to a baby and to a house. Little by little you'll get back your sleep and the time to work on your drawings and read the newspapers and all those books I saw stacked up on your night table. You'll be back in the world soon enough. Before you know it, you'll be looking over your shoulder, wondering how you managed to get from there to here in the blink of an eye."

"You sound like Henry," Kate said.

"What a racket he's got going here," her mother said, not unkindly, but in absolute astonishment. "He's made out like a bandit."

"You make him sound so undeserving."

"I'm your mother, cookie. I can't help wanting what's best, what's right, for you."

Kate stroked Darlan's palm with her finger, watched the slight smile that appeared at her daughter's lovely full lips. "And this isn't it?"

Her mother shrugged. "That," she said, "remains to be seen."

CHAPTER FIVE

Cynthia's new therapist was an extremely large, friendly woman named Blossom Weinstock. She was nearly six feet tall and fifty pounds overweight, and dressed only in loose, two-piece outfits of black or dark purple. Cynthia admired her deep, passionate laugh, her beautifully polished nails, the long silk scarves that were always knotted so artfully at her throat. Best of all, Blossom was a talker, a shrink who loved the sound of her own voice. She loved to think out loud, to toss out her theories like fastballs, one after the other, some outrageous, some absolutely on the mark. For Cynthia, spending an hour with her was exhilarating, and most often she left the office sweaty with excitement, her cheeks burning, the back of her neck cool and damp.

This afternoon, though, Blossom was clearly not herself. Her eyelids were puffy, her clear, strong voice seemed thick and choked, a scarf was hanging down loose and sloppy over her shoulders. She looked out at Cynthia from behind her desk now and shook her head slowly. "I'm a spiritual and emotional wreck today but let's just proceed normally and see how it goes."

"Are you sure?" Cynthia asked. She was depressed at the sight of Blossom's sadness, particularly disturbed by the scarf that drooped so untidily past her broad shoulders.

"I just got back from a memorial service," Blossom said. "A patient of mine, a woman in her thirties, two young children, a nice, sweet husband, the works. Truly a tragic story."

"Suicide?"

Blossom looked insulted. "I have *never* lost a patient to suicide," she said. "My patients wouldn't dream of disappointing me like that."

"Cancer?"

"A double mastectomy and they still couldn't save her." Blossom took a pencil from behind her ear and began tapping the eraser end against her knuckles. "So what's new with you?" she asked. "Have a good week?"

"Could you stop that, please," Cynthia said, gesturing toward the pencil, which fluttered furiously now between Blossom's fingers.

"Sorry." The pencil went back behind her ear. "Tell me about your week."

"As a matter of fact, the new semester just started," said Cynthia. "I daydream a lot about mesmerizing the students with my brilliance, but it never happens. The truth is, they're bored to death with me. They can tell how nervous I am, how much I want to please them. They don't like me for it, they just think I'm dull."

"L.S.E.," said Blossom with her eyes closed. "Low self-esteem. We've got to get a handle on it, Cynthia. You know it's still our number one priority."

"I don't want to talk about it."

"What *do* you want to talk about?"

"I can't look at you when your scarf is like that."

"What?" Staring downward, Blossom jerked on one end of the scarf and pulled it from her shoulders. She opened a desk drawer, stuffing the scarf inside. "Better?"

"You look unfinished," Cynthia said. "Naked, almost."

Blossom sighed. "I also look like I ought to drop fifty or a hundred pounds this weekend. How come *that* doesn't disturb you?"

"You know," Cynthia said, "I happened to have had a much-beloved cat who, unfortunately, grew overweight in his old age. He developed a layer of fat around the heart and that was the end of him."

"Is that a cautionary tale?" Blossom asked, smiling slightly. "Are you trying to scare me?"

Cynthia didn't answer. She was thinking of her cat, Slim, of his front paws and the tip of his tail twitching while he slept, of the tufts of hair that had grown out of his ears like an old man's, of the way he had nudged her in bed every evening, eager for her arm to swoop down around him and shelter him for the night. He had lived to old age and died at the vet's office with Cynthia's cheek against his face, while in the waiting room Henry sat flipping through the pages of a limp, soiled *Newsweek*. The sound of the pages being turned so casually intensified her sorrow and she hated Henry then for what she perceived as his heartlessness. But afterward, when she came out into the waiting room sobbing, he was gentle with her, insisting on driving them all the way out to Long Island to the beach, where they walked along the water's edge with their arms laced around each other, their shoes filled with sand, eyes turning tearful as they stared into the sunlight that wavered over the dark ocean. This was how he spent his life now, Cynthia imagined, walking end-lessly across the sand with his daughter against his chest, brushing his lips along the top of her head, whispering secrets and bits of songs into her hair. The thought of him like this was wrenching; the thought of all his sweetness, his generous good humor, given over to a baby, and, of course, to a wife—strangers she could not envision and would never meet. In the months since the baby's birth she had been plagued with curiosity and the slightest twinge of envy. She was unaccustomed to such feelings; they made very little sense to her. Self-absorbed as she knew herself to be, she had rarely been curious about the details of other people's lives. When she'd learned that Henry had remarried, she had nodded to herself, thinking, Absolutely, of course. It had been a relief to know that his happiness would be tended to by someone else. Beyond that, she gave no thought to Kate at all. What did it matter, really, if she were lovely and smart (as Henry had claimed in his letter), if her hair fell perfectly straight beyond her shoulders, if she wore shining silver jewelry around her neck and wrists? Cynthia hadn't wasted any time thinking of these things, but had tucked Henry's letter into a ceramic vase filled with silk flowers and gone back to the paper she was revising for a journal. Calling Henry, as she had six months ago, had been a disastrous mistake, an indulgence she deeply regretted. She had awakened that morning unexpectedly yearning for the sound of his voice, as keenly as if, walking past Pizza Heaven, she might have yearned for an enormous, sizzling slice.

They had been out of each other's lives for years and yet nothing was forgotten—it was all there to be sifted through like the tangle of gold and silver chains in her jewelry box, the jumble of single, loose beads and earrings; a disorderly heap she hadn't approached in ages. She tried to remember why they had been so wrong together. Certainly she had loved him, though he had never been entirely convinced. What he wanted from her was a flash of passion here and there, for her to be moved ardently by the sight of him, to look up from whatever it was she was doing and say, "Jesus, I have *really* got the hots for you, Henry!" That was the way he'd talked, openly, extravagantly, exuberantly. What a noisy presence he had been! He loved to talk, about anything at all, always needed an audience of friends or strangers encouraging him, drawing him out farther and farther, until finally he fell back, exhausted, having emptied himself of everything. She had never been the right audience for him, had never been able to listen hard enough. There was always a book in her lap, always a lecture she was re-thinking, just when Henry was off and running with whatever happened to be on his mind—the new stereo system he was contemplating buying, the Lotus Europa he had seen cruising down Park Avenue, the assistant he'd had a hand in hiring at the magazine where he worked as art director. "People *love* me!" he was fond of saying to her, implying, What about you? Why aren't I good enough for you? He was someone who talked a little too loudly, who stood a little too close to people when he spoke, who kept his hand on his listener's shoulder a little longer than he should have. In bed he labored too long to please her, refusing to give up, unable to believe that much of the time she simply wanted to be left alone. Before their marriage, she had been amazed and flattered by his attentiveness, by the way he threw himself into his study of her, as if a person could be learned like a foreign language. He discovered that she loved Bach and Cole Porter, and ran around town getting concert tickets and hard-to-find recordings. He saw that she had a sweet tooth and made her white chocolate mousse and peach sorbet and cookies flavored with orange rind—projects that took him forever and brought perspiration to the crook of his arm and the bend of his wrist. Even after they were married, for years it seemed that he was still courting her, still trying to win her over completely. Walking in the street, he took her hand and held onto it, held onto her, for longer than she liked. At home he seemed always to be at her side, as if he could not bear to have any distance between them. Enough, she told him finally. Hearing this, he seemed bewildered, and so she'd said, *Enough enough enough. It's just too much.*

"What?" he'd wanted to know. "What's too much?"

"You," she said. "Take a vacation, Henry."

"As in, 'take a hike'?" He had been sitting next to her on the couch in the living room watching television, a handsome middle-aged man whose legs were slung casually over hers on the coffee table, one bare foot stroking the tips of her bare toes. Slowly he moved himself away from her, to the other end of the couch. "I don't know what you're talking about."

"Just go easy on me."

"I don't get it. What am I doing?"

She did not tell him that the feel of his toes against hers made all her muscles contract in exasperation. "They're my feet," she said. "My toes. Don't you think that if I want to sit in my living room without having my toes touched I should be able to?"

Henry's face went white. "Are you crazy?"

"Don't you ever like feeling that you're alone? That there's no one in the world looking at you or thinking about you or wanting anything from you?"

"Not often," Henry said.

"Sometimes," she told him, "I feel so tied to you and it's like a noose around my neck."

"Shit," said Henry sorrowfully. *"You* are crazy."

This was what she remembered of her marriage.

She wept now for words exchanged in another lifetime, for everything she had ever asked of Henry, for all the years she had him tiptoeing around her, keeping his occasional love affairs quietly to himself. Going easy on her, just as she'd asked. She'd been thirty-five when they married, old enough to know better. She'd known that she was meant to spend her life alone, that solitude was her natural state. Don't be ridiculous, Henry told her. *Nobody* was meant to be alone. She had let him coax her into marriage, the way a mother coaxes her child into one little taste of cauliflower or mushroom. *See,* Henry said, *what did I tell you? Isn't this great?* Sometimes, when they'd had a party to go to, he led her to the edge of their bed and slipped a dress over her, trying not to sound too anxious as he asked, Which shoes now, the black or the tan? Snakeskin pocketbook? Opal earrings? No? No earrings at all? She was beautiful, he said, exaggerating, as usual. What pleasure he got looking at her in her lovely expensive things! He got a kick out of showing her off to people, but most often she stared at her feet when he introduced her to strangers. For God's sake, *look* at people when they talk to you, he'd whisper desperately, sometimes actually tipping her chin upward with his hands, gently, trying hard to control his anger and disappointment. He loved her but was incensed by what he referred to as her "nuttiness," her refusal to see things as he saw them. You'll miss me, he'd warned when their marriage ended. *You'll miss me bullying you out of bed and into the world. I'm a pain in the neck but I'm what you need.*

"Maybe so," Cynthia said out loud now. She wiped her eyes roughly with her knuckles.

Blossom stretched her arms high over her head, crossing her wrists and waving her fingers at the ceiling. "So you think that, like your cat, I'll develop a layer of fat around the heart and then kick the bucket?"

"It's just recently that I've been aware of missing him. I wake up in the morning and for an instant or two I'm surprised that he's not there."

"What kind of cat was he?"

"What cat?" said Cynthia.

"I think you've gotten away from me," Blossom said. "You're here, but I don't know where to find you."

"I want another shot at it," Cynthia said. "Of course now that he's found the love of his life, I can't imagine that he'd be the slightest bit interested. In fact, I don't think he wants to hear from me until late in the next century."

"Henry?"

"It was a mistake to have called him, but then again, it was probably a mistake to have divorced him. It was just my laziness, the easy way out for me. But of course Dr. Hochberg was all for it. I should have—"

"Shoulda woulda coulda," Blossom said wearily. "Let's not get started on that one. It can't possibly lead to anything worthwhile."

"I don't even know what I want from him. Sometimes, when I'm having trouble getting out of bed in the morning, I convince myself he's the only one who can get me going. I remember him standing on the other side of the bedroom, tossing my clothes to me from the dresser, clearly impatient, but never giving up on me."

"How romantic," said Blossom. "But believe me, it's no basis for a relationship."

"It *is* romantic, isn't it," Cynthia said. She imagined her clothing floating across the bedroom in slow motion, a beautiful silk blouse lingering in mid-air as Henry smiled at it, at her, saying, *See, what did I tell you?*

52

CHAPTER SIX

Watching Darlan drift into her afternoon nap in her playpen in the den, watching the dainty flutter of her eyelids and then their final descent that let me know she was out for sure, I couldn't resist a careful little whoop of delight: I was free! At least for an hour or maybe longer, if I was exceptionally lucky. Kate had been at her studio all day, working on spec on some new drawings for anniversary cards—giraffes with their necks intertwined, elephants holding champagne glasses in their trunks, a couple of pandas having breakfast in bed on wicker trays. The studio was actually an uninhabited cabin set deep in a wooded area just ten minutes from home, and Kate was without a telephone and even plumbing there. The thought of her peeing into an old coffee can (as she claimed to) always made me laugh, but in her eyes she was simply being resourceful. We hadn't been in touch since morning, and I was proud of how well I'd done on my own with Darlan. A few weeks short of her first birthday, she chattered incessantly and lurched about on thick little legs with great confidence. I was almost always grateful for her company, but the sight of her asleep at this moment threw me into a state of excitement. Tiptoeing out the door with exaggerated care, I considered the possibilities: I could go back to the biography of Oscar Wilde I'd almost finished reading, skim yesterday's *New York Times,* pay some bills, load up the dishwasher. As it turned out, the phone rang before I'd reached a decision, and I leaped to answer the nearest extension, which happened to be in the kitchen.

"It's me, Henry," said Cynthia. "Why do you sound so breathless?"

"We've got to stop meeting like this," I told her, only half-teasing. Her occasional calls over the past few months had always taken me by surprise, and I didn't really know how to explain them to Kate, who found them intrusive and unsettling. She just wants to talk, I'd told her lamely after Cynthia's last call. If she doesn't have any friends, let her call a loneliness hotline, Kate said.

"So what is it *now?*" I asked Cynthia. "Don't tell me you've suddenly been hit hard by the empty nest syndrome."

Cynthia laughed. "Wouldn't I have been an awful mother? Neurotic, inattentive, preoccupied—"

"Bingo," I said. "But don't be too hard on yourself."

"My low self-esteem is showing again, as Blossom would say."

"Does she know you've been calling here?"

"She's very much against it," Cynthia said after a pause. "She thinks I'm just looking for trouble."

"Are you?" I asked her.

"Why would anyone ever go looking for trouble?"

"Some people thrive on it," I said.

"They do?"

"Cynthia," I said, "I love not being married to you. I love the three hundred miles between us. I kind of enjoy being your phone pal but strangely enough, my wife is far from thrilled when you call. The hair on her head stands straight up in the air whenever she hears your voice. So I think it would be a great idea if we—"

"Let's get down to business," Cynthia said. "I'll be in Boston next week delivering a paper on suicide. Why don't you drive down and meet me and I'll take you out to lunch."

"Suicide?" I said. "That's not really a subject I have any particular interest in." My hands and feet were suddenly icy; I blew into one palm and then the other to try and warm them, but it didn't do much good. "And anyway, I'm busy all next week. I have to babysit," I added.

"Can't you hire a babysitter?"

"Never," I said, pretending to be horrified at the suggestion. "We don't believe in them, except in emergencies. And this lunch of yours doesn't seem to qualify as one of those."

"You really don't want to see me, do you?"

"It isn't that," I told her. Already I could feel my resolve weakening, my uneasiness giving way to excitement as I saw myself tracing with my fingertips the delicate outline of her mouth. I gazed around me at our newly remodeled kitchen, rubbed my fingers along a textured Formica cabinet, a smooth, sand-colored countertop. The shining surfaces of one brand new appliance after another filled me with satisfaction. Everything was perfectly positioned; everything looked exactly right. And it was.

I broke the news to Cynthia without apology: "Everything is exactly right," I said. "And I'm going to make sure it stays that way."

Hearing this, Cynthia sighed. "I'm talking about lunch, Henry. Salad, a main course, dessert. Does that sound dangerous to you?"

"There's danger everywhere," I said. "Hands meet accidentally across a little basket of hot rolls on the table and it's as if you've been struck by lightning."

"Don't be silly."

"I've been there, sweetie. Many times."

"I wouldn't brag about it if I were you."

"Don't," I said. "Don't make me apologize to you. We're done with all that."

"Absolutely," Cynthia agreed. "Meet me at the Ritz-Carlton across from the Common next Friday. How does one o'clock sound?"

"The baby's crying. I have to go."

"Oh sure," said Cynthia. "Why not go all out and say the house is on fire?"

"I'll be right back," I said, and left the receiver on the counter. I turned the radio up so Cynthia could listen to a flute and harpsichord sonata Mozart had tossed off at the age of eight.

Darlan was resting her chin on the rim of the playpen, looking forlorn. Her face was flushed and tear-stained; her curly, shoulder-length hair had a wild look. She perked up at the sight of me, holding her arms out in welcome. "Hi Daddy-Doo," she said.

"Some nap," I said as I lifted her out. "Really. How about having a little consideration for one of your Significant Others."

"Want bobby and blankey."

Rolling my eyes, I said, "Big girls like you don't drink out of bottles anymore. You may, however, drag your blanket around to your heart's content." I handed over the blanket, which she bunched up against my shoulder and then used as a pillow.

"Bobby," she said.

"I know a tiny little girl who had to have root canal

56

because she drank milk out of her bottle all day long. *Root Canal!* Is that what you want for yourself? Think it over, baby doll."

In the kitchen, holding Darlan against me, I picked up the phone, hoping for a miracle. "Cynthia?" I whispered.

"Mozart?" she asked me. "Very light and cheerful, I must say. And I appreciate your not subjecting me to Muzak the way everyone else does when they put you on hold."

"I've got to give the baby lunch," I said as I switched off the radio. "She's begging me for peanut butter on whole wheat and some sliced banana."

"Lunch? It's nearly three o'clock."

"You're right, she already had her lunch. It must be a mid-afternoon snack she has in mind."

"How do I know there actually *is* a baby?" Cynthia said. "You've never even sent me a picture."

I held up the phone against Darlan's ear. "Say hello to Miss Cynthia," I instructed her. Darlan opened and shut her hand a few times, her version of a wave. "It's strictly the spoken word she's after," I told the baby. "Come on and show your stuff." Bending her head, Darlan tapped a front tooth against the bottom of the receiver.

"I'm waiting," Cynthia said.

"She appears to have been struck dumb with amazement or something," I said. "At least for the time being."

"Bring her with you when you come down to Boston. The Ritz-Carlton is out, obviously, but I'm sure there's a Burger King that would be happy to accommodate all of us."

It occurred to me that she was actually serious, that she was so keen on this meeting she would actually have welcomed the sight of me with my daughter in my arms.

"Kate might like to come along, too," I said, testing her. "Any objections? Questions or comments?"

"That would be fine," Cynthia said evenly. "I've always been one for family gatherings." She knew I knew this was a lie, but I decided to let it pass.

"It's very unfair of you," I said, "to be so persistent. And to what end? Just what is it you think you're going to accomplish?"

"We'll have fun filling each other in on our respective lives," Cynthia said. "That's all."

Darlan yanked on my hair with one hand and pinched my neck with the other, signaling, I gathered, that she wanted to be put down. As soon as I lowered her to the floor, she headed straight for the cabinet under the sink, where she discovered a plastic bottle of Ivory Liquid, a spray container of Fantastik, an old stiffened sponge, a tall shiny can of Ajax. On her knees, she lined them up in the middle of the kitchen, then sauntered across the threshold and into the dining room. "Get back here, you," I called after her. "As for you," I said to Cynthia, "can't we exchange written reports or something? Why does this have to be done in person?"

"Indulge me," Cynthia said wistfully. "Just this once."

"Just this once?" I yelled as Darlan flipped through a magazine, stopping to tear out a page here and there. "Pardon me, but it strikes me I spent a lifetime indulging you."

"I know," said Cynthia. "And don't think I didn't love you all the more for it."

Lying in bed past midnight with my head on Kate's stomach, I listened to the funny little squawking noises beneath her skin, imagining a miniature ocean endlessly sloshing about in there. "What a commotion," I said. "It must be that big bowl of Coffee Heath Bar Crunch you consumed so greedily during the Eleven O'Clock News."

"I hate to say it, but I ate like a pig."

"True," I said, "but as pigs go, you're awfully attractive. I'm especially fond of that cute little corkscrew tail."

Pushing my head from her belly and drawing me on top of her so that eventually our lips met, she said, "I love it when you flatter me, Henry. Let's hear some more."

"I, on the other hand, would much prefer to humiliate you. Couldn't you be my love slave just for tonight?"

"Would I have to call you 'sir'?"

"Certainly."

"Then go find yourself another love slave."

"We never have any fun around here anymore," I complained.

"I'm sorry you feel that way, sir."

I rolled off of her and onto my back and stared at the ceiling for a while. "Speaking of fun, or the lack thereof, Cynthia called last week. She'll be in Boston on Friday and wants to take us out to lunch."

"You've got to be kidding," Kate said. "What's she doing in Boston?"

"Delivering a paper on suicide."

"That ought to be right up her alley," Kate said, springing from the bed. She was racing over to her dresser now in search of cigarettes. Her pack of True Blues, I knew, was hidden in the sock drawer, along with a book of matches and a tiny candy dish that she used as an ashtray. Lighting up, she looked over at me and shook her head. "What's on her mind, do you think?"

"Is this your idea of quitting smoking?"

"We all have our little failings, sir."

"Not me," I said. "I'm just about perfect." Approaching her now, I took the cigarette from her hand, snuffed its

59

life out in the candy dish, and led her back to bed. "I made a mistake," I admitted. "I was as firm with her as I could possibly be, but apparently I wasn't firm enough."

"Apparently not. And I still don't understand what this is all about."

"Me either." At least, I told myself, we knew it wasn't about love or sex—neither of which had ever been high on Cynthia's lists of priorities. "My guess is it's loneliness," I said. "And curiosity. She wanted to meet *you*, for God's sake."

"Well, that's out of the question," Kate said. "I've got too much work to do. I can't afford to spend an afternoon easing the loneliness of a loon I've never even met."

"She's not a loon," I said. "She's just . . . difficult."

Kate laughed out loud at this. "That's like calling a retarded child 'exceptional,' " she wheezed.

I waited for her to finish laughing it up and then I said, "Why do I get the feeling I'm not going to Boston on Friday?"

"Sure you are, sir. As long as you promise to report back every last detail."

"I don't know," I said. "What if her motives are impure after all? What if she drugs me, binds me and gags me and then performs unspeakable acts on my person? Then what?"

"Then I'll really want to know every last detail."

When I kissed her, her mouth tasted of ashes; even so, it was a long while before we came up for air. "I love you," I said. "Madly."

"I love you too, sir," Kate answered, and bit down hard on my lip, piercing skin, drawing blood.

CHAPTER SEVEN

I arrived at the Ritz at precisely one o'clock but couldn't seem to bring myself to open the door and go inside. "Cold feet," I murmured, and stamped them noisily on the pavement. I was the slightest bit tired from the hour-and-a-half drive down and from the walk across the Common from the underground garage where I'd parked the car. The day was windy and cold and blindingly bright at this moment, and my eyes filled with tears as I looked toward the sky. I asked myself what the hell I was doing here and waited for a reasonable answer to come to me, but it never did. A waste of an afternoon: I could have been home wiping peanut butter from Darlan's impossibly small, impossibly sweet fingertips, soaping up her pot belly in the bath, planting kisses at each of her ears. Instead I was stamping my feet in front of the Ritz, trying to keep warm in a limp, unlined raincoat that had clearly seen better days.

"Were you ever going to come inside or were you planning to stay out there all afternoon?" a voice said, sounding a little querulous.

"Frankly, I never *was* going to come inside," I told Cynthia, who put her cool powdery cheek against mine in greeting. She'd left her coat behind, and her silk dress blew outward in the wind, revealing a silken peach-colored slip underneath.

"Nice undergarments," I said, as she slapped her hands down against the dress.

"Ever the genteel gentleman, I see."

I shrugged my shoulders, refusing to apologize. "Seems like only yesterday," I told her, but the truth was, it seemed entirely unlikely that I'd ever shared anything more substantial than dinner and a movie with this small, elegant gray-haired woman whom I'd only known as a blond. I studied her pale eyes, her pale, pretty face, the delicate knobs of her collarbone. "Who are you?" I said in a whisper. This was the woman who'd loved me but had not wanted to marry me, a woman who, on three separate evenings preceding scheduled trips to City Hall, once came down with laryngitis, once, swollen glands, and once, a headache so fierce it made her vomit. She had been scared to death of marriage the way some people were scared of flying; it was as if she were in mortal danger. Her hands turned clammy, her breathing quickened, her mouth filled with dust. Her body was trying to tell us both something but I, at least, had simply refused to listen. We were finally married at noon on a miserably hot, steamy day in August. Throughout the taxi ride downtown, Cynthia kept insisting there was a ringing in her ears. Wedding bells, I told her, but she didn't laugh. It was 1960, and the judge's chambers weren't air-conditioned: He was in his shirt sleeves and drinking a Coke straight from the bottle when we arrived. Cynthia was unhappy with him on both counts and wanted to leave. Over my dead body, I told her, and asked the judge to hurry it up and get the show on the road because our plane was leaving for the Arctic Circle in less than an hour. The judge thought it sounded like a wonderful trip and asked if he could come along as our chaperone. He and I and the secretary who was to be our witness laughed together, and Cynthia claimed the ringing in her ears was getting worse. "Move it, Your Honor," I begged, and he opened his book and began reading. I kept an arm around Cynthia's waist and, in a whisper, praised her bravery, praised her for standing on her own two feet despite the ringing in her ears and the chorus of little voices that urged her to scram while she still had the chance. I stressed the positive, talking about how love made people stronger than they had ever been and how marriage strengthened love. I did all this in about sixty seconds, which was all the judge allowed before he stopped and asked for silence. "Will you kindly shut your trap?" he said in exasperation, and then a moment or two later Cynthia and I were actually, incredibly, husband and wife.

"So," I said now, "how did your little talk on suicide go?"

" 'Little talk'? If you mean the paper I delivered, it went extremely well, thanks. My colleagues seemed very impressed. Or at least I didn't catch a single one of them in the act of yawning." Hugging herself against the cold, she asked if I was ready to go in now.

"Oh, I'm not going in there," I said casually. "I'm on my way home."

"Don't *do* this to me, Henry," Cynthia said. "Don't joke with me like that."

"Look me in the eye and you'll see that I'm dead serious."

Cynthia stared at me briefly, laughed, and said she

63

was going inside for her coat. "You better be here when I get back," she finished, and disappeared.

While she was gone, a young black street musician set up shop in front of the hotel. He had a bass made of an upside-down washtub, a broom handle, and a long length of string. It sounded amazingly like the real thing as soon as he started to play. Winking at me, he sang something about lo-ove being a many-splendored thing. It wasn't my kind of music but his voice was as impressive as his playing, and I folded a dollar bill into the tin can at his feet.

"Thank you, scholarly sir," he said, and winked at me again.

"That's my ex-wife," I said. "She's the one with the PhD."

I let out a wolf whistle as Cynthia returned dressed in a mink hat and coat. "What's this all about?" I asked, running my hand up and down her sleeve a couple of times. "Nice fun fur."

"I read an article in one of the women's magazines that discussed how important it is to give yourself a little treat every now and then," Cynthia explained. She took my arm and led me across the way to Beacon Street, which was loaded with beautiful old townhouses all lined up opposite the Common. We swung up Charles Street and walked past small expensive shops, and restaurants with hand-lettered menus on parchment posted in their windows.

"No lunch," I said. "No way am I having lunch with a woman in a mink coat. It's just too risky."

"Quiet," Cynthia said, and now we were turning off Charles onto an extremely narrow cobblestoned street that swept sharply uphill. The houses here were skinny little things and just a trifle shabby. Pages of a discarded newspaper flapped like wings across the cobblestones and then sailed through the air over our heads.

"Well, thanks very much for the walking tour of this charming little neighborhood," I said as Cynthia unlocked the door of a corner house with white shutters that clearly hadn't been painted in this century. "It really was a lovely day so thanks again and let's do write from time to time. Bye," I said, and tipped an imaginary top hat in her direction.

Seizing my wrist, Cynthia pulled me inside and thumped the door shut behind us. "Just throw your coat over the bannister," she said. "They're very informal around here." This was a joke: following her through a darkened hallway and into the dining room, I saw china and crystal everywhere—arranged on open shelves, behind the glass doors of two cherry wood hutches standing side by side, and on the dining table itself, where there were four settings of scalloped, gilt-edged, impossibly rococo dishes decorated with birds and cherries and vines and God knows what else. A yellowish chandelier hung precariously above us, tinkling like wind chimes when it just happened to get in the way of my forehead.

"Where am I?" I asked, rubbing two fingers against the wallpaper, which was silk and patterned with muddy-looking water stains. At one of the place settings on the table was a handwritten note that said, "Cynthia dear— please treat us *very* carefully." I picked up the note and held it out to Cynthia. "I despise this person," I said.

"Put that back where you found it, please."

Crumpling the note, I shoved it into my pants pocket. "The author is a close personal friend of yours, I take it?"

"A very good friend. She and her husband just left for Florida for a month. Anyway . . . can I offer you a drink before lunch?"

I shook my head and trailed after her into the tiny kitchen. Taped to the dishwasher was a note that said, "Please don't run the dishwasher under any circumstance"; on the cabinet over the sink was another note saying, "Please don't use the dishes in here—paper plates can be bought just about anywhere."

"Well, they've certainly done their best to make you feel at home," I said. "It's freezing in here," I added, and asked if she knew where the thermostat was. When I went to investigate at the back staircase, I wasn't surprised to find an index card propped above the thermostat informing me that the temperature was to be kept at fifty-eight during the day and fifty-five at night. With the tip of my finger, I immediately pushed the heat up to seventy-five.

Walking back to the kitchen, I bumped my head on the chandelier again. "What are these people, midgets?" I complained.

"Have some lunch," Cynthia said in a soothing voice. She handed me a napkin and a paper plate with a scoop of cottage cheese set on a lettuce leaf; next to this was an enormous pile of pretzel sticks.

"Actually, I had my heart set on a little pâté and crackers."

Cynthia looked stricken. "You *love* cottage cheese," she said. "I went out and bought some for you just because I thought there was the remote possibility we'd end up here after all."

"Aha!" I said. "Your motives *were* impure. In fact, it occurred to me on the trip down that you might very well be planning to bind and gag me and then perform unspeakable—"

"Don't flatter yourself," Cynthia said, but my teasing clearly made her uncomfortable; she was eating one pretzel stick after another from my plate and then accidentally knocked a handful over the side and onto the floor. "Crumbs!" she cried. "And I don't even know where the broom is." I crouched down on the linoleum to help her, and our hip bones collided. About to lose my balance, I grabbed onto her knee to steady myself.

"Sorry," I murmured, and withdrew my hand. But it was already too late for me; there were goosebumps along my arms and my breathing was much too loud and obvious, a series of short, noisy spasms. Squatting down beside me, Cynthia's silk dress rose high on her thighs. "Pull your dress down," I said.

"You don't mean that."

"I don't?" I reminded myself that my days as a womanizer were long past; I didn't do this kind of thing anymore. I was a happy man, secure in my happiness, wanting for nothing in this world. I told this to myself over and over again, waiting for my excitement to wilt. My mind went blank and then suddenly I was imagining Cynthia entirely naked under her mink coat. Naked and willing and very persistent. Shamelessly, I saw myself on top of her, watching the coat flapping down over me in a passionate embrace. I was actually frantic now, like a high school boy getting it for the first time.

"Put your coat on," I barked at Cynthia.

"Don't talk to me like that."

"You're right," I said. "Forget it." I got up off the floor, taking Cynthia with me. "For twenty years we failed to make each other happy," I told her. "Believe me, now's not the time to start making amends."

"Come upstairs with me," Cynthia urged, but gently.

"No."

"It's what you want," Cynthia said. "You didn't get in your car and drive all this way just for a plate of sodium-free, low-fat cottage cheese." She took me up the back staircase in a hurry, her high heels dangling from their straps in her hand. The room she planned to seduce me in had a four-poster bed and a roll-top desk that was open to reveal a clutter of family photographs. There was a musty smell of ancient wallpaper and carpeting; I immediately opened a window half an inch and pulled down a series of dark green shades along one wall.

"Let's talk," I said, throwing myself down on the bed in exhaustion.

Cynthia sat upright beside me, holding my hands. "About what?" she said.

"You're the one who wanted us to fill each other in on our respective lives."

"Yours is full and mine is empty; it's as simple as that," said Cynthia.

"Oh, Lord," I sighed. "Here we go."

"Wait, I take it back: mine is full and yours is empty."

"That's better," I said, smiling. Then, "No men in this very full life of yours?"

"Oh, a freelance book critic here and there, you know. . . ."

"I hope these freelancers aren't gay or intravenous drug users."

"Really, Henry." She rolled her eyes at me.

"Just making conversation."

Cynthia faked a big yawn. "Well, I'm about all talked out, it seems."

"I guess I'll be running along, then," I told her.

"Break my heart and I'll never forgive you." Stretching herself out, she began to touch my face lightly, running a finger under my eye, across my eyelid, behind the curve of my ear.

"Still afraid of elevators and escalators?" I asked. My

hand slipped easily between her knees, then slowly made its way upward. "Dentists and hairdressers?"

"You know *me*," Cynthia said. "Chickenhearted in the face of all earthly dangers, large and small."

"There's danger right here," I pointed out, pulling her down on the bed. Lifting her dress to her neck, I set my hands to warm places I hadn't explored in ages. Her small breasts were a little droopier than I'd remembered and there was a delicate, lilac-colored vein running past her hip that I knew I'd never seen before. Overcome by curiosity, I tasted her shoulder, which smelled faintly of unexceptional perfume. Cynthia shivered underneath me, and without letting go, we exchanged places. I realized that what lingered still was a sentimental attachment to the soft flesh and slender hard bones pressed against me now. We were out of our clothes in an instant, it seemed, and I could have sworn that the heat of our embrace was a true measure of something that felt suspiciously like love. But this was impossible: How could I have felt anything even remotely resembling love for a woman who once claimed that her attachment to me was like a noose around her neck? I couldn't and I didn't. So there was no love here but Cynthia and I were on fire nevertheless, slippery with pleasure and desire and sweat and it must have been a hundred degrees in this unfamiliar room we'd taken over as our own. And then, just at the moment I was over the edge and coming, I remembered that I'd turned the thermostat up past seventy and I broke into laughter.

"I don't love you!" I hooted. Laughing like a wild man, I told her twice more that I was certain I didn't love her.

"That's all right," she said, undisturbed. "But what's so funny?"

"I don't know," I said, "I just feel so fucking joyous."

Cynthia slipped away from me. "I want another shot at it, Henry."

"Now?" I said. "I couldn't possibly. I'm exhausted, honey."

"Oh, not that," Cynthia said. "I wasn't talking about that."

"Wait a minute. I just know I'm not ready to hear this." For the first time, I began to think of Kate. Oddly, the mild guilt I felt seemed unconnected to the act of adultery; rather, it was as if I were a young husband who'd stayed out all night with the boys knowing full well I'd been expected back home by midnight. I was puzzled by the absence of profound remorse, and yet grateful for it, too: after all, who needed to feel awful over something so wonderful? And wonderful it was, like nothing Cynthia and I had ever experienced in all the years of our poor hopeless marriage.

"I have to tell you," Cynthia said with a smile, "that never in my life have I been happy. Well, maybe a moment here, a moment there, but nothing substantial, nothing long-lasting. But now, finally, I feel ready to go after it. I just—"

"Happiness?" I interrupted, knowing what was coming next. "People make such a big deal about it, but it's really just one of the things we're here to experience— don't forget there's also pain, fear, loneliness, whatever."

"Have you lost your mind?" Cynthia said.

"Not really," I told her. "I'm merely trying to point out that there are other options, that if happiness is out of reach, you can always—"

"What?" Cynthia said. "Settle for pain, fear, and loneliness?"

"I'm trying to be helpful," I said. "Why won't you let me?"

"What you're trying," Cynthia said, "is to let yourself off the hook."

"I suppose there's some truth to that," I said. "I'm sorry."

"*Some* truth?"

Winding a curl of soft hair behind her ear, I whispered, "You know what a bullshitter I am, Miss Cynthia. I love to talk talk talk. You never bothered to listen to me before; why bother now?"

"I need you," she mumbled, eyes fixed downward in shyness.

"That's only because I'm no longer available."

"Oh, really?"

"My marriage is my *life*," I told her. "It's there for me in the morning when I wake up, and it's there for me when I go to sleep at night. It's a lovely big strong thing, a miracle, really."

"Oh, I wasn't necessarily looking for anything like *that*," Cynthia said. "Full-time, you and I are disastrous together.'"

"What are you doing, offering me a part-time job?"

"It's just that I need to get a glimpse of you now and then." She lay her head on my chest; it was a burden I couldn't get comfortable with, but I didn't have the heart to shift her out of the way. "You never gave up on me," she said. "I miss that, miss having you there to let me know I might actually be someone worth holding onto."

"Well, I put up a good fight, anyway, all those years. And then you booted me out on my ear, with more than a little help from your friend the late Dr. Hochberg, I might add."

"He believed in a clean break," Cynthia said. "I was so indecisive, so anxious, I couldn't think for myself."

"What I'd like to do is break his head in a couple of places, the coldhearted bastard."

Cynthia lifted her head from me in surprise. "Even now?" she said. "At this late date?"

"Certainly." I laced my fingers together and cracked my knuckles in the air, ready to do battle with a dead man. After Cynthia had informed me she wanted me out, I remembered, I'd left immediately and without a word, slamming the door behind me in a heartsick fury. I crossed a street or two against the light, not really caring if I got hit or not; it made absolutely no difference to me one way or the other. I ended up at the 86th Street subway stop, only a few blocks from home, though this was a surprise to me: It was the tail end of the evening rush hour and I couldn't find a seat for myself. Hanging onto a metal strap, a businessman and his attaché case pressed at either side of me, it occurred to me that these two strangers were actually holding me up, that without them I would simply slip to the filthy floor beneath us. I was grateful and almost offered them my thanks, but something stopped me—perhaps the fineness of their camel's hair overcoats, or the shining brass locks of their attaché cases. I saw that this was all I wanted at that moment, to be kept in an upright position through no effort of my own, supported by strangers who did not even notice me. The train made its way downtown and the car emptied out a little at each stop and after a while I was the only one left standing. I sank into a hard metal seat and could not imagine ever getting up again. I could guess at what I must have looked like to the passengers sitting around me—a blank-eyed, shell-shocked survivor who had only recently been under fire. In fact, I didn't know if I would survive, and I wasn't sure that I cared. It came to me then just how easy it was to lose yourself, to find yourself slipping away to nothing. If a pair of guys in white had appeared at the next stop with a stretcher for me, I would have gone with them willingly, would have eagerly thrust out an arm to receive whatever drug they had to offer. It was terrifying to think of myself this way and I began to shiver in my down parka. I would never be warm again, I knew. This made me weep, and the woman sitting next to me looked at me with distaste and moved away. "Not that I blame you," I yelled after her, and surprisingly, the sound of my voice was a comfort to me.

The train stopped at Astor Place and I got out and walked around the Village in a daze, in and out of boutiques, book stores, shoe stores, record shops. I joined a line of a dozen or so teenagers who were waiting out on the street for something. I waited my turn along with them with extraordinary indifference, and when finally I arrived at the front of the line I saw that it was only a barber shop. I went inside and had my hair cut by a handsome young guy named Rod who wore a tiny gold ring through his nose. The hardest sort of rock and roll pounded from speakers mounted on the ceiling, but it didn't do a thing for me; I barely heard it. Pieces of wet hair fell past my eyes and onto the apron Rod had tied around me with a flourish. I fingered them sadly, as if they were something precious, pieces of my heart, perhaps. Afterward, I took the subway back home, because there was nowhere else to go. "You got a haircut," Cynthia said in surprise. She met me at the door and placed her hands at the back of my neck. Her fingertips were dusty and fragrant with the talcum powder Rod had smoothed along my skin. I lowered her carefully to the living room carpet then and we made love in a hurried, panicky kind of way. I was finally awake and I was furious, my old noisy self again. "I'm a pain in the neck but I'm what you need," I told her. She shrugged her shoulders at me unhappily. The next night I moved in with a friend, and later, to a residential hotel that served breakfast every morning—juice, toast, hot and cold cereal, and occasionally a dried-out croissant.

"What you did to me," I told Cynthia now.

"I know."

"You can't imagine."

"But here we are," she said. And here we were; utterly amazed, bewildered, a little lovesick. "I don't even mind it that you don't love me," Cynthia told me again. "I only want you to care."

"I do," I said, nervously, solemnly, but laughing the next moment because it sounded like a wedding vow. I studied the sweat that lined the creases in my stomach as I raised myself up on my elbows. "Do you have bathroom privileges?" I asked. "Or do you use the one in the restaurant on the corner?"

"I even have shower privileges," Cynthia said, offering me a half-smile. "Although of course I had to pay extra for them."

"A joke, right?"

"No joke: tub privileges are five dollars a day extra, shower privileges ten dollars a day."

"Give me a break," I said.

"Gotcha!" said Cynthia, and the smile she flashed me was bright with pleasure.

In the bathroom, I stepped behind a pale pink shower curtain that smelled like the inside of a new car; a sweet-ish, almost pleasant odor that filled the little room as soon as I turned the water on. I found an unopened bar of soap wrapped in paper stamped "Sonesta Hotel" and unwrapped it giddily, flipping the paper over the top of the shower.

Washing my chest and the hollows under my arms, and behind my neck, I sang, "... *On a bright cloud of music, shall we fly?*" I cha-chaed my way carefully along the tub's rippled floor with my eyes open wide. "Sex," I said out loud, drawing out the final sound in a long leisurely hiss.

A scrawny linen hand towel awaited me when I finally stepped out of the shower and onto a mouse-colored bath mat. I considered bellowing Cynthia's name but decided instead to do the best I could with the hand towel. Sitting on top of the toilet tank, I noticed, was a deep green fern whose fronds could have used a good dusting. And there among the fronds was a flash of white, an index card reading, "Please flush only once per 5-minute period." Of course I flushed the toilet three times in a row, then left the bathroom with the scrap of linen draped modestly across my thighs, looking like a very inadequate loincloth. Cynthia was lounging on the bed in her half-slip and bra, reading a book, when I returned.

"Ah, the sensuous sociologist keeping abreast of new developments in her chosen field, I presume?"

"Just browsing," said Cynthia. She threw me a towel that had been slung over the back of a rocking chair, and smiled at me as I dried myself off. I returned her smile, and as I was dressing it hit me that I was surprised she was still here. One of the last times we had made love, I remembered, she'd been gone by the time I'd finished with my shower—gone from the apartment, gone from the city, for all I knew, for all I'd ever know.

"Where were you?" I asked her now, reminding her of the time and place, letting her know that I still hadn't forgiven her.

"Oh, here, there, everywhere," she said lightly, infuriatingly, not even raising her head from the book.

"After all this time," I said, "what harm could it possibly do?"

"After all this time, what does it *matter*?" she said, and even though she was at last looking in my direction, I could hear in that trembly rise of her voice that the subject was closed, as it had always been; that she would never give that part of herself away.

"I hate you," I heard myself saying. "I mean, I hate this." Cynthia nodded, opened her arms to me in sympathy and consolation. Refusing to settle into her embrace, I turned my back to her saying, "Can't you ever give me *anything*?"

CHAPTER EIGHT

"Too much junk food," Kate's mother complained at the party, and Kate had to admit that she was right. Shopping for Darlan's first birthday, she and Tiki went overboard, sauntering up and down the supermarket aisles with their arms outstretched, unable to resist anything with too much sugar or too much salt. The aluminum folding table Henry had set up in the den was loaded with bowls of potato chips and salted nuts, jelly beans in gourmet flavors, M & M's, miniature marshmallows, and a dozen other things that Kate and Tiki managed to get their hands on the day before. On the floor was the guest of honor, rolling jelly beans across the carpet. She was wearing a pink dress with a picture of a slightly cross-eyed rabbit appliqued on the front, and tights that were wrinkled at the ankles. Her thirty-eight dollar pink patent leather shoes gleamed beautifully, as well they should have, Kate thought. It was Henry who'd insisted on buying them. Not in this lifetime, Kate had told him, but he went back to the store and bought them anyway, sneaking them into the house under his coat and handing them over the bars of the crib to Darlan, who licked their soles and then lost interest in them. Since he'd returned from Boston, Henry seemed a milder, paler version of himself, as if he'd used up all his passion somehow in a single afternoon. He'd lost his concentration, it seemed, reading the newspaper for three minutes at a time, then walking away from it and staring in silence out the living room window at the pitch-dark ocean. What do you see out there, what are you thinking, what *is* it? Kate asked him. It isn't anything, he answered, shrugging, sighing, falling back into his silence again. Perhaps, Kate thought, she should have been scared to death, but she wasn't; she simply had to remind herself that her marriage was rock-hard, stronger and sweeter than either of them. That it was imperfect was no surprise to her. It would survive its imperfections and it would endure; some things you know for certain.

Her father and Henry, she noticed now, had their arms around each other and were swaying slightly from side to side, both of them a little drunk on fruit punch spiked with vodka.

"Great party," her father said as she approached them. "Well worth the three thousand mile drive."

"That's three hundred," Kate said.

"Whatever," her father said. "What's an extra zero between friends, anyway."

"You really crack me up, Seymour," Henry said.

"Call me Dad, why don't you. After all, you *are* what is known in the vernacular as my son-in-law, am I right?"

"Gee, Dad, I don't know," Henry said, winking at Kate. "It's kind of like the pot calling the kettle black, I think."

"True," Seymour said sadly, then perked up. "Call me Sy, then, how's that?"

"I have no problem with that," Henry said. "In fact, I

have no problem with anything at all at this point in time."

"Really," Kate said. She eyed him sharply, waiting for him to falter, but he met her gaze without any difficulty.

"Hey, buddy," Seymour said. "May I call you Hank?"

"Feel free," Kate told him, knowing just how much Henry hated the name.

"Only my army buddies were allowed to do that," Henry said. "Were you ever in the army, Sy?"

Seymour looked at him in disbelief. "Was I ever in the army? They were only the greatest years of my life, Hank."

"No fooling!" Henry said reverently.

"Don't ask me about the time I spent down in Georgia eating hot watermelon, but Paris, that's another story."

This was where Kate made her escape, knowing she wouldn't be missed in the least. She looked around for Darlan, who was snoozing in Bunny's lap, minus her shoes and tights. She stooped to kiss her daughter's sweet big toe and then moved on to the table of food, helping herself to a single chartreuse M & M.

"Hey, man, you use drugs?" Tiki whispered in her ear.

"Are you kidding? My body is my temple."

"Yeah, well, maybe it's time to start abusing it," Tiki said.

"Where are your kids?"

Tiki pointed under the table, and Kate flipped up the cloth draped across it and caught Fudge, Spencer, Kathryn, and Jonathan in various states of undress, their mouths ringed with chocolate. Jordana, Fudge's best friend, was lying on her stomach, contemplating a bowl of pretzels.

"Having fun?" Kate said to no one in particular.

"They hardly ever keep their clothes on," Jordana complained, "and their mother doesn't even care."

"I'm putting you in charge, Jordana," Kate said. "You're the deputy warden for the afternoon. If it looks like there's trouble on the way, make sure you come and get me."

"You could pay me like a dollar an hour," Jordana suggested. "And then I could use the money to get my ears pierced."

"Couldn't you just do it out of the goodness of your heart?" Kate said, and let the tablecloth fall from between her fingers.

"All set?" Tiki asked.

Kate shrugged, and gave her a little push in the direction of the bathroom, which they locked themselves into in a hurry, immediately collapsing on the floor, their backs against the strips of shiny silver wallpaper that Henry and Kate had put up only recently.

"We're too old to be smoking pot," said Kate as Tiki lit up a joint. "Aren't we?"

"I don't believe I know the answer to that," Tiki said. "I'm the mother of sixteen children and I don't know the answer to anything."

"Great." Sucking in the smoke awkwardly so that her mouth made a squeaking sound against the joint, Kate caught Tiki's smile and began to laugh just as she exhaled; in an instant she was coughing like mad. Tears pooled in her eyes and in one desperate gulp she swallowed down the cupful of water Tiki held out to her.

"Next time," Tiki advised, "JUST SAY NO!"

Laughing some more, they kicked off their shoes and climbed into the tub, taking seats opposite one another, the only way they could arrange themselves. Kate drew her knees up under her chin and watched Tiki's exhaled smoke shoot straight toward the ceiling and out the louvered vent. "Something's up with Henry," she told Tiki.

"I hate to say it, but your new wallpaper has got to go," Tiki said, shaking her head sadly.

"For one thing, he's been staring at the ocean too much in this terribly distracted way."

"Maybe," Tiki said, "the getaway car is actually a getaway boat. He's planning to make his escape by water, I bet."

"And who's at the helm?"

"Oh, your standard beautiful young blond."

"He's already got *me*," Kate said. "Except for the fact that I'm neither blond nor beautiful, I fit the description of his dream girl exactly."

"Don't look so worried," Tiki said. "Can't you tell when I'm teasing you?"

"Actually," Kate said, "you've got it all wrong. The dream girl in question happens to be about sixty years old with a doctorate in sociology."

"Cynthia?" Tiki said in horror.

"She's had her eye on him for months. All those phone calls must have come to something after all," Kate said miserably. "Henry came back from Boston exhausted, worn out in a way that wasn't entirely physical, that went beyond that to a kind of sadness or confusion, I don't know. He fell asleep on the couch before dinner and would have slept there all night if I hadn't gotten him up and into the bedroom, finally."

"It was three hours of driving in one afternoon, of course he was worn out. I know you don't like to think of him this way, but he's not so young anymore. He's an old guy," Tiki said gently. "As in, 'See that old guy drifting down the street with that beautiful young girl?' "

Goosebumps prickled the flesh of Kate's arms, as if this were truly a shocking revelation to her. "That?" she said. "That's nothing. It hardly scares me at all, in fact."

Turning weepy suddenly, she slid down along the length of the tub, her feet nearly in Tiki's face. "Funny, of all the problems I never thought we'd have, this is the one I *never* thought we'd have."

"What?"

"He's in trouble," Kate said in a whisper. "In love. It's not what he wants, he doesn't even know how he got there, but he's there and he can't figure a way out."

Tiki's eyes were closing now and there was a half-smile at her lips as Kate rearranged her own arms and legs, took hold of the roach that was about to burn Tiki's fingers, and flipped it into the toilet. Tiki yawned, then set her mouth back into a fuller smile. "You know," she said dreamily, "I was stopped at a red light in the center of town the other day, and as I sat there thinking about all the different ways there were to get to a place, I thought, Isn't the human brain an amazing thing?"

"Amazing," Kate said.

There was a frenzied pounding at the door now, a pair of plaintive, urgent voices belonging to Spencer and Fudge. "I have to go so so so so badly," one or the other of them said. "Let . . . me . . . in!"

"Men are so predictable," Tiki complained.

"My guess is that we ought to get out of here and let your kids in," Kate said as the commotion outside grew louder.

"I mean unpredictable," said Tiki.

"What?" Kate said, flipping herself over the side of the tub and heading for the door.

"My point precisely," said Tiki. "So when it comes to men, you can forget about trying to read those peculiar little minds of theirs—it's just an exercise in futility, believe me."

Either Spencer or Fudge was hurling himself against

the door now, as if he meant business. "I'm going to whiz right here on the floor," he threatened in a panicky, high-pitched voice. "Open up!" Kate threw open the door and stood back as the boys marched through in matching sweatsuits. "Is my mom here?" Fudge asked sweetly. Kate pointed to the tub, and he leaned over the side saying, "I just wanted to see you, Mom." He patted her cheeks delicately. "Get up," he said. "Your children are calling you."

Stumbling from the tub, Tiki grabbed Kate by the elbow on her way out. "Take my advice," she said. "Keep the husband and get rid of the wallpaper. Or vice versa, whichever seems right."

Later, in the evening, Seymour decided the family was going out for Chinese food. At the restaurant now, Darlan was clipped onto the table in her Sassy Seat and throwing handfuls of damp rice to the carpeted floor beneath her. She knocked a glass filled with ice into Henry's lap and tossed broccoli and baby corn across the table at Seymour. Hands gummy with hoisin sauce, she turned to her mother and slicked Kate's hair back lovingly. "Mama-doo," she said.

"Babies," Henry said, sighing. "Can't live with 'em, can't take 'em to Chinese restaurants. What good are they?"

"They're hardly worth the paper they're printed on," Kate said.

"Hey, they're not *all* bad," Seymour said, but didn't elaborate. When the bill came, he and Henry fought over it good-naturedly, until at last Kate said quietly, "Let it go, Henry."

"That's what my shrink said when I told him I was in love with you. Just think where we'd all be today if I'd listened to him," Henry said. He opened up his wallet and took out a credit card, snapping it sharply against the table.

"I'd rather not contemplate the answer to that, to tell you the truth," Kate's father said, and handed the card back to Henry.

"Seymour," Bunny said in warning.

"Seymour, what?"

"And here I thought we'd made such splendid progress in a single afternoon," said Henry. "What a disappointment."

Kate's father shrugged. "Two steps forward, three steps backward, you know how it is."

Darlan had dozed off with a chopstick clamped horizontally between her lips. "Doesn't she look like a dog with a bone in its mouth?" Kate said, laughing as she took the chopstick away. But the sound of her laughter was met by a thick dumb silence. Now the fortunes arrived in a chipped little bowl at the center of the table, and one by one an arm stretched out to claim a cookie. "What's the story?" Kate said, gesturing to her father.

" 'A fool and his money are soon parted,' " he read as he cracked open the cookie and removed the sliver of paper.

"You're joking, right?" Kate said. All of them were laughing now, Henry loudest of all. His shoulders trembled; tears leaked from the outer corners of his eyes and slid toward his ears.

"Would I joke about something as serious as a fortune cookie?"

Henry slipped his credit card back into his wallet. "I graciously defer to you, sir," he said to Seymour. "Next time, I'll be the fool, I promise."

"Now there's a promise I know you'll keep," Seymour said.

Kate and her mother each got the same good news: "Someone is praising you to the skies." "Could that be you, Seymour?" Bunny asked.

"Doubtful," he said, but leaned forward to drop a kiss at the top of her head.

Henry made a show of crushing his fortune cookie to bits with a single squeeze of his fist. " 'Ask and you shall receive; this includes trouble.' Now there's a warning if I ever heard one," he said darkly.

"You better watch it, buddy boy," Seymour said, waving a finger at him.

"Anyone who takes this nonsense seriously ought to have his head examined," Kate announced, but her hands shook as she eased Darlan out of her seat and pressed the baby to her in a delicate embrace. Darlan's head, in sleep, was damp and heavy against Kate's shoulder, her upturned cheek rosy and unutterably soft. Kate caught Henry looking at them so lovingly that she had to turn away. *I've got your number, kiddo,* she told him silently. *How dare you gaze upon us with such unmistakable love!* He came around the table to help her with her things—a plastic-lined bag filled with diapers, a change or two of clothing, and books and toys, some of which had spilled out onto the floor.

"Scram," Kate said, but she needed his help and his love and everything else he had to offer, and she was pained by the miserable look that flickered across his face before settling in for good. And so she allowed him to gather her things together for her, to slip the bag across one shoulder and take her arm, leading her past her parents and out into the waiting area near the cashier's desk. Two Chinese teenagers in T-shirts and shorts were doing stretching exercises there; a Chinese baby in a stroller, wearing an enormous red beret that fell down over one eye, sat sleeping behind the desk.

"I'm on to you, buddy," Kate told Henry in a fierce whisper.

He nodded almost imperceptibly, dropping her arm as if it were on fire.

CHAPTER NINE

This was my fantasy: I'm still married to Cynthia, and it's one of those times when she's taken off for parts unknown. And, as usual, I'm beside myself with worry, despair, rage, frustration. I phone Dr. Hochberg, who is thrilled by the sound of my voice, only too happy to hear from me.

"Let's hear it, Hochberg," I say. "Where is she, and why?"

"Atlantic City, of course. She hopped on one of those express buses they've got running a hundred times a day to all those casinos. It's like this," he tells me, "whenever she feels a clinical depression coming on, she goes down to Atlantic City and hits the slot machines. A perfectly harmless way of dealing with things, in my professional opinion, at least."

"Does she ever win big?"

"That I wouldn't know. You'd have to check your bank statements on that one."

"Well, thanks so much for your breach of confidentiality, Hochberg. I really appreciate it."

"Oh, anytime," he says. *"Anytime at all."*

I was on the phone with Cynthia now, half-listening to her new excuse for flying to Boston in a couple of weeks. Darlan and I were in the master bedroom, Darlan trying her hardest to take a few steps in my oldest, floppiest loafers. Kate was safe in her studio, at work on a new line of sympathy cards or thank-you notes—all I remembered seeing was a dainty splash of lavender and of green against the palest beige. I could have done with a little sympathy myself; she'd cast a cold shoulder in my direction in bed five nights running, and I hadn't felt so bereft in years.

"I don't want to sound boastful," Cynthia was saying, "but it's an endlessly fascinating subject."

"Escalators?"

"Elevators," she said. "Human behavior in elevators. My paper's going to be of intense interest to a certain segment of—"

"Excuse me, but aren't you the one who has to take five milligrams of Valium prior to hitching a ride on any elevator at all? What could *you* possibly know about the subject?"

"I had student volunteers do hours of observing for me. And I surveyed over two hundred people with a three-page questionnaire."

"And I don't believe a word of this."

"It's true," Cynthia said in a tiny voice.

"My theory is, you're planning a trip to Boston strictly for an afternoon of unbridled sex and passion," I said as Darlan fell flat on her face and howled in disappointment.

"Your insight into the ways of the human heart really floors me, Henry," Cynthia laughed.

"God knows, I've been around long enough." I set Darlan back on her feet, watching as she made her way to my dresser and struggled to open my underwear drawer. Taking pity on her, I pulled the drawer out half-way. "Have a field day," I said generously. Shorts and under-shirts streaked through the air in a blizzard of pure white until the drawer was absolutely empty. "Good work, wea-sel," I said.

"I don't know what you're thinking," Cynthia complained. "You're playing on the floor with your baby, I imagine, madly in love with her, not really paying any attention to me. . . . What is it, Henry? This is the first time you've called me, and I'm terrified, scared to death at what I'm going to hear next."

"What did Blossom tell you you're going to hear?"

"What do you think, at seventy-five dollars an hour I'm going to sit around listening to her predict the future? I might as well have my palm read by Miss Erica at the Psychic Boutique around the corner, if that's what I'm after."

"What did she say?"

"Who, Blossom or Miss Erica?"

"You went to a fortune teller?" I laughed out loud: Darlan had slipped her head through one leg of a pair of shorts and was admiring herself in the floor-length mirror at the back of the door.

"Don't laugh at me, Henry, I find it intolerable," Cynthia said sharply. "Especially at a time like this, when I'm in pain and having trouble breathing."

"What kind of pain?"

"Oh, it's nothing, my head just feels as if it's filled with poisons and is going to explode at any moment."

"Relax your body and take some *niccce deeep* breaths," I said in a soothing voice, mimicking the extrav-agantly sprightly Lamaze instructor Kate and I could never quite bring ourselves to take seriously during class.

"How am I supposed to relax when I feel like this?" Cynthia shrieked into the phone.

"Calm down," I said. "I'm going to wait right here while you get a hold of yourself, which I know, without a doubt, you can do."

"I can't."

"Put the phone down and shake out your arms and legs until they feel completely relaxed, more like limp, really. Once you've got that down, the battle's more than half-won. Our Lamaze instructor always—"

"Lamaze instructor?" Cynthia screamed. "I'm not in labor, you jackass, I'm just in pain!" She threw the receiver down, and I could hear it banging repeatedly against a piece of furniture, could see the plastic curls of its cord loosening and tightening as it sprang up and down. I called out her name a few times, then waited with the phone slung over my shoulder. "Henry," she soon said. "Guess what, Henry."

"You're sorry you called me a jackass?"

"That, too."

"Apology accepted."

"I know you'll be surprised to hear this, but my head didn't explode after all. After a while I felt a little pop, and then a kind of lightening and—"

"And the rest is history," I said.

"Are you still interested in Miss Erica's prediction?"

"Shoot," I said cheerfully.

"She said I would receive a proposal of marriage which I wouldn't be able to accept."

"Any particular reason why not?"

"No further details available at this time," Cynthia said.

"Okay. What about Blossom?"

"You know Blossom," Cynthia said with a sigh. "Always the voice of reason."

"And what does the voice of reason say?"

"That you've got too much to lose."

"You?" I asked.

"*You.*"

"The woman knows whereof she speaks." Darlan was hard at work now re-stocking my underwear drawer; there was something almost ostentatious in her bustling diligence. My heart speeded up as I watched her marching back and forth, a single piece of clothing in hand each trip. Cynthia was right: I was truly mad for this child, grateful for the sight of her as she carried one of my shoes across the room so industriously and then thumped it down into the drawer. I grabbed her with both hands on the return trip, sure that I would never let her go. But I could not keep her even now; in a moment she had bolted from my embrace, and was off and running.

"Hey," Cynthia was calling, her voice emerging small and faded from the receiver at my feet. "Henry!"

"Sorry."

"But you're not," Cynthia said. "And my self-esteem is hovering at about zero now."

"I want you to remember what our marriage was like," I told her softly. "And for those of you who can't remember, I'm going to let you in on a little secret: it was murder. It was hard labor, it was me pushing and pulling and never getting anywhere at all. And now finally I've gotten somewhere, to a place I've been on the lookout for all my life. It took me forever to get here and I wouldn't dream of leaving."

"I know all that," Cynthia said impatiently. "I'm not asking you to leave behind everything you have, I'm just asking for a bit of you from time to time, just enough to keep me going."

"I feel like I'm some kind of super-duper high octane gasoline," I said, unable to keep myself from laughing at just the wrong moment.

"Why should I be surprised that you're laughing?" Cynthia said. "Give me one good reason why I shouldn't have expected it."

"I'm sorry," I wheezed, laughing even harder now. I wanted terribly to sober up, but I simply couldn't get a grip on myself. "I just can't."

"It's not even that I love you," Cynthia told me. "Not at the moment, anyway. It's just a feeling of attachment that I can't ignore."

The perfect response came to me out of nowhere and abruptly I stopped laughing. "Just think of me as that noose around your neck," I offered helpfully. "Someone choking the life out of you at every turn."

"No good," said Cynthia. "Think of that afternoon we spent in bed together. Now *that* was life-affirming, and I can't keep my mind off it."

"Try," I said.

"I can't."

"Listen to me: I'm a noose around your neck. I'm a pain in the ass who never left you alone, who could never let you be. You wanted, more than anything, to be free of me and when it finally happened, the relief was so exhilarating you felt like dancing on the ceiling."

"I did not," Cynthia said.

"Sure you did."

"You're always exaggerating."

"One more reason for you to steer clear of me." I'd sweated through my shirt by now, as if I'd been fighting for my life, hanging by my fingertips from one terrifying moment to the next. My stamina was dwindling; I had to hang up the phone before I was drained of all my good intentions. "Cynthia," I said, "here's the rough stuff: I called to tell you your shadow's not to darken my door again. Your voice, too. If you call I won't be able to speak to you, not even for—" There was a clattering sound as Cynthia dropped the phone. "What was that?" I asked when she returned.

"That was me, throwing up my hands in despair and defeat, a classic gesture of surrender."

"Do you want to know how rotten I feel?"

"Not really," Cynthia said. "On the other hand, it might be good for my self-esteem."

"Well, for what it's worth, I feel awful. Wanting something that's not quite good for me, and forcing myself to walk straight past it, always makes me feel awful."

"You didn't exactly walk straight past it," Cynthia pointed out. "You stopped for a good long look, I'd say. You just didn't like what you saw."

"Oh, but I did," I said, closing my eyes for one last look just as Cynthia gently disconnected us. Eyes open again, I saw Darlan standing on top of an upside-down wastepaper basket, her arms outstretched for balance, her mouth set in a brilliant smile.

"Look," she chirped, and when, a moment later, I whisked her off her pedestal and clasped her against me, she socked me one right in the nose.

PART TWO

CHAPTER TEN

I have not been well in many months but I don't spend much time thinking about the end of my life; right now I'm only concentrating on how to live with a failing body, with muscles that have gone slack, that will not do what I want them to do. My speech is slurred as a drunk's, my gait unsteady. According to the thousand and one doctors I've seen, I will not be getting any better, only worse. I have decided to grab hold of each day one by one, and to pretend, at least for now, that if I will get no better, perhaps I will get no worse. And so life goes on, as it always does, only slower and with a little sadness, a sadness that will in time deepen, grow to something enormous and all-encompassing, I suspect. The flashes of anger I feel from time to time don't really amount to much—after all, I remind myself, I've lived a long and generous life and have been cheated of nothing. My worries center on Kate and Darlan. How will they manage? I'm consoled by the knowledge that there is some money and of course the house, and that Kate can always get a job as a commercial artist. I don't want to talk about it, she tells me. Not yet, anyway. I earned her forgiveness gradually; we never talk of Cynthia anymore. In my mind, and in Kate's too, I think, she is a million miles away, so distant that it's as if she never existed at all. Kate and I have other things on our minds. We make love early in the morning, several times a week, if I'm lucky. My arms hang dumb and heavy at my sides whenever I stand up; in bed, where we are now, they will not do as I ask, will not circle Kate impassionedly, will not make their slow teasing way up and down the length of her. The pain of this loss brings tears to my eyes, tears I'm incapable of brushing away. Dumb faithless body, I think murderously. But Kate knows just what to do; she drags my hands to her breasts, closes my fingers around each nipple. We pretend I've made it there on my own, and there is pleasure in that. I'm still me, after all, still eager to be swept away to that keen, sharpened edge of perfect pleasure.

Kate begins to lick sloppily at me everywhere now, and, too soon, it's all over.

"Thanks," I say, when my heart finally slows.

"Don't ever thank me," Kate says gravely. "I mean it."

"Why not?"

"You never thanked me before; there's no need to do it now."

"Why?"

With a lavender tissue, she wipes away the milky trail that leads from the tiny sunken pool of my navel all the way to my hip. "I just don't want to be thanked," she says. "Everything I do for you is for me, too. I want you," she says. "I want our happiness. So don't think of me as selfless. I'm just me, doing what I do."

"Okay," I tell her. "I'll never thank you again for anything."

"Good," she says, and goes off to run the bath for me.

The day promises excitement: after breakfast, we're going to interview a friend of a friend, the first (and only) candidate for the position of live-in companion in our uneasy household. In exchange for room and board and a small salary, whoever it is we hire will stick to me like glue, helping me to a standing position whenever I need to get up, linking his arm through mine when we go for walks on the beach, bringing forkfuls of food to my mouth at mealtime, turning the pages of a book or newspaper for me when I ask him to. Although Day O'Neill, our number one candidate, is a stranger to us, we have, in fact, seen him in action: in a former life he'd been a piano player at one of those food courts in a mall in Portland. Surrounded by Everything Yogurt, Souper Salad, La Tablita, and Sushi City, he sat at his baby grand playing Gershwin, Cole Porter, Stephen Sondheim. I remember him there, his head thrown back in extravagant sorrow, playing "What I Did For Love," as his noisy audience sipped and swallowed and chewed. From there, I'm told, he went on to a succession of part-time jobs, none of them satisfactory, all of them meant to sustain him in his real work, which was writing mysteries. I suppose he supposes that if I'm not too demanding, he'll have plenty of time to devote to his new book. Fat chance: once I get my hands on him (so to speak) I'll have him at the piano playing "Embraceable You" all day long.

Kate approaches me now dressed only in one of my undershirts. She places her hands, which are wet from testing the bath water, under my arms, and helps me off the bed and into the bathroom. She brushes my teeth and gets me into the tub, soaps me up, rinses me off, gets me out and dressed, sighs with exhaustion and, perhaps, despair. Such is her life. Such is our life.

"Don't sigh like that," I say. "It makes me feel like packing it in, checking out without so much as even the vaguest of farewell notes."

"You do that, sweetie, and I'll never speak to you again," she threatens. "And incidentally, that wasn't a sigh, I was simply exhaling, if that's all right with you."

"Exhale anytime you want," I say.

"I fully intend to."

"Good," I say. "See that you do."

Stopping outside Darlan's room for a quick peek at her in her crib, we watch as she feeds herself from a plastic cup full of Cheerios, greedily pressing the cereal up against her open mouth. "HIJKLMNOP," she sings after she finishes swallowing. Feeling our eyes upon her, she scrambles to greet us, casting one leg over the top of the crib.

"This isn't a gymnastic event," Kate says, running to the crib to rescue her. "If you want out, just say so."

"Out," Darlan shrieks. Then, "ABCD."

"ABCD to you, too," says Kate. Holding the baby aloft, she flies her close to my face so that Darlan and I can nuzzle noses.

Nose against nose, Darlan's flesh and cartilage pressed joyfully against my own, I nearly swoon with pleasure.

I don't want to give this up. Not any of it. If it were possible, I simply would not allow this moment to pass to the next.

"Fuck it," I say out loud.

"Nice language in front of this here highly impressionable child," Kate says, but tears flash in her eyes. "Fuck it," she echoes softly.

"Fuckit fuckit fuckit," Darlan chants, clearly savoring the sound of it.

"Naughty," says Kate. "We don't talk like that in this house."

"Yes we do," Darlan says.

After her sodden overnight diaper is changed, we navigate our way to the kitchen, where Darlan is swung into her high chair and I'm helped into my seat at the table. Kate scrambles eggs and pours glasses of juice; beneath her knee-length T-shirt the shape of her behind is beautifully evident. In my mind I've already crossed the room and goosed her.

Holding a juice glass to my lips now with one hand, she strokes my temple with the other. I imagine seizing her wrist and kissing each fingertip one by one.

The doorbell rings midway through breakfast, and Kate shoots out of the room for a bathrobe before answering it. When at last she opens the door, full of apologies, Day hangs back, reluctant to cross the threshold. He's full of apologies of his own for arriving half an hour early.

"Excessive fear of being late," he explains. "I've tried so hard to shake it, but I've never been able to." He stares beyond Kate straight into the kitchen and waves at me.

"Come in here, you," I shout, ashamed, for an instant (as I always am in the presence of strangers), at the distorted sound of my speech. "You're not afraid of me, are you? I couldn't hurt a fly, much as I'd like to."

Day laughs. "Finish your breakfast. I'll sit in the waiting room and catch up on my reading, if you'd care to throw some magazines my way."

"How about a few crumbs?" Kate says. "I was just about to fry some bacon, nitrates and all."

Following Kate into the kitchen, Day shakes his head.

"It's not the nitrates," he says. "I'm a vegetarian. I don't eat animal corpses."

"Not even a tuna fish sandwich?" I ask.

"Not since 1978," Day says. "Hope you're not offended by that at all."

"No problem," says Kate. "In fact, I was just telling Henry that soyburgers garnished with tree ears were on the menu for dinner tonight."

"To which I objected strenuously, I might add." I wink at Day, who looks bemused and forlorn. He's tall and nicely built, with plenty of dark wavy hair that's a little too carefully combed, suggesting an excess of vanity. I don't know: something tells me he may just be a little light in his loafers, but I wouldn't bet my life on it.

"Does this mean I don't get the job?" he asks.

"What?" Kate and I say in unison.

"Discrimination against vegetarians is more common than you might think," he says. "You'd be surprised."

"We're an equal opportunity employer," I assure him. "We make it a rule never to discriminate against a man just because he has an aversion to animal corpses."

Taking my hand from the table, Day squeezes it hard. "It's a pleasure to meet you, sir," he says. He moves on to Kate, shaking her hand as well, and then to Darlan, who's ornamented both her earlobes with bright bits of egg. "And this must be Darling," he says. "Aptly named, I'm sure."

"Go away," says Darlan matter-of-factly.

"We'll see about that," Day says. He puts his palms to the floor, throws his legs into the air and walks on his hands to the threshold of the room. "Catch you later," he tells Darlan.

"You're a funny man," she says.

"True, although I did flunk out of Clown College a week before graduation."

"Your face is bright red," Kate observes. "Maybe you ought to come down now."

He lowers his legs one at a time, does a back flip to impress us, and then rights himself. Panting slightly, he removes a comb from the pocket of his jeans and goes to work on his hair. "Did I pass the audition?"

"How does a person flunk out of Clown College?" I ask.

"Let's just say it was a personality conflict."

"Make a note of that on his résumé, Miss Pickles," I say, turning to Kate.

"Duly noted," she says, and nods. "Did you pass Juggling 101, at least?"

Day goes for the bowl of fruit at the center of the table and soon has two oranges and a tangelo dancing beautifully in the air.

"Hey," says Darlan, standing up in her high chair in astonishment. "Hey, you funny man."

"I am *so* impressed," I say. "Do you do windows?"

"No, but I sing for my supper." The oranges and tangelo fall neatly into the crook of his arm. "Actually, I don't sing at all. But I play the piano—I guess you know that, don't you."

"Sure, we've seen you at the food court a couple of times. That sushi place wasn't bad, as I recall. Did you ever try their California Roll? Great seaweed, not the least bit fishy."

"You were wonderful," Kate says. "I put a dollar in that brandy snifter full of tips you had sitting on top of the piano."

"So that's where the dollar came from," Days says, smiling. He begins to peel the tangelo. "If you do decide to hire me," he says, "you'll have to keep lots of fruit around. And cheese—that's my other mainstay. Any outrageously expensive triple crème will do."

"Hah," I say. "In this house all you'll get is some nice processed American cheese. You still want the job?"

"In all fairness, I have to warn you that I'm very particular about my pasta, too. I have to have the thinnest angel hair you can find, the stuff you only cook for ninety seconds."

"You're a hard man to please, O'Neill. And you did, after all, flunk out of Clown College. I don't know about you, O'—"

"He's a terrific juggler," Kate interrupts. "I say he's extremely well-qualified and we extend an offer immediately."

"We haven't even given him a detailed job description yet. Ever pulled an old man out of a bathtub before, O'Neill?" I say. "It's not a pretty sight, let me tell you."

"Day," he says.

"And that's another thing. Where'd you get a name like that from?"

"Family name," he says.

"Can we please get down to business?" Kate says, then explains exactly what helping care for me entails. She ends by offering a figure slightly higher than she and I had settled on. I raise my eyebrows but do not argue with her. Listening to the job description, to all the ways in which I need assistance, is utterly disheartening. Can this really be me? I'm a man who can't unzip his pants, who can no longer piss without a helping hand. Things could be worse, I remind myself. I could be thirty years old with lots of unfinished business. I could be sexually inactive, blind, deaf and dumb, and in excruciating pain. I could be unloved, neglected, abandoned. Looking now at Day's eager, attentive face, I feel my mouth forming a smile. "You sure you know what you're getting yourself into?" I ask him. "You could be driven crazy by me, you know. Once I get going, it's very hard to shut me up. What if I'm just a big bore who repeats the same uninteresting stories over and over again until you're ready to scream? What then, O'Neill?"

"No problem," Day says pleasantly. "I have a Sony Walkman that's always charged up and ready to go. I simply clamp on the headphones, turn up the music, and your boring stories will fall on deaf ears."

"Actually," I say, "there'll be no need for the Walkman. I'm really a very entertaining guy."

"Me too," Day says.

"Two peas in a pod," says Kate. "Where does that leave *me*?"

"Free to go about your business without a care," I tell her.

"Or something like that."

"Come on!" I say. "This is going to be great! It's what you've been desperate for all these months, isn't it?"

"Right," Kate says, sitting down beside me and leaning her head on my shoulder. She runs a finger along my arm, all the way down to my wrist.

"Come on," I repeat. "Don't tell me you're feeling guilty."

"Right again."

"Snap out of it!" I yell. "This is your big chance to get more work done, to spend more time with Darlan when she's not at her play group, to do all the things you need to do. There's nothing to feel bad about. God knows, we have enough to feel bad about as it is. So don't let guilt stand in the way of anything. And listen, if the tables were turned, I'd jump at the chance for something like this."

"You would?"

"Are you kidding? I'm no martyr. I see a way to ease things, I go for it. That's just called being sensible."

"Excuse me," Day says. He gestures to Darlan, whose cheeks and forehead gleam with the egg that she's cheerfully smeared all over her. "She's got scrambled egg in her nostrils," he points out.

"She's just being a show-off," Kate says. "You know the type—anything to get the world to take notice."

"Get me out of here, O'Neill," I say as Kate makes a grab for the baby with a washcloth. "Under the arms and then pull up," I explain.

The four of us end up in the living room, listening to Day's command performance at the piano. He starts out with Chopin and Beethoven and then answers my request for Gershwin.

"Embrace me, my sweet embraceable you! Embrace me, you irreplaceable you!" I sing to Kate. I sound like a drunk, but it's the only sound I've got and it's good enough. She puts her arms around me and we dance the slowest dance in the world, maybe our last. The music keeps going, a gift from Day that we forget to thank him for. It's just the two of us in our living room, refusing to let go.

CHAPTER ELEVEN

Henry sits in the bathtub wiggling his toes, obviously enjoying himself. "You know you're okay if you can still wiggle your toes," he tells Day. "When that goes, along with the ability to get it up, you know you're *really* in trouble." The things Henry tells him! The things they tell each other! This intimacy came quick and easy, fostered by the very nature of what Day does for him; his hands so often against the flesh and bone of Henry's failing body. There's something about giving another human being a bath, Day thinks, that relaxes the barriers between people and encourages them to give away all sorts of secrets. It was during the course of one of the first baths he gave Henry, several months ago, that Day found himself revealing to him that he was bisexual. Henry did not seem at all surprised or alarmed, did not shrug off Day's hand or stiffen at his touch. He simply nodded, saying, "Good for you," when Day told him he'd tested negative for AIDS antibodies and intended to keep it that way.

"Kate says you're due to have your hair washed," Day tells Henry now, and soaps up his head with some expensive shampoo he finds in a corner of the tub. He scrubs his scalp gently, thinking of Douglas, an ex-lover who always wanted him to shampoo his hair for him, insisting there was something erotic about it, though for Day there wasn't.

"You ever wash another man's hair?" Henry asks, reading Day's mind as he so often seems to do.

"Once or twice," Day says.

"Who's the guy? Anyone you've ever mentioned?"

"Just someone named Douglas. He had this manic-depressive ex-wife who liked to come around during her manic phases and clean up his apartment. She was like a whirlwind, mopping and glowing at a hundred miles an hour."

Henry laughs hard at this, saying, "I myself happen to know quite a bit about depressed ex-wives."

"Cynthia?" Day says. "Head back now," he orders, and rinses out the shampoo with cupfuls of fresh water from the sink. "It sounds to me," he says, "that getting dumped by her was the best thing that ever could have happened to you."

"We had our moments," Henry says, and sighs heavily.

"Now don't you go all nostalgic on me," Day says. "Especially on the subject of ex-wives."

Henry tips his head back and laughs. "You've got one too?"

"Doesn't everyone?" Day helps him up and over the side of the tub, towels him dry and gets him into his bathrobe. "We were happy for a time, a year or so, maybe, and then I started picking up guys in Bloomingdale's on Saturday afternoons. She found out about it and decided to leave me to go to dental school in Philadelphia. And that was the end of that." Henry apparently thinks this is hilarious; he's laughing like a madman, absolutely uncontrollably. "Get a hold of yourself," Day says. "It's not that funny."

"I love it," Henry says when he finally simmers down. "Especially the part about dental school."

"She did have exceptionally good teeth, I'll say that for her. Very white and very straight."

"Isn't it always like that," Henry says. "Optometrists always wear glasses, dentists always have good teeth."

"You're crazy," Day says, shaking his head. They go into the bedroom now and inspect the clothing Kate has laid out for Henry across the bed.

"What is she, my mother?" Henry says irritably, staring at Kate's choices: cuffed chinos, pink oxford shirt, polished loafers, braided belt. "Why does this have to be dress-up day?"

"I guess it's because your daughter's coming."

"All the more reason for me to be dressed as I usually am. I don't want to be standing there like some phony in a pink shirt and fancy pants. Let's get my sweatpants and sneakers and one of my sweatshirts with the sleeves cut off. Let Nina see my true casual self."

"Whatever you say, sir," Day says, and snaps his heels together sharply. Just after he's gathered the sweats and slipped Henry's bathrobe from his shoulders, Kate appears.

"Excuse me," she murmurs, and her face goes red, as if she's intruded on an intimate scene. Day realizes that the three of them have never found themselves together like this before—with Henry entirely undressed, and he and Kate standing around in embarrassment, not knowing where to focus their gaze.

"Hand me a fig leaf, will you?" Henry says, and all of them laugh at once.

Day helps Henry into his underwear and listens as he and Kate argue, predictably, about his clothing.

"You haven't seen each other in over twenty-five years," Kate says. "Why wouldn't you want to look presentable? And what's Nina going to think when she sees you looking like such a slob?"

"That I'm an extremely casual guy," Henry says. "Which indeed I am."

"I just want so much for things to go well between the two of you," Kate says. "I can't tell you how panicky I feel."

"You're the one who got us into this," Henry complains. "And may I remind you that I don't appreciate your making midnight phone calls to her in California behind my back, no matter how noble your intentions."

"It's your chance to fall in love with each other all over again," Kate says. "Now please please please get yourself into this shirt which I ironed so professionally and with such high hopes while you were in the bath." She holds the shirt out as if it were an object of great beauty, worthy of long and close examination. "Notice the points of the button-down collar," she teases him. "The monogrammed cuff, the—"

"Enough," Henry says. "But just remember that you owe me one."

"One what?" says Kate as she guides his arms so gently into the shirtsleeves.

"I'll think of something," Henry warns.

Later, when Day and Henry take their slow walk along the beach, their arms linked, Henry finally admits how frightened he is of seeing his daughter again.

"Scared stiff, to be exact," he confesses. "Although I must say I was a good father, patient, great at coming up with answers to all those unanswerable questions children always ask, great at sitting through all those Disney movies without falling asleep—*Cinderella, 101 Dalmatians, Song of the South*—you name it, I saw it. We were great together, Nina and I. Not much arguing, but a lot of talking, a lot of nestling in my lap without my even having to call her over to me. And then everything went bad, like mayonnaise left out too long in the sun. After her mother and I separated, I tried to keep up with Nina but it didn't work out. Her love for me evaporated, and after a while I just gave up trying to win her over again. I just gave up! Can you believe it? What a dumbass, lazy, inexcusable thing to do! So what am I supposed to say to her now? 'I'm sorry for going along my merry way and leaving you behind'? It's such an enormous failure in a father's life, impossible to live with, you'd think, but I managed to do just that, to glance back over my shoulder now and then and feel only a pinch, a spasm of pain, over what had been lost. And every so often there'd be a nightmare, getting me like an elbow in the stomach, something that would wake me at dawn and knock the air out of me for a few minutes. But I took it in stride, that elbow in the stomach, because that's always been my way."

Day senses that Henry has more to say, but his step is slowing, his speech slurring more than usual, as it does when he's tired. "Let's look out at the water for a while," Day suggests. The afternoon is lit only by a weak May sun, and yet it's unseasonably warm and muggy. Day can hear the good-natured shrieks from a volleyball game farther down the beach, can see the leaping figures and the flight of the ball across the net and back again. A borzoi and its master, both with excellent posture, parade by, and a mutt wearing a black bowtie clipped to its collar, followed by an aging hippie, his gray hair tied behind him in a limp ponytail. Three little boys, a trio of shirtless ten-year-olds sipping at cans of Pepsi, stroll past. Day wants to call out to them to put their shirts back on; the sight of their pale, narrow rib cages saddens him.

"Kate says she doesn't take much notice of the ocean anymore," Henry says, sounding disappointed in her. "She says it's like a piece of furniture she's had around forever and rarely uses. It's just something that's there, that's all. 'Just something that's there'?" he says in disbelief, shaking his head. "In the days when I was still driving, I almost always took the long way home, the drive along the ocean. Not Kate. She always takes the shortcut, coming around the back way to get home five minutes quicker. When I first brought her up here, when we were still living together in the city, before I retired, she claimed to love the smell of the ocean, the sound of the tide drawing back, the vastness of the sky. But when I got the idea of winterizing the house, of trading the city for all of this, she actually went pale. I had to work hard at talking her into it, at getting her to come here. I think she's made a pretty good adjustment, actually. But not to take pleasure at having the ocean right at our doorstep! Doesn't that seem crazy? Sometimes, when I find myself kind of passively staring out at the water, worrying over something, I don't know what, it comes to me that what I'm looking at is precisely the same sight that the Indians who were here a couple of hundred years ago saw. It's a real consolation to me that the ocean is unchanged, that it's all here just as it once was and just as it'll always be."

Hearing this, Day shivers. "It's a spooky thought," he says. "But each of us, I guess, finds comfort where we can."

"So you don't see it my way," Henry says, then falls silent.

A volleyball is suddenly rolling along the hard, damp

sand at Day's feet, bumping to a stop against his toes. He hoists the ball with both hands into the air and hears someone calling his name hoarsely. It's Tiki's husband, Rob, inviting them to watch the game.

As they head off in the direction of the net, Day is surprised to see that Kate is one of the players, along with Tiki, a divorced friend of hers named Nancy LeClerc, and a couple of neighbors—two fat teenage boys who, given their size, are astonishingly quick and light on their feet.

"Where's Darlan?" Henry asks Kate, after giving everyone a smile and a nod. "I thought you two were going to the supermarket or something."

"Done," says Kate, and spikes the ball over the net. "She's at Tiki's, with all the kids and a team of babysitters specially trained in the care and feeding of teeny tiny delinquents."

No smile from Henry. "I didn't know you played volleyball."

"I don't," Kate says. "I mean I didn't. I mean I haven't, not since high school."

"She's good," Rob calls out. "And with a little practice she's going to be real good. We're getting teams together for the summer and she's been drafted."

"Oh, I don't know," says Kate. "What do you think, Henry?"

"Are you asking for my permission?"

Kate makes a fist of her hand and serves the ball with a noisy punch. "Not really," she says. "I only wanted your opinion."

"In my opinion, a little physical exercise is always good for the soul," Henry says stiffly.

"What about Day?" Nancy says.

"What *about* me?" Nancy and Day have had a not-very-successful blind date, most of which was spent on a dissection of her failed marriage. After Day had given her a single, uninspired good-night kiss on the cheek, she asked him if he'd been tested for AIDS. Wiping the imaginary print of his kiss from her face, she'd burst into tears. "It's just so hard," she told him, and Day had to agree, promising that he'd call her again soon. But he hasn't and he won't. She's too fragile for him, too desperate for happiness. Staring at her now, her expression so hopeful and expectant, Day wants to shake his head at her gently, let her know she's looking in the wrong direction.

"Let's see you show your stuff," Nancy urges. "Come on, Day."

"Not me," he tells her. "And anyway," he says, tightening his grasp on Henry's arm, "I'm on duty."

"Take a leave of absence," Rob shouts. "We want to check out your serve."

"Go on," says Henry. "If I could give you a push, I would."

"You would not," Day says.

"You're right, I wouldn't," Henry says. "But that's just because I happen to be feeling like a selfish old man at the moment. Be that as it may, I want you to feel free to go ahead and enjoy yourself."

"Yeah, feel free," Kate says. "And remember: the employer is always right."

Settling Henry on the hard sand in his good clothes, feeling more than a little like a traitor, Day joins the others. His first serve goes straight into the net, but he's given another chance. He knows he's blown it as soon as the ball leaves his hands.

"Strike two," Rob calls meanly.

Third try and he's over the net finally, his palm and knuckles stinging, his heart beating like mad. It's a terrific serve, swift and high, absolutely unreturnable.

"Way to go, Day!" Kate shouts, and rushes over to hug him, and for the first time since he's known Henry, for the very first time, he realizes later, he's actually forgotten all about him.

CHAPTER TWELVE

Peeking out our living room Levolors, watching Nina emerge from the cab, what I notice first about her is her long, long legs and big feet, both courtesy of her mother. She's dressed in white cotton leggings, white jacket, a pink, billowy, knee-length T-shirt, and shoes that look like ballet slippers. Her dark hair is cut punk-short and gleams with some kind of styling mousse, I suppose.

"Get away from the window," Kate hisses, and just then the doorbell sounds.

"Goddamnit, I left my speech in my other suit," I tell her. "My opening remarks were in one pocket and my reading glasses were in the other."

"You'll just have to improvise," Kate says, laughing. "You know, say what's in your heart."

What's in my heart: guilt, terror, excitement, more guilt, more terror. And in my throat a salty lump that refuses to dissolve. I swallow hard one more time, feel the lump rising high in my throat before it settles back in its familiar place. I watch as Kate struggles to the front door, Darlan wedged stubbornly between her knees. The door opens; there is laughter as Nina bends to greet her half-sister.

"Is your name Princess?" she asks Darlan. "No? Kitten? Petunia? Peaches? It's none of the above? Is it Duke?"

"Duke!" Darlan exclaims. "That's a dog's name."

"Oh, *I'm* sorry," Nina says. "I thought you were a little dog."

"I'm a ghorl."

"No you're not. You're a cute little dog. Isn't that a tail I see?"

"Where?" Darlan says, and abruptly bursts into tears. Reaching downward, Kate swings her up from the floor as Nina backs off.

"Whoops," Nina says. "I guess I went a little too far."

"You look like someone at a loss for something to do," I say as quickly as I can. "Stop wasting valuable time and come over here and give your old father a kiss." Miraculously, in a flash, she's at my side, her hands on my shoulders, her mouth at my cheek. My face burns at her touch; my feet tingle and sweat. My arms just hang there, as if they belonged to someone else.

"Haven't we met somewhere before?" Nina says as she takes a step backward to check me out. She says nothing at all about my slurred speech, for which I'm grateful.

"You're too skinny," I tell her. "Other than that, you're just fine."

Nina continues to look me over, staring hard at my face, searching for clues, for something familiar. "I don't remember you," she announces finally. "I mean I do, but not with any clarity. Or maybe it's that I remember things you did, but not you. You took me to see *The Shaggy Dog* and *Flubber*. And to the Empire State—"

"Never," I say. "I would never take you to a movie called *Flubber*. I always maintained the highest cultural standards with you. I read *Little Women* to you, a chapter a night. Do you remember that?"

Nina nods. "But I also remember *Flubber*. And after we went to the Empire State Building, you bought me a poodle made of glazed popcorn, wrapped in pink cellophane. It had a candy eye that you wouldn't let me eat. I wanted that candy eye more than anything in the world but you kept saying the sugar was bad for my teeth, and finally you broke it off and threw it in the trash."

"I'm awfully sorry," I tell her. "You can have all the candy you want now."

"Too little too late," Nina says, looking me straight in the eye.

Embarrassed, I smile at her for a moment, hoping for forgiveness, but on the subject of the candy eye, at least, she's resolute.

"Don't smile at me," my daughter says.

"I was just thinking how pretty you are." And she is: clear turquoise eyes, lovely fair skin, a tiny, perfect nose. "Excuse me," I say, "is that the nose you were born with?"

"Absolutely," she says.

"The eyes too?"

"I'm getting a little tired of this, Henry."

"They're turquoise, for crying out loud. And call me 'Dad.' "

"Okay: the nose is mine, the eyes aren't. Any more questions of a highly personal nature?"

I'm exhausted suddenly and need to sit down. Turning around to ask for Kate's help, I see that she and Darlan have vanished.

"Are you all right?" Nina asks. "You look awfully tired."

"I didn't realize we were alone."

"You didn't see Kate and the cutie pie sneaking out the front door?"

"I guess Kate decided we could use the time together."

"Sweet of her," Nina says.

"I have to ask you to help me sit down," I say. "The couch right over there." With her assistance I lower myself onto a corduroy cushion, thinking, in my vanity, If only she could have seen me on the racquetball court, on the golf course, swimming laps at the 92nd Street Y in the city! I'm a big strong guy, I want to say. Never sick a day in my life.

"It's not what you think," I tell her. "I mean I'm not what you think. What you're seeing isn't me. I'm the guy women couldn't pass up. I was sixty-eight when Kate married me, and no one was holding a gun to her head, believe me. She couldn't *wait* to marry me. My shrink, a guy my own age, used to listen to me in disbelief—his tongue was hanging out, he was so envious." An exaggeration, but I smile at the thought anyway.

Nina returns my smile. "Good for you!" she says. "So how come you were so lucky?"

I have my answer ready in an instant. "I have great personal charm, you know. People kind of naturally gravitate toward me. They *love* me!"

"I see," Nina says, rolling her eyes, as if there were a third person in the room who could appreciate her sarcasm.

"Okay, forget *that* theory. Maybe it's my exceptionally high self-esteem. People respond to that, you know. Especially women. They see a man who knows his own worth and they find that very attractive." But then I remember the deep depression I was in when Kate and I first met. I was a sorry mess of a human being, dragging myself back and forth to work on the subway, unable to eat or sleep well, falling victim to anxiety attacks that left me weak and trembly and tearful. I kept bumping into things and scraping up my shins, burning myself on the toaster oven, dropping pots and pans on one foot or the other, and once actually breaking a toe. At night, after dinner, I lay for hours at a time across my bed, my arm flung over my eyes, shutting out light, hope, everything. So it couldn't have been my high self-esteem Kate was so hooked on at first.

"Damned if *I* know," I tell Nina. "What's *your* theory?"

Nina shrugs. "We're strangers, you and I," she says. "It's almost as if we've never met."

Strangers! The word gets to me like an ax thrown straight at my heart. I search frantically for anything I can offer up as proof that once I'd been at her side, that once, briefly, we'd lived a life together. The memories I'm able to unearth are strange, charmless ones, not for retelling: Nina's cake at her first birthday party sliding from the plate, landing right-side up on the carpet, her mother removing the lint from it with a pair of tweezers; Nina in a kindergarten play speaking her lines in a monotone, her eyes glued to the stage floor, her shoulders hunched; Nina, age four or so, biting my hand right through a leather glove because I insisted she take off her wet boots before we entered the living room of our apartment.

I tell her these stories anyway, proof that we are not, after all, perfect strangers.

"But you don't remember me!" she cries. "Me! Who I was, what you felt for me."

"I remember exactly who you were," I say. "You were tough when you didn't get your way, infuriating. You never gave up. Never. You were two and a half or three, and wanted a chocolate egg once for breakfast, and I said no. Your hurled yourself at me, tried to knock me over, you were so angry. You were shrieking and dancing around like a little madman, utterly enraged. I had to send your mother out of the apartment finally because she couldn't bear it. And finally you collapsed. You didn't give up; you simply fell asleep. On the kitchen floor. I got down beside you and stared at you in amazement. My beloved child, so willful and tough. I listened to you breathe, watched the rise and fall of your belly. It was chilly and I covered you with whatever was in reach—a dishtowel that was hanging over a cabinet door. I sat there with you on the kitchen floor, mesmerized by the sight of you, unable to leave your side." I look up at Nina now, sure of what I will see: a face I have known forever. "It's you I remember. What you were. What you were to me."

"A pain in the ass, it sounds like," Nina says, but there are tears in her startling turquoise eyes.

"Kids are," I say. "But then we all are, in our own way. We do the wrong things, say the wrong things, then go back and do it wrong all over again. But sometimes, if we're lucky, we get it right and it's wonderful. Like this marriage of mine. I struck out twice, but in my old age I finally made it to home. Look at me! Baby, I'm doing just great!"

Nina is staring at me as if I've truly lost it. A couple of tears are trailing down her face, spilling off the edge of her jaw and onto her T-shirt.

"Stop that," I say. "And there's a tissue in my pants pocket for those of us who might need it."

"I wasn't going to come," Nina says as she goes into my pocket. "I told that to Kate. I wasn't thrilled getting your Christmas cards; I didn't even like thinking about you all these years. I was sorry to find out you weren't in great shape, but what did that have to do with me? But Kate was so determined not to let go. I actually hung up on her, and she called me back the very next minute. I challenged her at every turn, but after a while I saw that she was stronger than me, that she was perfectly willing to stay up all night and have it out with me. 'You win,' I told her finally, and then I went off with my boyfriend and got myself a little drunk. And here I am two weeks later, sober as can be and—"

"Boyfriend?" I say. "I thought you were still married to . . ." My head is reeling at the thought of all that effort of Kate's just to get Nina here. My gratitude, though, is mixed with humiliation: I can just imagine the pathetic portrait of me she must have painted. And the weary sound of Nina's "You win," her sigh traveling cross-country in a single moment.

"John Meyer!" I say triumphantly. "Am I right? Now what's the story on this husband of yours?"

"We're separated," Nina says. "He got a non-speaking part in a Michelob commercial and it went to his head."

"I thought he did something with computers."

"He did. He used to design software, but after the Michelob commercial he got a speaking role in a Honda commercial and actually quit his job. He started tweezing the fuzz in the space between his eyebrows and blow-drying his hair in a way I found offensive."

"So you left him?"

"I asked him to move out. Listen, I'm a toxicologist. I do experiments on rats' brains. How can I relate to a person in a TV commercial who gets pleasure out of saying, 'Save hundreds more on factory options! Now!' Dressed in a gorilla costume, no less."

"Rats, gorillas, I don't know, there must be a connection somewhere," I say.

Nina shakes her head. "He's not the person I thought he was. It's a terrible disappointment."

"And your boyfriend?"

"We're doing research for the same drug company. We speak the same language."

"Ah," I say. "The language of little white rats. How romantic."

"You're alienating me, Henry. I flew across the country to be with you and here you are making fun of my love-life."

"Call me 'Dad,' " I say, then smile, for only an instant, at the memory of hearing those same words from Kate's father.

"I can't," Nina says. "I'd like to, but I can't. Maybe later. Maybe later it'll just slip right out very naturally, without either of us even—"

"I haven't earned the right to the title, is that what you're telling me?"

"Listen, I have something for you," Nina says. "A gift, I guess you'd call it." Rummaging around in her bag, she comes up with a tiny package wrapped in deep blue tissue paper and tied in purple yarn. She opens it for me and holds out a card, about the size of a business card, trimmed in what looks like gold dust. "It's from the turn-of-the-century," Nina explains. "The man in the antique store said these little cards used to come in cigarette boxes, kind of like fortunes."

"Read it to me."

"You've got to read it yourself."

"Can't without my glasses. You know, middle-aged eyes and all that." They're on the mantel, resting on the nose of a fake marble bust of Mozart. Nina brings them to me, slips the wire side-pieces along the curve of my ears. She frames the card between her fingers.

"Read it again, with feeling," she says.

" 'May the fiery trials of adversity lead us to scenes of bliss.' "

"Well?"

"Well," I tell my daughter, "perfect bliss would be better, of course, but I'll take it any way I can get it."

CHAPTER THIRTEEN

At the dinner table, Henry sits with a long white trail of paper towels tucked in the round neck of his shirt, the paper reaching all the way down into his lap. Nina is at his side, cutting up pieces of chicken breast and baked potato, feeding them to him at a pace too quick for Henry to manage.

"Slow down," Day says. "Give him a chance to swallow."

"Sorry," says Nina. She leans across the plate for a napkin, a sip of ice water, anything at all, and the whole plate of food slips off the edge of the table and onto the kitchen floor, breaking into pieces. "Good work, Nina," she says.

"You're a naughty ghorl," Darlan says cheerfully.

"Girl," Kate says.

"She's my big girl," Henry says. "And she's not naughty."

"She *is* a naughty ghorl," Darlan insists.

"Girl!" says Kate. She's on her hands and knees, collecting bits of chicken and potato mixed with shards of china. Ever since Nina's arrival two days ago, Kate has been on edge, annoyed with everyone, Nina most of all. Henry and his daughter have been getting along famously, exactly as Kate had hoped, and yet there is something unsatisfying about this, she has found, something that makes her body stiffen with displeasure at the sound of their laughter, at the sight of a fork or a spoon or a glass in Nina's hand rising so eagerly to Henry's lips. Deliberately now, as she starts to lift herself up from the floor, Kate steps lightly on the toes of Nina's foot in its ballet slipper, lightly, but just hard enough to cause Nina to cry out in pain and surprise. "I'm sorry," Kate murmurs, but she knows she would do it again, given the opportunity. She is, she realizes with alarm, jealous; what else could it possibly be? It is as if they are rivals for Henry's affection, or, more accurately, his gratitude, the two of them competing for the chance to wipe away the crumbs lingering at the corner of his mouth, to comb his hair for him with the perfect gentle touch, to flip the pages of his newspaper with just the right timing. And, too, Kate realizes, she is envious of their ancient history, the deep past that the two of them, Henry and his daughter, seem to delight in bringing to the surface: memories of movies they saw together, books he read to her, songs he sang to her as she drifted toward sleep thirty years ago. It's utterly senseless and stupid, Kate tells herself, all this resentment she feels toward Nina, and yet there it is.

"She's a naughty naughty naughty ghorl," says Darlan in a sing-song, and then Kate is beside her, lightly slapping her daughter's silky little wrist just for the pleasure of it.

Darlan looks at her curiously, without anger. "I'm calling the police," she announces, and drags her chair to the telephone mounted on the wall. "Hello, police?" she says into the receiver. "My mom slapped me." She nods her head slowly. "Okay, goodbye."

"What did they say?" Kate asks her.

"They said I was *not* naughty, what do you think."

"What do I think? I think it's important to be nice to people."

"*You're* not nice."

"Wrong!" Henry calls out. "But she'd be even nicer if she'd bring me a new plate of food."

"I'll get it," Nina says. "After all, I'm the one who—"

"I'll get it," says Kate, and is already at the counter, carelessly, furiously, cutting up food into pieces far too large for Henry or anyone else.

"How am I supposed to eat this?" Henry says, looking down now at the plate in front of him.

"I know," Kate says. "I mean, I don't know. I'm sorry."

"You're tired," Henry says. "It's a long day."

"It's always a long day."

"I want to kick you, Mom," Darlan says, approaching Kate with a smile. Sticking one leg out in the air behind her, stretching out her arms for balance, she says, "Or else I want to be a ballerina."

"I vote for the ballerina," Kate says as Darlan lowers her leg to the floor. "Clearly a much better choice."

"I don't love you and I want to shoot you," Darlan says. She climbs into Kate's lap and pinches her cheek. "Okay?"

"You don't have to love me but you definitely may not shoot me."

"But I want to."

"Don't you love me even the littlest bit?"

"Not really," Darlan says.

"Well, then, I'm leaving."

"Wait," Henry says. "You can't leave. I happen to have the number of the parent abuse hotline right here in my pocket. Give them a call and see what they have to say."

"And what do I tell them?" Kate says. "My life is being threatened by a two-year-old?"

"Don't forget the part about her unconditional love being withdrawn," Henry says.

"Maybe I better write all this down."

"You know," Nina says, "John and I once thought about having children. But it was just an idea we considered, you know, like putting a skylight in our kitchen or a sauna in the second bathroom. In the end we decided it just wasn't necessary."

"Like the sauna and the skylight?" Henry says.

"Actually, we had the skylight put in after all. Sometimes we would stand in the middle of the kitchen, holding hands and watching the moon at night and—"

"That is really sick," Kate hears herself say.

"It was actually very romantic," Nina says.

"That wasn't what I meant." Darlan's fingers are at Kate's face again, delicately stroking her eyelids and then her brow. "This doo up doo dee dah day," Darlan sings.

"What *did* you mean?"

"I think," Henry says, "it was your choosing the skylight over the ch—"

"Never mind," says Kate.

"You don't like me very much," Nina tells her. "But it's not a problem; I can handle it." She is cutting Henry's food into smaller and smaller pieces, and feeding them to herself dreamily.

"What are you doing?" Henry asks.

"Of course I like you," Kate says. "I invited you here.

I bent over backwards to get you here. Why wouldn't I like you?"

"I have no idea," says Nina. She puts Henry's fork down. "You tell me."

Abruptly, Day rises from his seat, pushing his half-finished dinner toward the center of the table. "I think I'm about to go for an extremely long walk," he announces.

"Sit," Kate says. "This isn't going to get any worse. It's just—" She throws up her hands. "Just that I'm not coping too terrifically all of a sudden, that's all. And it's a surprise, really, because I'm someone who's always been able to deal with things. When we first realized Henry was sick, when we were off to three, four doctors in a row and listening to the same bad news phrased a little differently each time, I thought, This is impossible, I can't face this, this wasn't meant to be. And then after a while I let myself see just where we were. We're on a slippery slope, Henry and I, and it would be foolish to deny that. But let me tell you, I've been digging in my heels like crazy, and I'm doing okay."

"She is," Henry says. "And so am I. We're doing just great."

"God, I hope so," Nina says.

"What about you?" Henry asks her. "Are you happy you came?"

Nina doesn't answer, but rubs her jaw soundlessly, as if to ease the pain of a toothache. "It's like I found you, only to lose you," she says finally, in a whisper.

"Nah," Henry says. "I'm not going anywhere til I'm good and ready."

"I want to go wish you," Darlan says, sliding off Kate in a hurry. "Where are you going?"

"Nowhere," Henry says. "I'm going nowhere at all."

"Are you going to the bank?" Darlan asks.

"Nope."

"To the sukermarket?"

"Supermarket," Kate says. "And no, he's not going there, baby."

"The cash machine?"

"Nope nope nope," says Henry.

"I want to go wish you," Darlan cries. Her face is bright with fury now; she stamps her feet and waves her arms frantically.

"Kind of reminds you of a war dance," Henry says. "A feather and a headband and a little fringed skirt and vest and she'd be all set."

Tipping her chair back on two legs, Nina smiles. "Children are so natural," she says. "Listening to them cry is like looking at a sunset—a wonderful natural phenomenon. It's fabulous, really. I feel like I could listen to her for hours."

"What the hell are you talking about?" Henry says.

"I don't know, I just think it's great that children are so free, that they can express themselves any way they please. Look at her go! Look at her stomping around like that! It's wonderful, isn't it?"

"Does this have anything to do with your living in California all these years?" Henry says. "Please tell me it does."

Nina seems puzzled. "I don't think so," she says. "But it may very well have something to do with the fact that I'm about to get my period. It's always the same thing—every month, at just about this time in my cycle, I'm almost always blessed with some real interesting insights, which I'm able to articulate at great length. John couldn't stand it. He used to hook himself up to headphones, turn on the CD player, and just kind of tune me out."

"Hard to imagine why," Day murmurs.

"Well, everyone has his or her tolerance level, that point beyond which they simply—"

"All right, that's it," says Kate. She strides across the floor to Darlan, who, though clearly in a rage, appears to be tapdancing, her tiny, jerky steps performed with real flair. Kate seizes her by the shoulders and says, "How about a Devil Dog?" Darlan comes to an immediate halt. She breathes heavily for a few moments, then pushes her hair from her face with both hands.

"Okay," she says. "One Devil Dog and one orange Gummy Bear. And one red one, how about that, Mom?"

"We don't have any Gummy Bears," Kate says in a tiny voice. "You finished the last one yesterday, I think."

Darlan shakes her head. "I want to show you," she says. Climbing onto her chair at the telephone, she lifts herself to the countertop and flings open the cabinet doors above. "Here you go," she says, taking down a small plastic bag. "One red and one orange."

"Thank you, Lord," Kate sighs.

"Amen," says Henry.

Leafing patiently through Henry and Kate's wedding album, Nina says, "I love weddings on the beach. How come I wasn't invited?"

"No relatives allowed," Henry says. "Just a small number of very close friends."

"Come on," says Nina, "not a *single* relative?"

"Put it this way," Kate says, coming around from behind the couch and sitting down beside Henry, "those relatives who were invited chose not to attend."

"Idiots," Nina says. "That kind of narrow-mindedness is just so hard to fathom. Your own parents, for crying out loud!"

"Well, they've made real progress since then."

"Yes indeed, her father's just crazy about me," Henry says. "Or at least he was for about nine minutes once when he was slightly drunk. We exchanged war stories and danced cheek to cheek, as I recall."

"Not the most joyous of weddings, but the food was great," Kate says. She finds a photograph of the two, ten-pound poached salmon they'd had to keep in their bathtub overnight, half-covered in ice, olives at their eyes, wedges of lemon at their gills. She cannot remember eating a forkful of anything that afternoon, only the awful humidity inside and outside the house, her feet sliding around in her shoes, the perspiration trickling down between her breasts, while Henry worked the room with such ease, shaking hands, patting shoulders, agreeing with everyone that yes, he was the luckiest guy in the world.

So quickly, it seemed, so cruelly, his luck had run out. Her luck. Marrying him, she had not let herself linger too long over the possibility of disaster, the infinite variety of terrifying possibilities. While it had been true that Henry wasn't young, it had also been true that he was healthy and strong. And there was always, so comfortingly, the example of her grandfather to point to: at ninety-one, he lived entirely alone, without complaint except for a touch of arthritis that flared in his fingers and toes now and then and that was, to hear him talk about it, more of an inconvenience than anything else.

So. What is left for her to take comfort in? There is Henry's lively presence, his warm, eager self that will not submit to despair, either his own or hers. In bed he does not wait for her to make the first move, but turns toward her with excitement, armed with kisses that go a long way. He is determined to make the most of everything, absolutely everything; who is she to deny him the pleasure?

He will leave her, as they both knew, always, that he would. But why so soon, she wants to ask him. Why does it have to be so soon? All along she had been counting on a good strong measure of happiness that would last and last. She could not foresee, cannot foresee, the end of it. She cannot imagine Henry vanishing, disappearing from this life of theirs. She has heard somewhere that, while dreaming, a man cannot envision his own death. It simply isn't possible. And so it is with Henry's; her imagination cannot take her that far.

She kisses the side of his face now, the cool smooth rosy flesh that she loves so dearly. "Is that me?" she says, staring at a photograph that shows her standing alone at the linen-covered table which holds the two beautifully poached salmon of their wedding feast. "I look so young," she marvels.

Henry laughs uproariously at this. "Baby, you *are* so young," he says.

She smiles back at him, as if to say, Of course. She will not let him in on her secret, that there is nothing like this downward swing of luck to send you flying, straight through to your old age.

CHAPTER FOURTEEN

I know just what Seymour's thinking as he stands in the doorway of my home giving me the once-over. *Henry, you poor son-of-a-bitch,* he's thinking.

This father-in-law of mine is uninvited, but here nevertheless. Here to check up on me and, more importantly, his daughter.

"Cut it out, Seymour," I say, knowing he can barely understand me and my impossibly sloppy syllables. Listening to me, his mouth falls open in an astonished "O." "Close your mouth, Seymour," I tell him. "And come on in and have a seat."

Kissing her father in greeting, Kate says, "I told you not to come, Daddy. I asked you not to come. Begged you not to come. Am I right?"

Seymour shrugs. "You know fathers," he says. "They read between the lines, and after that, there's no stopping them."

"And will you be staying for dinner?" I ask him.

"Dinner?" he says, looking to Kate for confirmation. "Did he say 'dinner'?"

"Watch his lips and concentrate, and before you know it, you'll be doing fine," Kate advises.

"Check-out time is traditionally eleven o'clock around here," I say. I'm enjoying myself enormously, taking pleasure in his discomfort. It's easy enough to feel this way, knowing that all along he's disapproved of me, disapproved of my hold on his daughter. But I can't help feeling sorry for the guy, who clearly can't believe what he sees. And hears.

"What of your lovely bride?" I say. "Couldn't convince her to come along?"

"Don't look at *me*," Kate tells her father. "Concentrate."

"Bunny," I say, deciding to give the guy a break.

"Bunny? She's furious at me for doing exactly what you asked me not to do. But she sends her love and also some sour cream brownies. The kind with the chocolate chips in them. Let's see, they've got to be somewhere in my overnight bag here. Kate," he says, his voice growing louder and more deliberate, "would you mind helping me put them away in the kitchen?"

"In the kitchen?"

"Isn't that where you usually keep your food?"

"Usually but not always," Kate says blithely. Like me, she's enjoying herself, standing there with her sly smile, her hands cupped behind her back, as if she were hiding something.

"Kate," Seymour says.

"What is it?"

"KATEI'MBEGGINGYOU!" her father shouts, red-faced.

"Begging me for what?" Same sly smile, broadening now into a grin. "And no yelling."

"What I'm begging for," Seymour says, "is two minutes alone with you."

"Don't mind me," I say. "I only hear what I want to hear, anyway."

"Henry, I'm sorry," he tells me. "I am *so* sorry." He looks dazed, a man who's had the breath knocked out of him and can't figure out what hit him.

"Take him into the kitchen for some Valium and a nice big glass of water," I tell Kate.

"Just water," Seymour murmurs.

This, perhaps, is their whispered conversation in the kitchen:

> Seymour: He looks awful.
> Kate: What do you mean?
> Seymour: You want to know what I see when I look at him? A man who's not long for this world, that's what.
> Kate: Why are you telling me this?

When they return, two or three minutes later, I say, "What a surprise. I wasn't expecting the two of you back until midnight."

"The water was excellent," Seymour says. "First-rate, really. Very refreshing."

"That Kate is such a gracious hostess," I add.

"Daddy has this idea that we should move back to New York," she tells me, rolling her eyes none too subtly so I can tell just what she thinks of this. "Where all the good doctors are."

"Thanks, but I prefer to die in my own bed, which has a great set of box springs and provides an excellent view of the ocean." I say this extraordinarily slowly and as distinctly as possible, so Seymour won't miss a word.

"Don't talk like that!" he cries.

"Believe me, I wish I could do a whole lot better. You can't imagine how frustrating it is."

"Not that," Seymour says. "I mean, don't say things like that."

"Ah," I say. "It's my content you object to, not my style. Come to think of it, it's *me* you object to. It's always been me, hasn't it?"

"Never," says Seymour. "It's always been the situation."

"You know, you remind me of a father-in-law I once had, this goes back almost forty years. He—"

"Thanks," Kate interrupts, "but I think we'll pass on that one."

"Fine, then let's just concentrate on the one and only father-in-law I've got. Listen Seymour," I say, "you can stay for dinner and a sleep-over, but only if you promise to butt out of my personal affairs. Please restrict your comments to the weather, sports, WW Two, the weather . . ."

"You said that already," Kate points out. "Wouldn't you like to come to the bathroom and freshen up?"

"Why? Does my nose look like it needs powdering?"

"It's just that you've been sitting there so long I thought you might want to move around a little." Kate approaches and starts to give me a hand out of the chair.

"Avert your eyes, Seymour," I say.

"What?"

"Even better, close them."

"Can I make a wish?" Seymour says.

"Absolutely, providing you don't wish for the impossible."

"This is killing me, goddamnit," we can hear Seymour grumbling as we leave the room.

In the bathroom, Kate washes my face without her

customary gentleness, rubbing the washcloth across my cheeks impatiently. "Really," she says, then falls silent.

"I want him out of here by sunrise," I say. "I don't want to get up in the morning and find him sitting at my breakfast table all nice and cozy, reading the newspaper and asking for seconds of French toast."

"He's my father, Henry."

"All right then, he can stay for the French toast and then that's it, out he goes."

"When Nina was here in the spring she stayed for nearly a week."

"Nina," I say, "was fun to have around. She was entirely accepting of us." Here Kate gives me a look that makes my heart sink. "Nina *wasn't* fun to have around? How come I'm hearing this now for the first time?"

"Do you have to pee?" Kate asks. She takes down my pants and aims me in the right direction, then looks away. At this moment, it strikes me that if only I could pee without supervision, I'd be the most contented man in the world. In the universe.

"Shake, please," I say, and sigh as my wife shakes off the two drops shimmering at the tip of my penis. "Do you know how much I hate this?" I ask her.

She nods silently.

"Don't tell me it's nothing in the grand scheme of things," I say.

"It's something. Just something neither of us had bargained for." She brings my pants back up, tucks in my shirt. I stand in front of the mirror above the sink and check myself out. My face is a little slack, my eyes a little droopy, but I can still see myself. What, I wonder briefly, will it be like, when I can no longer recognize myself, when the arrangement of flesh and bone seems entirely unfamiliar, seems to belong to someone else?

"Hold me," I order Kate.

She is washing her hands; I cannot be understood over the sound of rushing water. "One minute," she says.

"Hold me!" I cry. Her arms are around me, her wet hands cool against my back. She rubs her cheek across mine and then lifts a hand to my hair. "I don't want to just vanish," I say. "Don't let me disappear like that."

"No," she whispers in my ear. "You're still here. With me." She holds me tighter, with both hands, as if it were in her power to keep me safely rooted to this earth, to this life. But I'm fading day by day, losing strength, losing my hold on everything. The slippery slope beneath my feet is growing steeper; I can feel myself sliding downward at a faster pace every day.

"I don't want to go so fast," I say out loud. "I need some time to catch my breath."

"I'm here," Kate says. "Right here next to you, holding on." Arms pressing against my waist, squeezing me tighter and tighter, she lets go and laces my arms around her. With all my strength and will, I concentrate on hugging her back, on returning, in kind, the ardor of her embrace. I think of mothers lifting two-ton trucks to free their children pinned underneath, of Hindus walking a path of fiery coals, sleeping upon a bed of nails. Surely what I'm attempting is a breeze next to these things. And yet hard as I try, I've nothing to show for it, not a thing.

"Nothing!" I say, as disappointed as I have ever been.

"What?"

"Just another one of my fantasies," I say, shaking my head.

Then the door is flung open and Darlan rushes in, saying, "Mommy and Daddy, Daddy and Mommy, Grandpa's going to take me to Toys Я Us to get a bicycle."

"You already have a bicycle," Kate says. "And where's Day?"

"Talking to Grandpa. He's going to Toys Я Us, too."

"No one's going," I say. "You don't need another bicycle."

"And besides, the store is closed," says Kate.

"Is it nighttime?" Darlan says, as we all emerge from the bathroom.

"You tell me," I say.

Darlan smiles. "It's not nighttime and Toys Я Us isn't closed, you silly."

"Yes it is," I say. "They closed early today for ah . . . inventory." Kate laughs appreciatively.

"What's that?" Darlan asks.

"A special holiday."

"No," Darlan says. "Grandpa said I could go there *today* to get a doll stroller."

"You *have* a doll stroller."

"A shopping cart."

"Got one of those too."

"I have everything!" Darlan says in amazement.

"That's right, you do," I say.

Darlan makes a run for Seymour, shrieking, "Grandpa, guess what, I have everything!"

"Impossible," Seymour says. "What exactly do you mean by 'everything'?"

"Did you meet Day?" Kate asks.

"He's in the kitchen eating bean curd and something I can't identify."

"He's a terrific guy," says Kate. "Absolutely indispensible."

Seymour nods. "Need any help paying his salary?"

"Seymour," I say, truly horrified. "Quiet!"

"I'm merely—"

140

"The answer is thanks but no thanks."

"Don't be so stubborn," Seymour says. "You have to let me help you."

"I don't *have* to let you do anything!" I tell him. When I get excited like this, my speech worsens; it's clear he hasn't understood me. Kate quickly translates, but what she says is "It's sweet of you to be so generous. Really." I listen in disbelief; it's the first time she's betrayed me like this. And, I realize, it's undoubtedly not the last. What power she has! To rearrange the words coming from my mouth, even to invent new ones!

"Did I say that?" I shout. "Is that what I said?"

"Take it easy," Seymour says. "I didn't mean to start a war, for God's sake."

Actually, I'm no longer angry with him; at least he has the courage to say what's on his mind. It's my wife I'd like to strangle, if only I could get my hands around her throat. Looking at her stricken face now, I see that this power of Kate's is a revelation to her, that the possibility never occurred to her before. I shoot her a look of warning, and immediately she lowers her eyes.

"You listen to me, you," I say. "You're playing dirty, and I don't like it."

Silence.

"You pull that on me again and I'm out of here." I can see Day packing up my things for me, loading up the car, the two of us heading nowhere in particular, maybe just south on 95 or, perhaps, straight into the ocean; it's all the same to me.

"All right," Kate says. "I'm sorry."

"Good. Now come over here and kiss me."

"I don't know that I'm *that* sorry."

"Fake it," I say. The kiss that she drops so reluctantly upon my forehead is absolutely unacceptable. "No good,"

I tell her. "You'll have to do it over again." This time she kisses me on the mouth, lingering long enough to win my forgiveness.

"You young people," Seymour sighs.

Later, after dinner, after he and Darlan and Day have returned from Toys Я Us with a Strawberry Shortcake tricycle, after everyone in the house is asleep except Kate and me, she tells me, jokingly, what she suspects is Seymour's plan: to move us all back to New York, whether we like it or not.

"What a lunatic," I say, half-believing in the possibility.

"I think he's considering having us kidnapped by professionals."

"You and Darlan, maybe, but me he'd leave behind."

"Could be."

"Do you think we ought to be sleeping with a couple of baseball bats under the mattress?"

"Mmm," says Kate. "Go to sleep."

But I'm up for hours, on guard, waiting for the sound of footsteps, for the shadowy figures of Seymour's henchmen bending over our bed, ready to make a grab for us.

In the morning, I confront Seymour at the breakfast table. "Don't get any ideas," I tell him.

"What's that supposed to mean?" he asks, munching on Day's special cinnamon toast.

"A man's home is his castle," I remind him.

"Yes indeed."

"So just don't get any ideas."

After his departure, we find a check made out for a thousand dollars propped up against a bottle of perfume on Kate's dresser.

"Tear it up," I say.

"I will not," Kate says.

"Then I'll do it." Kate smiles at me. "With my teeth," I say. "I'm nothing if not resourceful."

"An extra thousand dollars is nothing to sneeze at, Henry."

"That may be," I say, "but I'm a highly principled man when it comes to this kind of thing." I walk over to the dresser, lean one shoulder against it, dip my head, and after a couple of trys, take the check between my teeth.

"We're not millionaires," Kate reminds me, and then I find myself opening my mouth and watching with regret as the check drifts to the floor.

"Seventy-two years old and taking money from my father-in-law," I say mournfully. "And to think that only minutes ago I was a highly principled man." I feel like getting into bed, yanking the sheet up over the top of my head and spending the rest of the day there, in misery and solitude. But then, I think, A little company might be nice. It's one in the afternoon on a hot, hot summer day and the house is cool and still, except for the satisfying hum of air-conditioning. My father-in-law is about to board a plane; Day and Darlan, heads tilted upward, are watching the airport sky from the departure gate.

I look toward our bed longingly. "My guess is that if you listen extremely carefully, you can read my mind," I tell Kate.

"It's one o'clock in the afternoon," she says, but there's a little smile playing at her lips.

"I know. Funny how the phrase *carpe diem* keeps going through my mind."

"Ah," she says. "Great minds *do* think alike."

In bed, I'm all greed and selfishness, taking everything that comes my way, offering not a whole lot in return. I'm not sure why this is so, except, perhaps, that

I'm so in the habit of taking, of accepting, all day long, that I've actually grown lazy.

"Ask me for something," I'm begging Kate now. "There must be something."

"It's all right," she says.

"It's not all right." Don't be so selfless, I want to say. You're breaking my heart.

"No talking," Kate says, and slips me inside her. But who knows if this is really what she wants, or if, once more, she's simply on automatic pilot, responding to me and what I so clearly need, with hardly a thought of herself at all. It wasn't always this way; just a few months ago, she was still eager to show me precisely what she wanted, leading me urgently here and there along her body. It is as if she has ceased to care about herself, about her own pleasure; working so hard to please me, she's lost track of her own desire.

Abruptly, I pull myself away from her now, saying, "You can't *always* be thinking of me first."

"What?" she says.

"It's like a bad habit you've got to break."

"I don't care!" she cries.

"You have to care," I tell her. "Start being a little selfish, it's good for you."

"My mind's too cluttered right now; I've got so much to sort through, I can't even *think* about what I want."

"Tell me," I say, but the truth is, I'm relieved at the long silence that follows. We snuggle up into each other, our knees touching, our breath heating each other's faces. When, in a while, she asks me what it is I'm daydreaming about, I smile and say, "Trading away the present for the past, what else?"

"What else," she answers, and soon we begin to make love, slowly and sweetly and without a sound.

CHAPTER FIFTEEN

At Thanksgiving dinner at her father's house, Nina sits with Darlan on her lap, absently stroking her half-sister's wild dark hair.

"Make me a pony tail," Darlan says. "Two pony tails, how about that?"

"Finish eating first," Nina says, but Darlan has already flown from her lap and is racing in her patent leather party shoes from the room. She's back in not much more than an instant, it seems, carrying a plastic bag full of barrettes and cloth-covered rubber bands, ribbons and toy jewelry and makeup. Nina smiles patiently as Darlan climbs on top of her and runs a plastic tube of lipstick across her lips, then brushes her cheeks and the bridge of her nose with a powder puff from a toy compact.

"Pretty," Darlan murmurs, and goes for Nina's eyelids now with five colors of pretend shadow, daintily skimming a tiny wand across her palette, one color at a time.

"My two girls," Henry says with a sigh of satisfaction. This is not what Nina hears from her father's lips:

what she hears is a series of oohs and aahs that she cannot make any sense of at all. "My two girls," Kate translates, her voice cool and absolutely uninflected, as if the words meant nothing to her. But she is smiling at Nina and Darlan now from across the table, letting them know that she, too, is pleased by the sight of them in their shared seat. Gratefully, Nina returns her smile. She studies her father, whose face has taken on, in the months since her last visit, a slightly vacant, almost childlike look, as if he does not entirely comprehend the world around him. According to Kate, this look is deceptive; it's a slackness of muscle and no reflection of the man himself. Still, it's hard to believe he's all there, that it is merely flesh that has gone soft. Nina watches as Day's steady hand raises a forkful of turkey and cranberry sauce to Henry's mouth, watches the gleaming bit of sauce that clings to his lower lip then drops down somewhere around his collarbone, and trails along his napkin in its slow journey toward his lap.

"Got it!" Kate says, swiping at it with her linen napkin.

"Can't take me anywhere," Henry says, according to Kate's translation. "Did you see that Ann Landers column where all those idiots were complaining about having to see people like me eating in public? One of them said restaurants should have special sections set aside, hidden by screens or something, so the rest of the world wouldn't have to be in danger of throwing up their dinners."

"Awful," Nina says, with a shake of her head. "But what can you do."

"Henry and I had a great time composing a letter," Day says, laughing. "There were so many four-letter words in it we finally had to throw it away."

Henry squints into the distance, bites down on his

lip, trying to remember. "Dear Asshole in Arkansas," Kate translates. Henry goes on talking, on and on, but Kate, it seems, is no longer cooperating.

"This is X-rated stuff," she explains to Nina. "I just can't. Not in front of everyone." At this, Henry's face glows red with anger and frustration. He howls like a man in pain, and Nina is startled to find herself in tears.

"Can't you just say it, goddamnit!" she cries. "What's with you, Kate?"

"What's with *me*? What's with *you*?"

"Look," Day says, "this is crazy. This is Thanksgiving," he finishes lamely.

"Butt out, O'Neill," Kate says. "Is this your family? Is this your home? You're hired help, buddy, in case you've forgotten."

Henry, who has fallen silent, now looks at Kate in utter amazement. "Ah," he says. He turns to Day, leans his head against Day's shoulder. "I."

"I know," Day murmurs.

"Hey everybody," Darlan calls out. "Everybody, hey, I'm under the table."

Slowly Nina sinks down beneath the tablecloth, where she wipes at the tears that have dampened her face. She hunches over so that her head doesn't collide with the bottom of the table, and pulls Darlan into her lap. "It's nice under here, isn't it," she says.

"Can I go home wish you?" Darlan asks.

"Maybe another time," says Nina, listening to the conversation swirling furiously above her head, to Kate's rage, Henry's unbearably drawn-out syllables, Day's cool muted responses. "Maybe when you're a big girl," Nina says.

Darlan slips the fingers of both hands in her mouth, sucks on them thoughtfully, then sets them against Nina's cheeks. "I'm a college ghorl," she says. "So I can go home wish you, right?"

"Do you know who I am?" Nina says, placing her hands over Darlan's. "Do you know?"

"You're Nina, silly."

"I'm your sister."

Darlan shakes with laughter. "You're not my *sister*."

"Why not?"

"Because you're too big. You're a very big ghorl."

"I know," Nina says.

"You and my mom are two big ghorls together," Darlan says. "So you're my mom's sister!" she cries, excited at her discovery. "Right?"

Smiling, Nina shrugs her shoulders.

"And you love me," Darlan says.

"I do," says Nina, stunned that this is so, that there is actually something between them after all. Something to be grateful for, she thinks. This child of her father's old age, soon, like Nina, to be fatherless—of course there must be a bond between them. A bond based on loss, if nothing else. More than thirty years span between their childhoods, light-years, really. Contemplating this, Nina has to smile. The last few years of her father's life seem a series of adventures, full of danger and risk. She's got to hand it to him: the man was fearless in his old age, seizing happiness and love with such ease, making a go of it one last time, absolutely unafraid. She wonders if, looking back, her father sees that it was all too good to be true, that, like a dream, it was never meant to last more than the blink of an eye. Even so, would he have traded away that brief bright happiness for a dozen more years of the most ordinary, uneventful life? She doubts it, but who knows. Perhaps, facing the end of everything, all he wants is a reprieve and would do anything to get it.

"You love me," Darlan is saying, "because I'm your brother, right?"

There's a commotion now as, Nina sees, Kate's feet pull back abruptly from their place under the table, her chair shifting back too, slamming hard against the wall, Kate herself stalking off and out of the room. And then Day's feet have disappeared, and there's the sound of him hurrying after her, calling, "Don't you think I've had enough of *you*?"

Tentatively, on her hands and knees, Nina emerges from under the table, followed by Darlan, who perches herself in Henry's lap, closing his arms safely around her.

"Hi," Nina says, and instantly feels a great embarrassed silence between them. "I thought you might be a little lonely," she offers, after a while.

"Yah," Henry says. And then he talks his heart out, telling her everything, pretending it is still within his power to make himself understood to anyone at all. Instinctively, Nina nods at the right moments, dipping her head slightly here and there, patting his swollen fingers and wrists, agreeing, a dozen times over, with whatever it is he's so determined to tell her. The effort exhausts her, but she keeps up her end of it for as long as he needs her to.

"So," she says as Henry slips at last into silence. She cups her hand at the edge of the table and sweeps some crumbs into it. "Darlan tells me I'm her brother."

Henry laughs, rolls his eyes, comments briefly.

"True," says Nina.

"That ice cream with the cookies in it," Darlan says, tugging on Nina's sleeve. "I want that."

"I want that, *please*," says Nina.

"I want that please and you have to open the refrigerator for me."

"Back in a minute," Nina tells Henry, "okay?" Feeling, with a touch of shame, as if she's been liberated, Nina walks ahead into the kitchen, Darlan at her side. She immediately stops short and stares, completely bewildered, at the sight of Kate in the farthest corner of the kitchen, her back against the refrigerator door, her eyes shut tight in concentration as she bends forward to receive Day's kiss. His palms are flat against the refrigerator, for balance, but Kate lifts hers to his shoulders, kneading them fiercely, as if to cause him pain. It's a kiss straight out of the movies, Nina thinks—deeply passionate, requiring swelling music, and close-ups—and in the instant before she is overtaken by anger, she feels sick with envy. The room is charged with romance and possibility and a great deal of heat; Nina, too, is sweaty and overheated and suddenly very thirsty.

It is Darlan who breaks the spell, barreling toward the refrigerator, announcing, "I want ice cream all melted up in my bowl with the pink flower on the bottom, okay?"

Kate lets out a low moan of grief, and thrusts Day against a cabinet. "Ice cream?" she says. She sweeps her hair across her face and holds it there like a veil.

"I don't want to know anything about it," Nina hears herself say. "I'm just a stranger passing through on my way to the refrigerator."

"I never expected to find myself here," Kate says. Her hair is draped over her eyes now, her head lowered. "You can understand that, can't you?"

Day has claimed three or four walnuts from a small pewter bowl on the counter and is juggling them masterfully. He will not, cannot, take his eyes from the spinning circle of nuts in front of him.

"It's none of my business," says Nina. "And anyway, I don't give a shit. What you do in your spare time is—"

"Nina," Kate says. Approaching her, Kate reaches out a hand to touch the sleeve of her sweater.

Nina takes a step backward. "Don't touch me, please," she says.

"I just don't want you to think that this has anything to do with love."

The walnuts are flying faster now, a dizzying blur that has everyone mesmerized. Without warning, Day lets them drop to the floor and then walks out of the room, having said not a single word. In a moment he and Henry are talking together, though it's impossible to hear what it is they are saying.

"You don't know anything about my life," Kate says softly. "The feel of it, the taste of it. It's not a life like everyone else's. I can't hope for a whole lot. I'd like to, but that would be foolish. It's like everything is shrinking, shriveling up. Henry's life, our life together, is narrowing, the opportunities for pleasure growing fewer and fewer."

"Can I have a banana?" Darlan asks. "And then I'm going to put a tape in the VCR."

"I forgot about your ice cream; I'm sorry, sweetie," Kate says. She hands Darlan a banana from the refrigerator and says, "Hug me?"

Darlan shakes her head. "I have to watch a tape now."

"Too busy to hug your one and only mom?" Kate says, bending to the floor and opening her arms.

"Just for one minute and that's it," says Darlan, and steps into the circle of her mother's embrace.

Watching them, Nina feels herself softening, her body going limp with resignation. "You're waiting for me to say I have no right to judge you, is that it?"

"Something like that," says Kate, as Darlan makes a run for it and disappears.

"I don't know why I'm taking this so hard."

"It was just a kiss," Kate says in a whispery voice. "The first that's come my way in a long while. And it came out of nowhere, in the middle of an argument, just when I was thinking murderous thoughts."

"Want to know something even crazier?" Nina says. "We've *been* through something together! We've been through something together and nothing's quite the same; do you know what I mean?"

"You're scaring me," Kate says. She pushes up her sleeves to reveal the gooseflesh of her arms, the little hairs sticking straight up in terror. She is trembling now, her outstretched arms shaking so violently that Nina simply seizes her by the wrists and cries out, in a stranger's high-pitched voice, "Stop!" They stand there together in silence for a moment or two, regarding each other with surprise, and, Nina thinks, something very nearly like affection, and then, without a word, they float apart.

CHAPTER SIXTEEN

Lazing about in the living room, listening to Day at the piano, I tap my foot in perfect rhythm. *"I'm bidin' my ti-ime, cause that's the kind-a guy I-i'm ..."* Day sings along with me and even though I have to admit we don't sound too terrific together, there's no stopping us.

"What a guy, that Gershwin," I say with a sigh when the song ends.

"Yup," Day agrees, and swings into "That Certain Feeling" just as Kate steps out into the room in a short black dress, cut in a V almost to the waist. She's wearing see-through black stockings and high heels, and she dances toward me with Darlan, who's in her pajamas and all set for bed.

"That certain feeling, The first time I met you, I hit the ceiling," I sing.

"You did not," Kate says as she dances away, twirling Darlan under her arm jauntily.

"Did so. And oh what a vision you were in your sweatshirt and sneakers!"

"That may be, but look at me now!" says Kate.

Abruptly, in the middle of the song, Day switches to "Old Macdonald," which sends Darlan racing to his side and aboard the piano bench.

"Hey," I protest. "What happened to 'That Certain Feeling'?"

"It faded fast," Day says. "Predictably, they grew bored with each other and started pursuing separate but equal activities—softball for him, aerobics for her, jogging for him, Jazzercise for her, you know how it is. . . ."

"And?"

"Same old song," Day says. "He got stuck paying alimony and child support and she went to Club Med and found herself a scuba diving instructor who taught her a thing or two about life."

"I am *so* depressed," says Kate, taking my arm and leading me through the room to the coat closet. "Who are these people, anyway?"

"I have no idea," says Day. "Just go out there and enjoy your dinner. Where are you going?"

"The Count of Antipasto. I've been warned the Veal Puttanesca is wonderful."

Day swings around to face us, screwing up his mouth horribly. "A calf is bad enough, but a *young* calf!"

"You're just jealous," I tell him. "As well you should be. Look at me," I say, "my lovely young bride here on my arm, the two of us heading off to a romantic dinner . . ."

"Don't rub it in," Day says, turning back to the keyboard. *"They're writing songs of love, but not for me,"* he sings in a tragic voice.

"You're breaking my heart, buddy boy," I say as Kate gets our coats and we start toward the door.

"Wait!" Darlan calls after us. "I need kisses and some water."

"Here are your kisses," Kate says, scooping her up

from the bench and then almost immediately setting her down again. "The water you can get from Day."

"No, *you*."

"Mommy's too old and tired to walk all the way into the kitchen."

"I, on the other hand," says Day, "am young and filled with boundless energy."

"No!" Darlan says.

"Who wants to ride on my shoulders and touch the ceiling?"

"I!" says Darlan, raising her hand. "I!"

Closing the door behind us, Kate ushers me out into the chilly winter night and into the passenger seat of the GTI, then belts me in. I watch her stepping daintily in her high heels around the carport, hear the rustle of her coat as she settles in behind the wheel. The cold, and the full moon and spray of stars above us remind me of the night Darlan was born, a hundred years ago, it seems. I remember warming Kate's ice-cold hand against my chest, listening to her tell me she loved me.

"Don't," I say now as she turns on the motor.

"What?"

"Let's sit here and neck a while." I lean toward her and lick the corners of her mouth, savoring her moan of pleasure before she kisses me back. I ask to see her breasts and watch with excitement as she opens her coat wide and reaches down into the V of her dress. In the moonlight, her breasts are silvery, mysterious. She puts my cold hands over them delicately. "Time to get into the back seat," I say, and see my old self scrambling like mad right over the top.

"Where will I be without you?" she whispers.

I let my tears fall soundlessly on her breasts and then I get a hold of myself. "Sell the house," I say. We've been over this before, every month or so taking a shot at it, but we always end up somewhere far short of acceptance, staring at each other in disbelief, eyes glittering at the thought of each of us alone in the pitch darkness. "Move back to New York, make a life for yourself in the big city," I tell her. "And whatever you do: no funeral. Keep my ashes on top of the piano so I can really feel the music. And don't forget to dust the little container I'm in. Keep it all shined-up and looking good, okay?"

Kate's nose is running; she sniffs a few times and rubs her tears into her cheeks. "Very funny, Henry," she says.

"On the other hand," I say, "who knows? Maybe I'll surprise us all and live forever."

"Promise me we'll never have this conversation again," Kate says. She arranges herself back into her dress, then takes my face in her hands. "I'm a very practical person," she says. "But this is something that's beyond me, that I just can't bring myself to seriously contemplate, not for more than an instant. Sometimes I catch myself just as I'm about to give in to the truth and then I think, No, nothing's inevitable, not even this. As if there were a possibility of a reprieve."

"From the governor?" I say.

"*You're* no help," Kate says.

It's the end of my life but I'm not ready. I'm a greedy son-of-a-bitch—I want every last moment that's coming to me, and more. My body is a miserable useless wreck, faulty machinery that only gets in the way. I'd dump it in a flash if I could and hitch a ride with the next soulless, able-bodied guy who comes along. What a childish fantasy! But oh what a lovely thought!

"What's that dopey smile all about?" Kate says.

"Nothing—I just had a great idea for a movie, that's all," I tell her.

*   *   *

This Count of Antipasto is a dark and nearly silent place, so dark I can barely read the menu that's placed before me by a young, cheerless waiter dressed in some kind of weird velvet get-up.

"Got a flashlight?" I ask him.

"Pardon?" he says, and when I don't respond, he begins to mumble the specials for the evening. "And I'm Vincent," he finishes. "I'll be back to take your order shortly."

"Vincent what?" I ask him before he gets away.

"Vincent Spatinuda," he says with surprise after Kate translates for me.

"You seem depressed, Vincent," I tell him. "A little down in the dumps, I'd say."

Not comprehending, he shrugs his shoulders and disappears into the gloom.

"This place gives me the creeps," I say, looking around at the handful of other diners sitting quietly in their seats, at the fluted white columns laced with plastic greenery, the muddy-colored still-lifes in their broad gold frames. "It's Saturday night, for crying out loud. You'd think there'd be a little more action going on. Really."

"I heard from a couple of different people that the food was excellent. In fact, Nancy LeClerc—you know, Tiki's friend—told me that she always comes here on first dates for a nice, quiet, kind of romantic time."

"Romantic?" I say, and just then the Muzak goes on, playing something vaguely sorrowful and familiar. "Too bad she and Day never hit it off. It might have been a nice thing for both of them, something to ease the loneliness, I mean."

"That's old news," Kate snaps. "That was months ago, one lousy date that led nowhere."

"Take it easy," I say. "You're the one who set it up, weren't you?"

"It seemed like a reasonable possibility. Obviously, I was wrong."

"I don't know what he's thinking these days," I tell her. "He hasn't been confiding in me the way he used to. I miss that, actually, hearing what's on a guy's mind. Now mostly it's me, talking my head off when the mood strikes."

"Talking about what?"

"Oh, you know, the simple pleasures, wine, women, song . . . whatever."

"The past, you mean," Kate says.

"Old people have been known to spend their time that way. It makes them feel better. And worse, too."

"All those failures and disappointments," she says, not sounding very sympathetic.

"I've had my share," I tell her. All at once I realize that the Muzak that's been haunting me is a series of theme songs from cancelled TV shows—*M*A*S*H, Hill Street Blues, St. Elsewhere*. Listening to them, I feel close to tears, nostalgic for the not-so-distant past. Details of my own past suddenly seem shadowy, out of focus, but I can see Dr. Craig, my favorite from *St. Elsewhere*, marching through the hospital corridors, shoulders held back stiffly, mouth curled in a perfect sneer. When the waiter comes to take our order, tears are sliding past my face, and I can't speak a word. Kate puts a hand on my shoulder and orders for us both.

"What is it?" she says as soon as Vincent has left.

"*St. Elsewhere*," I say with a sob.

"What? I can't understand you." She gets it the second time around by reading my lips, and looks at me with relief. "What *about St. Elsewhere*?"

"It's the music," I say. "I must be getting sentimental in my old age."

"Are you all right?"

"Sure I'm all right," I tell her. "I'm just a little weepy tonight."

"Do you want to go home?"

"Are you kidding? This is our night out on the town. You're in your sexy black dress and I'm in tears, in mourning for one of my favorite TV shows. But there's romance in the air and I'm staying put."

"Re-runs!" Kate says, smiling, wiping my face with her fingertips. "I bet it'll be in syndication heaven before you know it."

"I should live so long," I say with a sigh, but smile back at her.

She's feeding me the croutons from a Caesar salad when a little girl about six or seven wanders over to our table, stares at us, and decides to stick around for a closer look. "What's the matter with *him*?" she asks. "Why's he wearing a bib like that?"

"He's kind of a messy eater," Kate says.

"Oh. I'm Taylor," she adds after a while. She fools with the salt and pepper shakers on the table, which, oddly, are old Perrier bottles with holes punched in their caps. She makes them dance, clicks their heels together noisily. "Could I have some of that?" she says, pointing to the bread basket at the center of the table.

"Breadstick?" says Kate. "Sure. But you know, Taylor, I'm wondering if your mother and father have any idea where you are right now."

"There's just my mother," Taylor says. "And Howard. I told them I was going to get some mints in the little bowl they have up front there."

"Then maybe you ought to do that and then go back

to your table. You wouldn't want your mother to worry about you."

Taylor reaches into the back pocket of her dungaree skirt and pulls out a shiny bundle of keys held together on a broad pink ribbon. She swings them slowly in front of my face for a while, as if she were trying to hypnotize me. "See these?" she says finally. "Guess what. They're the keys to my mother's boyfriend's apartment."

"No fooling," Kate says, and the two of us laugh.

"Yes, and he likes me very much. He's a hairdresser and once he braided my hair in a thousand braids and it stayed that way for years, the whole summer. And once he took us to Niagara Falls. That was in the summer, too, and we all stayed in a room that had a teeny refrigerator in it and a lock on it. You had to get a key to open it up and then you could drink what was inside it, like beer and soda and stuff like that."

"So what did you think of the falls?" Kate translates for me.

The girl raises her eyebrows at me. "Liked it," she says. "Once a boy who was my age and was only wearing a bathing suit fell in but they pulled him out and saved him and he was okay."

"True story!" I say excitedly. It happened shortly before Cynthia and I had been there, and hearing the story from a taped recording that boomed, first in English and then in French, from the speaker system on *The Maid of the Mist*, we'd shuddered beneath our rubber raincoats, Cynthia clutching my arm in terror. She wasn't much of a traveler, and two days into our trip she was already homesick and full of complaints. Icy spray from the falls dampened our faces and hair, exhilarating me, but as I lifted the hood of Cynthia's raincoat over her head, it was just in time to hear exactly how awful she felt. It's one of the eight wonders of the world, for God's sake, I told her, but she couldn't wait to get off the boat and back to the hotel for a hot shower. Her shower would have to wait, I insisted, and from the falls I dragged her to some lovely formal gardens on the Canadian side. Set behind a low stone wall was a fragrance garden for the blind, plants with unusual texture and aromatic foliage: scented geraniums, summer savory, bayberry, sweet basil. We watched as a young blind guy bent down on his knees in the garden and lowered his face to the ground, looking like a solitary Moslem praying in bright sunlight. He was the only blind person in the garden, and a small group of tourists stared at him in silence. It was Cynthia who went to his side as he began to rise, a bit unsteadily, from the ground. She brushed off the clumps of earth at his knees and led him back to the concrete path where the rest of us stood. I looked on in pleasure and surprise, thinking, This was Cynthia, someone who feared escalators, elevators, getting out of bed in the morning, meeting the gaze of strangers and even friends. Maddeningly self-absorbed and yet capable of acting generously after all. Seeing her wipe the dirt from a stranger's knees filled me with hope; we would continue with our trip and our marriage, joyful and unafraid. Wrong, and wrong again. It turned out that she was too anxious to stay away even one more day and so we drove home that night, Cynthia dozing in the passenger seat, offering neither comfort nor companionship, and me hunched fiercely over the steering wheel, whistling, singing along with the radio, talking to myself to keep awake, uttering out loud an endless list of grievances against my sleeping wife. How can you love a woman who doesn't know the first thing about making you happy, who doesn't feel the need or desire to even look into the matter? Talking aloud like this on a summer night in a speeding car, my voice strong and clear, I grew bolder and bolder. "This love is senseless, you idiot!" I roared out the open window. "There's nothing in it for you!" I hollered. "What?" said Cynthia, awake but only barely. Go back to sleep, I told her in annoyance. I'm too busy to talk to you. In a moment she had dozed off again, and I fell silent, my throat sore and dry. I took a hand off the steering wheel and ran two fingers across her mouth. She sighed and drifted toward me, leaning heavily against my shoulder. I cast my arm around her and smiled at the thought of the two of us nestled like teenage lovers in the front seat of a Plymouth on the Thruway. Where was my anger, my pride, all the reserves of strength and good sense that I knew were mine? Out the window, down the tubes, vanished into the mild night air.

No wiser now than I was then, I find myself in thrall to her again, desperate, all of a sudden, to know what she is doing at this moment, what she is thinking. I'd like to kiss the smooth pale stalk of her neck, behind her ear and the back of her knee. What's the big attraction, I ask myself, with this woman who used up twenty years of my life and then showed me the door? Who knows? Who will ever know?

But here is Kate beside me, patient and loving, the love of my life, the one person who's surely going to mourn me when I'm gone from this earth. Is it possible I'm unworthy of her, of her devotion? The thought is unbearable and I dismiss it immediately. I brush my face against her hair, breathe in its sweet light scent. I see her breasts, silvery in the moonlight, see my limp hands resting on their softness. I don't know why, but we haven't made love in some time, two months or so, and I miss it. Perhaps we've stopped because I'm too clumsy and leaden, and often too tired. But I'm never too tired to look at her, to ask to have my hands placed against her warm flesh. At night we drift toward sleep folded together in an easy embrace. Sometimes, before dawn, I awaken in a cold sweat, my hands and feet icy, my heart thumping. Like the rest of us, I'm scared to death of dying. To all these shrinks with their bestsellers and phone-in shows and advice columns, all these guys trying to tell you it's simply a part of life like anything else, I say, Horseshit! Is the end of the world simply a part of life? Any idiot knows the answer to that one. The only real plans I've made, the one thing I've got my heart set on, is a bowl of raspberries and cream right before I fade out for good. I don't care if they're out of season and $9.99 a half-pint, I want them anyway. Kate laughed when I told her this, then wept. Put it on your shopping list, I told her. I'll never forgive you if you screw this one up.

Our food arrives now and the little girl is still hanging around, still talking up a storm about her mother's boy-friend. "Where the hell is her mother?" I ask Kate. "Wouldn't you think she'd be frantic by now?" I study my dinner in this ridiculous, inadequate light—as far as I can tell, angel hair in three colors with shrimp and broccoli mixed in here and there. "Just pop one shrimp in my mouth and then go ahead and eat your dinner," I say.

"I hate broccoli," Taylor says. "I hate all vegeta-bles." She pronounces it "veg-e-ta-bles," causing Kate and me to smile at each other.

"Where'd you learn to talk like that?" I ask.

"Oh, hi How," says Taylor, as a big tall guy with the blow-dried look approaches. "I'm going to get my mints now." She grabs his hand and squeezes it. "This is How-ard," she tells us.

"And these must be your keys," says Kate, pointing them out on the table.

"We've heard so much about you," I say.

"Taylor tells us you're a hairdresser," Kate says, as Howard gives me the once-over. "Do you work in town? I could probably use a good haircut one of these days."

"A hairdresser?" Howard looks startled, runs his hand over his hair. "That's a laugh," he says. "I'm in construction, actually. Her father's a hairdresser, or at least he was, last I heard, maybe that's what she meant." He lets go of the little girl's hand. "Is that what you meant, Taylor?"

Taylor shrugs, toes the carpet with the pointed tip of her cowboy boot. "I want to stay here," she says. "With this lady and this man."

"You have to come back and finish your dinner," Howard says.

"No."

"Do as I say, Taylor."

"Why?"

Lowering his hands to her shoulders, clamping them down on her, Howard says, "Because I'm sort of your father and I said so, that's why."

"Oh, man," Taylor groans.

"When you're big, you can do as you damn please," Howard consoles her.

"Excuse me," I say. "That's not entirely true, as we all know."

"Is he drunk?" Howard asks. "What's going on?"

"Nah, he's just a messy eater," Taylor says.

Kate lines up her silverware all in a row, puts the pieces in size order, then arranges them exactly as they were. "He's ill," she says, and I hate hearing this, hate the way she casts her eyes downward as she talks. I ought to be immune to this sort of conversation by now, but I'm not: it's still so hard to take.

"I'm actually doing pretty well," I say, "all things considered."

"Gee, that's too bad," Howard offers, eyeing me sorrowfully. "I hope you'll be feeling better real soon. Come on, Taylor," he says. "Your food's probably ice-cold." He shoves her a little to get her going, and she has to grab hold of the edge of the table to keep her balance. "He is so a hairdresser," she says in a frantic whisper as he leads her away.

"Next time," I tell Kate, "just say that I'm drunk."

"I will not." She twirls some angel hair around her fork and guides it into my mouth.

"Drunk is easy," I say. "It's short and to the point and doesn't inspire the least bit of sympathy. In fact, here's an idea: why don't we just hang a sign around my neck that says 'He's had a few too many'? That way you won't have to say anything at all. You can just point to the sign and roll your eyes or something."

"Henry." She's coming at me with a tiny flower of broccoli and the gleaming tail of a shrimp. I chew them slowly, then ask for a sip of wine. "I'm not used to you sounding so bitter," she says.

"Did you see the way he looked at me?" I say.

"Who?"

"Howard the hairdresser. I can't stand that kind of sadness in a stranger's face, sadness for *me*. I'd prefer he think I was hitting the bottle once too often."

"No you wouldn't."

"You bet I would."

"Fine. I'll go to a stationery store tomorrow and get some oaktag and Magic Markers."

"A T-shirt might be nicer, actually—you know, like the one you had made up for me that said 'I'm the Father' across the front."

Kate smiles. "What a big braggart you were! It was such fun watching you parade around in that shirt, showing off in front of everyone like that."

"I was sitting pretty, all right," I say with a sigh. "On top of the world."

"You were one lucky son-of-a-bitch," says Kate, reminding me of the truth of the matter, just in case I'd forgotten it.

Monday morning, as soon as Kate and Darlan are off to work and to play-school, I sit down at the kitchen table with Day and break the news to him.

"I've got a little assignment for you, buddy," I say. "Get out some paper and a pen and start writing."

"You're not revising your will, are you? If you've decided to leave me a lump sum to the tune of fifty grand, I have absolutely no objection whatsoever."

"You never give up, do you?" I tease him.

"Never."

"Be that as it may, Madame Secretary, get ready for some dictation."

"Is this business or personal?" he says as he takes what he needs from a cabinet drawer. "Semicolon or comma?"

"Very personal," I say, "and none of your business. Ready? 'Dear Cynthia, As you undoubtedly know, life is a series of surprises, some more welcome than others. I know that when we last spoke, I left you with the distinct impression that our paths were never to cross again. However—' "

"I quit," Day says, and his pencil goes flying over his shoulder. "You can notify personnel immediately."

"Calm down," I say. "And pick that pencil up off the floor."

"Don't be a jerk, Henry."

"I am not a jerk. I am simply a man with a few loose ends to tie up. Now read that back to me from the beginning."

" 'Dear Cynthia, I am not a jerk. I am simply a man with—' "

"Cut the crap, wise guy," I say.

"I'm your friend, Henry. I just don't want you to do something that might end up being hurtful to any number of people."

"What do you think I'm planning to do—fly to New York in my private plane and seduce her one last time?"

Day retrieves the pencil and lays it across the pad of paper. "She has no part in this, she has no rights to anything here. She gave all that up when she booted you out on your ear, Henry. After twenty years, or whatever it was."

"I don't want her reading my obituary in the *Times* without any warning; it's not right." I envision her picking up the paper one morning, casually running her eye down a column of names, passing me by and then backtracking, eyes fixed on that familiar arrangement of letters. Tears come instantly and she runs to call her shrink, who says, Hop in a cab and we'll talk for fifty minutes. And when she arrives Cynthia can only say, It was Hochberg who did us in, the bastard.

"Hochberg!" I say.

"Hochberg?" Day says. "Who the hell is Hochberg?"

"Just the shrink I happen to hold personally responsible for the death of my marriage. My marriage to Cynthia, I mean."

"Oh, *that* Hochberg," Day says.

"Interested in the details?"

"Nope."

"Good. Let's get back to work."

"As your friend and personal advisor, it is with a heavy heart that I pick up this pencil and—"

"Duly noted," I say. "Now stop stalling and assume the position for dictation."

Crossing his legs and propping the note pad against his knee, Day says, "Inexplicably, I find myself in the mood for a coffee break. How about we take a ride into town for some croissants? My treat, of course, given the circumstances."

"My blood pressure's soaring," I say. "It's already gone through the roof. In fact, if I were still capable of making a fist, I'd waste no time in shoving it down your throat."

"I take it the croissants are out, then."

"You guessed it, buddy."

Day sighs theatrically. "Dear Cynthia," he says, "It is with a heavy heart that I . . ."

For more than an hour we bicker over the contents of the letter, tirelessly moving around parts of speech, re-ordering sentences, even consulting a thesaurus when Day insists I've chosen a wrong word. Too melodramatic, he says. A light touch is what we're after.

"You'll have to forgive me," I tell him, in kind of a mean-spirited way. "I keep forgetting you're the writer here."

"Just because I've barely written two chapters' worth in almost a year, doesn't mean I'm not a writer," he says, clearly insulted. "Maybe I'm not an author, but I'm still a writer."

I can easily imagine my hand rising up to pat his shoulder fondly. "I know," I say. "And you're right: saying 'Despite everything, I sometimes think I still have the hots for you' *is* a bit much."

"A bit much?" Day says. "It's a lot worse than a bit much." He gives me a look of such reproach that I'm chilled by it. "Grow up, Henry," he says.

Even so, he drags the portable typewriter out of his room and sets up shop on the kitchen table so I can watch every move of his fingertips.

"Great typing job," I say when he finishes. "Not a single typo."

He ignores my praise, refusing to even look in my direction. "You want to sign it?" he eventually asks. Slipping a pen through my fingers, he moves my hand slowly across the page. My signature comes out large and childlike, appearing to reflect a severe case of arrested development. I read the letter through twice more and watch as Day folds it carefully into an envelope. I have him drive me to the post office, the letter hot and burdensome in my lap, burning through my coat and the fabric of my pants, all the way through to my skin.

CHAPTER SEVENTEEN

These are Henry's symptoms: fever, a bit of a cough, difficulty breathing. In the emergency room, the resident—whose nameplate reads "D. Randall Radin"—murmurs "dyspnea" and scribbles on his clipboard.

"What?" says Kate.

"Labored breathing, that's all that means."

Kate seizes him by the elbow. "Help him!" she says urgently. "What are you waiting for?" The resident winces, at the sound of her voice or at her touch, perhaps both, and removes Kate's hand from his arm. He slips a see-through, green plastic oxygen mask over Henry's nose and mouth, and clicks his ballpoint pen restlessly. In the next cubicle an elderly woman is taunting her husband in a loud and cranky voice.

"So you do the laundry and the cooking and the marketing and everything else, too. So what. What do you want, a medal?" she says.

Her husband peeks out through the partially drawn curtain separating them from Kate and Henry. "Fifty-four years we've been married," he tells them with a wink.

"You know the expression 'There's a sucker born every minute'? Well, right here you've got yourselves a first-class example of one."

"I'm trying to take a history here, Mrs. Dubrow," the old woman's doctor says, drawing the curtain closed. "How old did you say you are?"

"Fifty-five," Mrs. Dubrow answers.

"I see," the doctor says. "So you were an infant then, at the time of your marriage, am I correct?"

Kate smiles and takes Henry's swollen fingers in her own. "You look a little like you're in outer space," she tells him. "In that mask, I mean."

"I bet he feels like he's in outer space," Dr. Radin says. "Anyway, we're probably going to end up keeping him for a while. My guess is pneumonia. We'll take a chest X-ray and some blood tests, but I'm pretty certain that's what it is." He pauses, watching them both for an instant. "Don't look so frightened," he says.

"Me?" Kate says.

"Both of you. We'll treat him with antibiotics and send him on his way. If all goes well, of course," he finishes.

"I've always made it my business to steer clear of hospitals," Henry says when the doctor removes his oxygen mask. "And up until recently I've done a pretty good job."

The doctor nods at Kate's translation. "I hear where you're coming from," he says. "And we're going to try and spring you from this place just as soon as we can."

"This is the hospital where my daughter was born," Henry says.

"You?" the doctor says, pointing to Kate. "I don't think so. This hospital's only about fifteen years old."

"I don't think so either," Henry says, smiling.

"Allow me to identify myself," Kate says. "I'm his wife. I told you that when we came in here, in fact."

"His wife?"

"As in, the person he's married to."

"Holy shit," says Dr. Radin slowly.

Henry's face is luminous with pleasure. "I love it love it love it," he says. "It gets them every time."

After Henry is settled in his room and Kate is asked to leave for the third time, she makes her way back downstairs to the emergency room's waiting area, where Day and the overweight Hell's Angel sitting next to him are drinking from cans of Diet Coke and staring out into the parking lot.

"A friend of yours?" Kate whispers.

"How's Henry doing?"

"He's breathing a lot easier, actually."

"Literally or figuratively?"

"Both, I think," says Kate.

"And you?" Day asks.

"Young and healthy, as usual."

In the parking lot, Kate stands in front of the GTI with her keys in her hand. She looks on in fascination as a man dressed in panty hose and white boxer shorts under his open coat, a shoulder-length wig askew on his head, speaks animatedly to his companion. A pair of sequined high heels and a black curly wig rest on the hood of his Buick, which is parked nose to nose with the GTI. "Listen to my poem," he says. "Roses are red, violets are blue, I'm schizophrenic and so am I."

"Swell," says his friend, and slaps the curly wig onto his head. "We'll stick it on a T-shirt and make millions."

"That's where I saw it," the man in boxer shorts says. "You never listen to me, Leonard. I talk and talk and virtually nothing sinks in. Sometimes I think a hearing aid is in order."

"Sorry," Leonard offers.

" 'Sorry'? What do you think it's like when you try to explain your life and no one's listening, especially the person who should be listening hardest."

"Get into the car, Angelo," Leonard says. "And put a lid on it, will you."

Kate watches, absorbed, almost in a trance, until they pull out of the lot; exhausted, she stands alongside her car, keys still in hand, unable to decide what to do next. She does not see Day approaching from the passenger side in his long gray coat, hands shoved deep in his pockets, his gaze fixed so steadily upon her.

"Poor Angelo," she says, and her eyes glitter with tears as Day's arms open, and then close, around her.

Driving home in the vanishing winter light that makes her feel utterly forlorn, she ignores Day's attempts at conversation. When at last he gives up and lapses into silence, she finds that unbearable too. She studies the clouds of their breath, the glow of the illuminated dashboard, the position of her pale hands against the steering wheel.

"Want to know something?" she says. "When I first met Henry, I went after him like there was no tomorrow. I saw him in that classroom, mourning his lost marriage, and I thought, Now there's a great-looking guy who could use a shot in the arm. And I gave it to him. I followed him home and took off my clothes and brought him back to life. And all of that was meant to be, of course. No one can convince me it wasn't. But this," she says, "what's happening now, is something else entirely. It's like we've taken a wrong turn somewhere, lost our way, and that's that. He tells me he wants his ashes kept on top of the piano, and I'm supposed to nod my head and say 'On top of the piano? Certainly. Unless of course you think the bookcase might be nicer somehow.' " She looks at Day, glares at him in exasperation. "This is a conversation that's for real? This is my life?" When Day doesn't answer, she begins to laugh. "So I'll move back to New York and take a Grief Workshop with a bunch of other loonys. Grief 101 and then a follow-up course a few months later. Grief 102: How to Get Your Act Together and Find Happiness in a World of Relentlessly Swinging Singles."

"There's no food in the house," Day says gently.

"Am I supposed to care about that?"

"We've got to stop off at the supermarket."

Slowing at a red light, Kate searches in her purse for her wallet and throws it across the seat at Day. "I can't make any decisions right now. I'll drop you off at Price Chopper or something, and you can go in and buy to your heart's content."

"I'm warning you," Day says. "Send me in there and I'll come back with tofu and rice cakes and maybe, if you're lucky, some red pepper thrown in for color."

"Don't threaten me, big shot," says Kate, giving in to his smile, to his hand resting sweetly at the back of her neck. In the supermarket, she allows him to lead the way and to fill their wagon with things he knows will please her. He knows her so well, she thinks; if they were married, he could not know her any better, really. He has seen her at her worst, staggering into the bathroom in the early morning in her pink-and-white seersucker robe, hair in her eyes, nose shiny, her mouth sour. He has witnessed her infrequent arguments with Henry, her impatience with Darlan, her lapses in housekeeping. He has heard the sound of her weeping, berating her child, insulting her husband. He knows just how far from perfect she is. Oddly, in all the months he has lived with them, he has rarely shown anything but a true sweetness and patience. She does not know if he has ever felt like fleeing their household in search of his own happiness, and cannot believe that he has not, that he is as content as he seems. Once, a long time ago, she and Henry discussed their suspicions that he might be gay, but they soon lost interest in the subject and that was the end of it. He has been a part of their family for nearly a year and yet in many ways is still a stranger. She wants to ask him who he really is and where that kiss came from. It was the kiss of a lifetime, mysterious, completely unexpected, absolutely stunning. Like a teenager, she relives it from time to time just before she falls asleep, remembering its heat, the way her skin blazed for so long afterward. Telling Tiki about it a day or two later, she waited for that sickish feeling of guilt and remorse to overtake her, but it never did. There's a restlessness in her groin now as she stands behind Day in the check-out line in this extravagantly large, chilly supermarket, noisy and crowded so close to dinnertime. She is, she tells herself, like everyone in the lines all around her, just an ordinary person, full of her own sorrows and looking for a way out.

When, a moment later, Day turns around to ask her about the price of a carton of orange juice, she is already gone, running through the parking lot to ease the restlessness that has spread now to her limbs, her hands, her feet, her heart.

Tiki hands Darlan over gratefully, saying, as she shakes her head, "This little cutie pie, she ain't what she used to be, let me tell you."

"Little Miss Sweetness and Light?" Kate says, without irony. "What happened?"

"Oh, a few minor skirmishes here and there, but we'll forgive her." Tiki kisses Darlan's forehead, then asks about Henry.

"It's probably pneumonia. But he's tough, he'll be home in a few days, I bet."

"Worried?" Tiki asks. "What am I saying, how could you not be?"

Kate shifts Darlan lower down against her shoulder, fluffing out her fine wild baby hair with one hand. "We'll see," she says.

"Come cry on me anytime you like," Tiki offers.

"Not me," Kate says. "That's not my style."

"You're not made of steel, are you?" Tiki says as one of her kids passes by with bright red Jell-O oozing from the fingers of his fists like blood. "Or are you?"

"Yeah, and I can fly, too. And the only thing my X-ray vision can't penetrate is lead."

"Stay for dinner," Tiki says. "We'll get a pizza or something."

"I can't. But thanks."

"I'm begging you," says Tiki. "Can't you see I'm desperate for the company of grown-ups?"

"You'll do a whole lot better without me tonight, kiddo." Darlan begins to wriggle in her arms and Kate lets her slip slowly down to the floor. "Believe me," she says, "I'm hardly fit for socializing with humans."

"This is me you're talking to," Tiki says. "I'm barely human myself, most of the time."

"We'll talk soon, I promise."

Walking homeward across Tiki's frozen lawn, Kate and Darlan hold hands and swing their arms high and low. "Brush brush brush brush, plaque plaque plaque plaque," Darlan sings tunelessly.

"What a lovely song. Where did you learn it?"

"My daddy," Darlan says. "I talked to him on the telephone."

"Interesting," Kate says, as they walk through the door into light and warmth and the sound of Day at the piano.

"Oh, I love my daddy so," Darlan sings to Day's music. She unzips her jacket and struggles out of it, then flings it to the ground. "How long are we going to keep him?" she asks.

"I don't know what you're talking about, sweetie pie," Kate says, and picks up the jacket. Absently, she cradles it in her arms.

"When do we have to give him back, I mean," Darlan says.

"Give him back where?"

But Darlan has already lost interest, and disappears down the hallway and into her room, slamming the door behind her like an exasperated adolescent.

Stretched out on the living room floor, head propped against her palm, Kate contemplates the cluttered Scrabble board with a yawn. "Are four-letter words permissible?" she asks Day. "Because if they're not, I'm out of luck."

"What kind of four-letter words?"

"The nasty kind."

"Let me consult the official Scrabble rules," Day says, and grabs the cover to the box. "Let's see, it says right here in traditional black and white that if there are no players under the age of seventeen, the game may be rated X, i.e., full frontal nudity and coarse language acceptable.''

Kate sits up, folds the Scrabble board in half, tilting it sharply so that the tiles slide to the floor in a jumble. "Sorry," she says. "I just checked the score and saw that I was losing by almost fifty points and suddenly it was clear to me that drastic measures were called for. And anyway, I have a much more interesting game in mind. Truth or Consequences: ever hear of it?''

"Nope.''

"Well," Kate says, smiling, "it goes like this: tell me about your marriage, or face the consequences.''

"Which are?''

"That's easy, I tie you to a kitchen chair and force-feed you Steak Tartare.''

Clapping a hand to his forehead, Day closes his eyes, as if in pain. "Is my face ashen?" he says. "My palms clammy?''

"So what's the scoop on this marriage? Or shall I head for the freezer and defrost some chopped sirloin in the microwave?''

Now it is Day who lies back, hands clasped underneath his head. "Do I have to keep my eyes open?''

"Open or shut, suit yourself. All I ask is that you speak directly into the tape recorder.''

Eyes shut, Day begins, "Let's just say it was short and relatively sweet, rather like my wife, actually. For about a year or so I was pretty contented, and then came the call of the wild, and the marriage was history.''

"You split for the Yukon?''

"Bloomingdale's," Day says. "The word was out that Bloomingdale's on a Saturday afternoon was the perfect place for . . .''

"For what?''

Day breathes in and out noisily. "For guys like me to pick up guys like me," he says. "So I hung around forever in the men's department on the first floor, pretending to look longingly at some very expensive cotton sweaters, and sure enough, my social life got very complicated. Elizabeth didn't want to try and work things out, she just wanted to go to dental school, preferably in another state, and devote herself to the care of other people's teeth. When she got out of Penn, she came back to New York to start her own practice and of course I ran into her on the street. She was wearing an engagement ring, and a wisdom tooth around her neck on a gold chain. Her life was in great shape but she still felt compelled to tell me I was a fucked-up guy."

"And are you?" Kate says. She has listened to his story without a great deal of surprise, and yet she feels an inexplicable disappointment, as if he has let her down somehow. His sexual preferences are his own business, after all: surely he does not owe her an apology or explanation. So why does it seem as if she has just been given a piece of bad news? Suddenly she feels awkward in his company, uneasy at the sight of him lying so casually on her living room floor, his head resting on a silk batik pillow given to her as a wedding gift.

"I may have been then," he says, "but this AIDS thing has gone a long way toward helping me get my priorities straight. I just can't afford to indulge every little urge I happen to feel. So, in fact, I don't indulge any of them, not those particular urges anyway. It's been clear for a long while that I can't go back to that life I had in New York, that it's just too dangerous."

"So where does that leave you?" Kate says.

Day smiles, opens his eyes at her. "Safe, healthy, confused . . ."

"Lonely?" Kate asks.

"You'd think so, wouldn't you, but it's not really like that. I feel so bound to Henry, to you, this family; it's what consumes me, really, what keeps me going."

"For now, at least," Kate says in a whisper.

Day nods. "For now," he says.

As she rises wide-awake from her bed at 2:42 in the morning, Kate lays her hand across her heart, feeling its swift, terrified flutter. She makes her way in darkness to the kitchen, where she stands at the refrigerator and drinks Coca-Cola straight from the bottle, the inside of the refrigerator door icy at her back. Her bare feet are icy, too, and something sticks to the bottom of one of them: an old Cheerio that she examines in the refrigerator's light and then tosses in the direction of the sink. Except for the three nights she was in the hospital when Darlan was born, she has not slept alone in years. "Get used to it, kiddo," she tells herself, in a voice so soft she may only have imagined it. She wishes now that Darlan were one of those kids who sleepwalked night after night to her parents' bed, appropriated space for herself, and stayed until morning. A bad habit, of course, one that absolutely had to be broken, but what a comfort, Kate thinks—a sweet warm presence to savor all through the night.

She smokes a cigarette, her first in ages, and strains to see the smoke in the pitch dark. She unloads half the dishwasher, quietly stacking plates on the countertop. And then the room floods with light and she is blinking at Day in his sweatpants, his bare chest a surprise on this winter night.

"I smelled smoke," he says, and takes the plate that she is holding out in front of her like an offering.

She focuses on the dark field of hair that ornaments

his chest. "I can't sleep," she says. "I mean, I can't sleep alone, it's just not a natural state for me."

"Are you hungry?"

Shrugging her shoulders, she says, "Want to share a candy bar?" In the cabinet, she rummages around until she finds a Nestlé's Crunch, which she splinters into odd-shaped pieces and abandons on the counter. She walks past Day, then steps back and twists a curl of hair from his chest around her finger.

"Thanks, I'd love some," he says.

"What?"

"Some hostess—you offer me a candy bar and then forget all about me." He reaches beyond her to the counter and slips a piece of chocolate into her mouth and then his own.

"I can't sleep," she says. She admires his broad wrists, the well-developed muscles of his upper arms, the bones of his hips that she sees peeking out over the rim of his sweatpants. She knows that he sees her looking, and she begins to tremble.

"I'm here," he says. Hands at her shoulders, he steers her through the doorway, through the familiar space of her darkened house and into his bedroom.

"I just want you to hold me," she says as they fall upon his bed. But she says nothing as he lifts her night-gown over her head and lets it drop to the floor. Lightly, he runs his hands everywhere along her body, and she listens in amazement to the sound of her own pleasure. "Let me see you," she says. Shrugging off his sweatpants, he smiles at her. "You have a beautiful body," she cries out, grateful for the sight of it, for the feel of hard muscle and the flesh drawn tautly across it. In truth, she does not know whether he is beautiful or not, whether the propor-tions are exactly as they should be; she only knows that his body is perfect in its youthfulness and that he can do anything she asks. She knocks on the ridges of her hips, feels the lovely soft flesh of her inner thighs, squeezes a breast gently. Like Day, she is perfect too, and this is what makes her forget the sorrow of her life, all sorrow, as she seizes Day and gives herself up to the pleasure she has all but forgotten for what seems as long as a lifetime.

She awakens to bright, almost blinding sunlight, and the sound of the telephone ringing. She is back in her nightgown, back in her own bed, though she has only the vaguest memory of getting there. Darlan is at the foot of the bed with her paintbook, a long, skinny paintbrush in one hand, a custard cup half-filled with water in the other.

"I'll get it," Darlan says, and reaches for the phone.

"Where do we paint in this house?" Kate yells. "Do we paint in bed or do we paint on the kitchen table?"

"The kitchen table," Darlan says into the phone.

"Who is it?" whispers Kate.

"Who?" Darlan says.

"Find out, please."

"I have to paint first, one picture and that's all, how about that?"

Sighing, Kate picks up the receiver and listens as a woman claiming to be Cynthia instantly launches into a story about a trip to Toronto, lost luggage, and the bumper-to-bumper traffic she was caught in on her way back from the airport.

"Cynthia?" Kate says. "Hold it a minute."

"You have to listen to me. So they finally find my luggage and I get in from the airport, vaguely car-sick from all that stop-and-go traffic, and here's this unbearable letter from Henry waiting for me, and what am I

supposed to do? Unpack my suitcase, pack up an overnight bag, go back to the airport, get on another plane
and—"

"Calm down," Kate says.

"You don't know me," says Cynthia. "It seems to me
you have no right to tell me to calm down."

"It was just a suggestion," Kate says mildly. "Feel
free to ignore it."

"I'm sorry; we don't really know how to talk to each
other, you and I, do we? Do you think I might talk to
Henry, instead?"

"He's not here," Kate says, and pauses. "He's in the
hospital."

"Am I too late?" Cynthia says. "Oh Lord," she moans.

"Too late for what?"

"I don't know, to see him again, to talk to him again
one last time, I suppose."

Kate sits up straight, uses her hand as a visor to shield
her eyes against the sunlight, as if she could see Cynthia
more clearly without the sun in her eyes. "Of course
you're too late," she says. "Ex-wives don't, as a rule,
have visiting hours around here."

"I won't intrude on your life," Cynthia promises. "I'll
stay overnight in a motel and I'll fly back the next day.
We don't even have to see each other—I'll leave just as
you're getting to the hospital. We'll be like two ships
passing in the night, if that's what you want."

"Whose idea was this?" Kate asks.

"It's right here in this letter. Very neatly typed, I must
say. Do you want me to read it to you?"

"Spare me," Kate says. She slides a finger across her
front teeth, then bites deeply into her fingertip, stopping
just short of causing herself pain. "Look," she says, "I've
never been an ex-wife, never had an ex-husband. I don't

really know how these things work. I imagine there's a residue of pain, and love, too, but frankly, I don't really care. I'm not interested in any of it."

"It's the end of his life," Cynthia says softly. "There are certain things he needs to do, I suppose. It wouldn't be right to stand in his way."

"But I'm jealous," Kate hears herself murmur.

Cynthia laughs at this. "Don't be," she says. "Our marriage was a serious mistake. There was nothing right about it, ever."

"That's old news. And it doesn't cheer me up in the least."

"Well, I was so glad when he married you," Cynthia says. "It was such a relief; it was like I was off the hook, finally, and now it was someone else's turn to pay attention, to do the work of making him happy. And there was no sadness at the thought of never seeing him again, only relief, how do you like that."

"So why *do* you want to see him again?" Kate says. She thinks of Henry's trip to Boston almost two years ago, of Henry and Cynthia in the sack together one last time, and it suddenly strikes her as preposterous, the idea of two utterly mismatched people on fire like that in the middle of the afternoon. Not only preposterous, but something that has absolutely nothing to do with her. Just as she and Day together have nothing to do with Henry, with her undeniable love for Henry. She doesn't know if what happened last night will happen again, or even if it is something she hopes for. This morning she feels renewed, strong, close to happiness; she will simply be grateful for what her time with Day has brought her.

"I don't know," Cynthia is saying, "maybe I won't come after all. I don't know if I'm up to it. It could be very unnerving seeing him like that, just too stressful for someone like me. I'm not a very strong person; I could never do what you're doing, seeing someone through a terrible illness. Undoubtedly, I'd be a miserable failure at it."

"Listen, could you cut to the chase, please. I have to tell you I'm starting to lose patience with you, Cynthia."

"Then help me. You have to help me decide what to do."

"Flip a coin," Kate says, looking at the deep, ceramic ashtray at her bedside that's cluttered with change and paperclips and keys. "Be scientific."

"You don't want me to come, do you?"

"Of course I don't want you to come."

"Okay," says Cynthia. "Heads I call the airlines, tails I stay home and torture myself."

Kate hears the slap of Cynthia's palm across her knuckles, imagines the dull face of the quarter or nickel or dime that has come to rest neatly between her hands.

"Oh Lord," she hears Cynthia wail. "What if I fall to pieces when I see him? What if we have nothing to say to each other? Maybe it's better if I just send flowers and a deeply felt note."

"Roses would be perfect," Kate says brightly. "Or birds of paradise, maybe, something sturdy that will last."

"Valium," Cynthia says. "If I'm going to come I need a new prescription, even if I'm only going to stay overnight."

"I thought you were sending flowers and a note."

"I did say that, didn't I? Oh Lord, I'm in such a quandary. Let me put the phone down so I can wring my hands; maybe that will make me feel better."

"Or I could wring your neck *for* you," Kate mumbles. "That would make *me* feel better."

"I'll get back to you in a little while," says Cynthia. "Or maybe tomorrow."

"Next week, next month, take your time," Kate tells her. "And remember, you can always say it with flowers." She hangs up the phone and heads for the kitchen, where Darlan and Day are at the table, heads bent over the paintbook. Day's hair is wet from the shower and looks almost blue-black; she breathes in the lingering fragrance of his shampoo, and holds back the kiss she would like to drop at the top of his head. She is shy in his presence, she realizes, and wonders if he feels this same hesitancy at facing her, if he will keep his head lowered forever. And then she remembers she has reason to be angry with him, and her shyness vanishes.

"Excuse me," she says, giving Day's shoulder a sharp tap. "Informed sources report you type a very neat letter. I just got off the phone with Cynthia."

"What?" he says, and looks up at her slowly.

"So Henry dictated and you typed. It must have been quite a project. What did it take, a whole afternoon?"

"I tried to talk him out of it but he wouldn't budge. I'm sorry," Day says. "It's what he wanted."

"You should have ripped it up when you went out to mail it."

"I couldn't. We drove to the post office together."

"The post office? I'm surprised he didn't go all out and Federal Express it."

"You're over-reacting," Day says. "How about if I make you a mushroom omelet before you go to the hospital. I have some great-looking mushrooms I was going to save for my dinner, but since you're so pissed off at me I think I'll sauté them for you right now."

"Mushrooms," says Kate. "Thanks to your wonderful typing skills, Henry's little Looney Tune is probably coming to town."

"I like Looney Tunes," Darlan says. "And I like mushrooms, too. But I don't like black olives—too spicy."

"You're kidding," Day says. "I really don't think Henry ever expected her to come. He said she'd have a crippling anxiety attack on the way to the airport and would turn right around and go home."

"Oh, God, I hope so," Kate says. "And you better hope so too, because if she sets one foot in this house, I'm never going to forgive you."

"Really." Day makes a playful grab for her and pulls her downward and into his lap. She falls awkwardly against him, hits the top of her head on his chin.

"Not a good idea," she says, gesturing with an upward sweep of her head toward her daughter, and scrambling off of Day.

"My daddy's in the hospitable," Darlan says. She brandishes her paintbrush threateningly in her mother's face as Kate leans toward her. "And he's not going to talk to you *any more*."

"Sure he is," Kate says, her heart thumping. "Why not, sweetie?"

But Darlan chooses to play it cool. "Daddy and Mommy, Mommy and Daddy," is all she says.

CHAPTER EIGHTEEN

One of the nurses, the skinny one with the cold hands, is standing over me with a quizzical look on her face. "You were humming in your sleep," she says. "The strange thing is, it was a real song—something I've heard before, Cole Porter, maybe."

I smile at her, instantly remembering my dream. In it, I was standing around on a dance floor somewhere, snapping my fingers, savoring that wonderful sharp clear sound for a while. Then I began to dance with Kate, tricky numbers like the mambo, the rumba, the hustle—dances I've never been able to do in real life. Around me in an admiring circle were Cynthia, Nina, and Darlan, each of them clapping in rhythm, each waiting their time at bat with me. They all got their turn in the comfort of my arms, and I was the smoothest of operators, sweet-talking each of them as I shook my hips, spun and whirled across the dance floor.

"Open up, please," the nurse says, and deposits a green, oval-shaped pill into my mouth. "You have a visitor," she reports. "A lady friend. Do you want me to comb your hair? A little after-shave might be nice, too." She pretties me up with those cold hands and holds a mirror to my face.

"Not so bad," I say, and in walks Cynthia. She's wearing the same silk dress she had on in Boston, high heels, and a silver necklace and earrings. She's as pale as ever, and as soon as I begin talking, she grows even paler. "Don't be afraid," I say. "It's just me behind these Foster Grants." It's hopeless to continue without an interpreter, of course, but I'm not about to sit here like a dummy when I have so much to say. "Come on and pull up a chair," I offer. "I have to admit I'm truly surprised to see you."

"Don't go," Cynthia begs as the nurse is about to pass through the doorway and out of Cynthia's life forever. "I'm really having terrible trouble here."

"It's Greek to me, too," the nurse tells her. "Just talk to him and I'm sure you'll manage fine."

Hearing this, Cynthia bursts into tears. "Tissue box on the little table next to the bed," the nurse calls out over her shoulder, and then disappears.

"Perk up, Cynthia," I say. "It's bad for the patient when a visitor carries on like this. And extremely selfish of you, I might add."

Incredibly, she starts to smile. "Subtitles," she says. "It's like watching a foreign film without the subtitles."

"There you go," I say, "getting right into the spirit of things." With my foot, I reach out over the edge of the bed and give the chair next to me a kick. "Don't be shy," I say. "Come on over and sit down."

Cynthia takes her time, walking slowly with her hands behind her back, head lowered, like a condemned prisoner on her way to the scaffold. But before sitting down, she brushes her lips lightly against the corner of my eye, and I take this as a good sign. "I shouldn't have come," she tells me, and stands right up again.

"Now don't start *that*," I say. "Jesus, Cynthia."

"I got your letter and I was absolutely floored, Henry. You tell me there's not much time left, that you have this burning need to see me, that I can't deny you one last look. So I call and your wife is very rude to me and I can see that this is all a huge mistake. But here I am anyway and now it turns out you can't even talk to me. You know, Henry, I went to my friend Miss Erica at the Psychic Boutique and as soon as she saw me she said, 'You need to see an old and dear friend.' And that, frankly, was what made me get on the plane this afternoon."

"Thank God for Miss Erica," I say.

Cynthia stamps her foot in its high heel. "I have to know what you're saying!" she cries. "Doesn't this hospital have interpreters? Can't they train people to learn your language? What's the matter with this place? What's the matter with *you*?"

"My wife understands me," I say, then laugh at my choice of words. "I mean, she understands me and my speech, too."

"How can you laugh?" Cynthia says. "How can you stand to live like this? How?"

"It ain't easy," I say. But still, I'm not ready to let go yet. My chest continues to hurt with every breath, but that's going to get better. And then worse, no doubt. So what's in it for me? I want to hang around a while longer, feeling Kate's breath upon me when I awaken in the morning, watching Darlan parading so confidently past me, listening to Day's music filling my house, my life. This is what I have; these are my pleasures, and I savor them. The past is done, done and done; so be it. But there's plenty for me there, too. It's like watching old

190

movies in my head; the vivid colors have washed out, the bright sounds of those other lifetimes have softened, but not entirely. I've had a long romance with life—*of course* I'm reluctant to let it all go.

"Wake up, Cynthia!" I tell her. "You're talking to a man who's had three marriages, two daughters, and a satisfying career out in the world. You're talking to someone who's really *lived*! This isn't some Sad Sack full of regrets, who can only go over and over all the old mistakes, feeling like a fool and worse. This is me!" I bellow. "Me!"

Of course she's frightened by all this noise coming from a guy sitting in his pajamas and bare feet in a hospital bed. She looks terrified, in fact, as if at any moment I might get up and hurl myself or maybe even both of us through the window. She thinks I'm in a rage, but it's only the frustration of a man who loves to talk and can't get his audience to understand even the simplest of things.

Very tentatively, she puts her hands on my shoulders and then pushes me back against the pillows. "Are you in pain?" she says in a trembly voice. "Do you need help? What can I do?" I shake my head, and now she places my hand at the back of her neck, which is startlingly white and very damp.

"You scared the S-H-I-T out of me," she says with a small laugh. "In all the years of our marriage you never once yelled like that." She pours herself a paper cupful of water out of a plastic pitcher, sips from it a while, then holds it up to my mouth.

"Sure I did," I say. "You're an infuriating woman. I must have blown my cool God knows how many times. But I don't want to get on the subject of you and your numerous failings, I just want to get a good look at you and listen to the sound of your voice."

Sitting down, she picks up my hand and laces her fingers through mine, as casually as if she were a woman to whom this sort of thing came naturally, which certainly it did not. Most often, I remember, she preferred to keep her distance, and so at this moment, as she brings our hands to her lips and slowly kisses each of my fingers one by one, I nearly swoon with astonishment and pleasure and, perhaps, love.

"You know, Henry," she says, "you were right about one thing, at least. Remember that day in Boston when you told me that happiness was only one of the things we were here to experience—that there was also pain, fear, loneliness and everything else? Well, it's actually been a great comfort to me. I typed it up on an index card and tacked it on the bulletin board over my desk. There's a good deal of wisdom in it, really, and I'm just glad I came to my senses and finally realized it."

"I can't believe you fell for that bullshit," I say, shaking my head at her so that she gets the point. "For a person with a PhD, you really can be awfully dumb sometimes. My advice to you is just rip that card right out of your bulletin board and tear it up into a thousand pieces." I think of that wild afternoon, the two of us in a frenzy over each other in an overheated room belonging to strangers. And then there was Cynthia, clearly wanting more than I could give her, just as I had wanted from her during all those endless years of our impossible marriage. Where did I ever get all that energy, I wonder now. I can see myself driving home from Boston, speeding the way I loved to, throwing coins into the receptacles at the toll booths so jauntily, you'd think I was speeding along in more ways than one. It seems that I'm looking back at a much younger self, someone who still thought that everything—absolutely everything—was within reach. I've grown old in the two years that have passed since then, and it's still a surprise to me. But in my dreams I'm snapping my fingers, dancing up a storm with all my women, every muscle of mine beautifully at work. Heads turn in my direction whenever I'm on the dance floor; I'm incandescent, giving off heat and light, transformed by love into something dazzling.

"I don't want to leave you," I hear Cynthia saying. "It seems that I've left you so many times. That I was always leaving you. I could have been nicer," she concedes, freeing my hand at last. "More generous, more yielding."

"Can't argue with you there," I say. "And it's a pleasure to know you've finally wised up."

"Did I ruin your life?" she asks timidly.

This makes me laugh so hard, my chest and middle actually ache. "What a question!" I say. "You're very self-important, you know that?"

"I gather you're making fun of me," Cynthia says, stony-faced. She goes to the window and leans her back against the ledge. "It's good for you to laugh, I'm sure, so I'm not saying a word."

"You never did have much of a sense of humor," I tell her. "You've got to learn to lighten up, Cynthia." At this moment Kate appears, dressed in her rattiest sweats and sneakers. She and Cynthia get a good look at each other and then Kate crosses the room and shakes Cynthia's hand.

"Dr. Livingston, I presume?" she says.

"Where are *you* off to?" I ask as her cool lips graze my cheek. "Or should I say back from. You look a little sweaty."

"And in dire need of a shower. Just got back from volleyball practice. I was going to shower first but then I decided to skip it and get over here to see you instead."

"Volleyball?" Cynthia says hesitantly.

"We play in the auxiliary gym at the junior high, usually at night, after all the kids have cleared out. We were having these impromptu games on the beach all summer and then we just thought we'd . . ." Kate's voice trails off. "Maybe I'll go home and take a shower and come back after dinner."

"That's not very sociable of you," I say. "She's going to think you're just trying to make your escape."

"Damn straight I am," Kate says cheerfully.

Cynthia has been shifting her gaze back and forth from Kate to me and back and forth again, as if she were trying to follow a tennis game. "Invite her for dinner," I urge. "As a favor to me. One last request from a dying man," I say with a wink.

"That is really low, Henry, appealing to me like that," says Kate. "You ought to be ashamed of yourself."

"Come on, ask her if she has any plans for dinner."

"No thanks," Kate says.

"You're having fun, aren't you, knowing she doesn't know what the hell is going on here."

"It's kind of hard not to," Kate says, smiling.

"Will you take pity on her, for crying out loud. She's a fragile person, in her way. It took a lot for her to fly up here."

"La dee dah," Kate says. "Life is hard for all God's creatures, large and small, great and dumb, sensitive and insen—"

"Kate!" I roar, hurting my throat and chest, and absolutely exhausting myself.

"I hear you," she says. "You don't have to yell."

"Just wanted to make sure."

Kate nods at Cynthia. "Are you all right?" she asks. "You look a little shaken." She pours Cynthia some water and offers her the cup. "Interesting necklace," she says, reaching over and fingering the little porcelain face hanging from a silver chain around Cynthia's neck. "Looks familiar," she adds.

"Edvard Munch," Cynthia says. " 'The Scream'?"

Instantly, Kate lets go of the necklace and steps back from Cynthia. "What's it doing around your neck?" she says, horrified.

"It speaks to me," says Cynthia.

"I see," Kate says. "So it's like a little friend to you, is that it?"

"I didn't say it talks," Cynthia snaps. "I said it speaks to me. Of the human condition, I meant."

"Personally," I say, "I much prefer the string of pearls I gave you on our tenth anniversary."

"You gave her pearls?" says Kate.

Cynthia swings the porcelain face up and down along the chain and says nothing.

"Listen, I'm still waiting for you to extend that dinner invitation," I say. "What's taking so long?"

"There's no food in the house," Kate tells me. "Nothing suitable, anyway."

"Just scramble up a couple of goddamn eggs and put a glass of wine in front of her. It's not the food that's important, it's the gesture, that's all." It comes to me now that I'm feeling like one of those ghosts in the movie *Topper*, imperceptible to everyone in the world except for a single person. I know that Cynthia can see me, of course, but I feel invisible nevertheless—as if, in her eyes, I simply no longer exist. "Tell her I'm not invisible," I beg Kate. "Tell her I'm here, even if she doesn't believe it."

"Henry wants you to know he's still here," Kate says quietly. "He thinks you don't know that. That because you can't understand what he's saying, you're dismissing him, I guess, no longer thinking of him as someone to be reckoned with."

"And stop feeling sorry for me!" I add.

Kate translates this word for word, getting the inflection exactly right, and making all three of us laugh. And then we fall into an easy, companionable silence that I soon feel an irresistible urge to shatter. "Will you look at us," I say. "Just look at us. Aren't we doing just great?"

Five days later, when I'm released from the hospital and into Kate's arms, she seems less than joyous, and I can't figure out why. "So you're not happy at the prospect of having me home again," I finally say. "What's the deal here?" We're sitting under the carport in the GTI, neither of us ready to make a move toward the door. We stare through the windshield at the frozen brown grass of our backyard, at the extravagant swing set of treated pine that we put together for Darlan during her first summer. Unfortunately, the termites eventually had a feast with it, and the broad beam from which the swings and two kinds of gliders still hang is now partially eaten away. In the summer, a time I may or may not see, Kate will put up something new, something of shining steel and plastic. It had taken us forever, I remember, to make any headway at all with the old set, and finally we had to call in Tiki and Rob, who worked alongside us under a blazing sun, the four of us laughing and cursing at our own ineptitude and drinking so much beer it was a miracle we ever managed to finish the thing. Later, pushing Darlan in her swing for the first time, I felt like the youngest of fathers, just venturing out into new territory I had only recently claimed for my own. The baby in the swing was mine, I told myself in amazement. And too, the big strong girl in a bathing suit and T-shirt who was looking on with such pleasure. An ordinary scene in an ordinary backyard in summer, but not to me; to me, at that moment, it all seemed so unexpected, so utterly astonishing, that I actually felt faint with something that could only have been happiness. I did not argue with Kate as she led me inside into the air-conditioned house, claiming it was too much sun and too much beer that had gotten to me. I could not admit, even to her, that this life we were sharing sometimes seemed only imagined, so dreamlike that it was sure to vanish without a trace.

"I'm thrilled to death that you're home," she tells me now.

"Well that's a relief."

"It's Cynthia," she says.

"My Cynthia?"

"Your Cynthia. She seems to have settled in for the long hard winter."

"Where's your proof?" I ask. "Got any witnesses?"

"She had Day take her into town and then she went off on a shopping spree, all of it clothing. She bought nightgowns and underwear," Kate says with a small shudder. "The woman's got plans, let me tell you."

"Talk to her, then. Find out what's on her mind."

"I *know* what's on her mind," Kate says. "The worst of it is she's on leave this semester. She's going to be doing more research on her old favorite."

"Suicide?" I say. "So what's she hanging around here for?"

"Who knows? Maybe she's hoping to drive me to it and then study its effects on those who are left behind."

"She's harmless," I say. "Quit worrying."

Kate folds her arms across her chest, taps the fingers of one hand against the sleeve of her coat. "She's your ex-wife, Henry. How harmless could she be?"

"And this too shall pass," I say after a while.

"Oh sure," says Kate. "She slipped out of the Sea Breeze Motel at midnight the other night, complaining the mattress was too soft, the room smelled old, the towels had rust stains on them. And there she was on our doorstep, looking very small and bewildered, so of course I opened up the couch in the den for her, gave her our best towels and my ten-dollar bar of Shalimar soap, and then went to bed with what I thought was a sinking heart but actually turned out to be acid indigestion."

"Your Shalimar soap? I bought that for you for Christmas. And it was twelve-fifty, for your information."

"Well, you'll just have to buy me another one. I told her she could keep it."

"What did you do *that* for?" I ask.

"I don't know. I thought it would add to my anger and resentment and in fact it did."

"Now that makes a lot of sense."

"Listen," Kate says, "here's the thing: I'm not getting out of this car until I have your permission to send her packing."

"Be my guest," I say, and we both have to laugh. But then I see that there are tears in her eyes, and suddenly I'm aware of how worn-out I am, how utterly fatigued this short car trip has made me feel. I can't wait to get into bed and drift away to someplace dark and soundless, my mind a perfect smooth blank.

"What is it?" I ask Kate, hoping for no answer at all.

"It isn't good," she says, and then tells me that according to my internist, I was extremely lucky to have gotten through the pneumonia, that probably we could expect future bouts, that probably, and here she pauses, things were going to happen.

"Blah blah blah," I say, trying to sound cavalier. As if it were gossip she were passing along to me, rumors that were easy enough to dismiss. But as she helps me out of the car and leads me to the front door, I know enough to savor the ice-cold air against my face, the whitish winter sky above us, the dark severe look of the ocean. "Let's go down to the water," I tell her. When she starts to protest, I say, "One last time." And so we make our impossibly slow way toward the water's edge, a hundred feet, or, perhaps, a hundred miles, in the distance. "Take off my shoes and socks, please," I say. We're still in dry sand, and I knead my toes into it, go deep into the cool gravel, listening to the squawk of the seagulls as Kate holds me up against her without a word. Wiggling my toes, I feel young and powerful, capable of greatness. I watch their movement in the sand, thrilled at what I can still do.

"We have to go," Kate whispers, and of course she's right, and so I let her ease me down and clean my feet as best she can. She struggles with my socks, and then my shoes, and even though it takes forever to get back home and through the front door, I don't feel at all grateful when, at last, we arrive. As the door shuts behind us, I have the spooky feeling that this is it for me, that the only way I'm going out again is on a stretcher or in a body bag. My heart seems to have slid down into my stomach, where it pulses madly, and there's a ringing in my ears. The first person I see is Cynthia, down on the living room floor playing Candy Land with Darlan. "Help me," I call out to her. "I need some of your Valium quick!"

"Oh hi Daddy," Darlan yells as she runs to me. "Are you better yet?"

"Worse!" I cry. "Much worse!"

With Cynthia's help, Kate gets me onto the couch and lays me out along the cushions. "What is it?" she says. "You're scaring me."

"I'm having an anxiety attack," I say. "And any minute now I'm going to have a heart attack and die."

"No you're not," Kate says. "You're home—you know, where the heart is and all that. This is where you're happiest, where you always want to be. And look at that," she says with insincere cheeriness, gesturing to the homemade banner taped above the entranceway to the kitchen. It reads "WELCOME HOME HENRY!!!" and underneath the letters are four perfectly round grinning faces—belonging to Kate, Darlan, Day and Cynthia, I suppose.

"Very nice," I say, "and very much appreciated, but where's my Valium?"

"I don't know anything about any Valium," Kate says. She pulls off my socks and begins to rub my feet, which are clammy and studded with little bits of sand and a few dark specks of seaweed.

"*She* does," I say, nodding toward Cynthia. "She lives on the stuff."

"It's a controlled substance," Cynthia informs us. "I can't just go handing it out to any old person who happens to ask for it." Kneeling beside me at the couch, she massages my shoulders, but hesitantly, wondering, perhaps, if she ought to ask my permission first.

Darlan watches over the proceedings for a moment, then decides to join in. She pinches my cheek with a surprising fierceness and I cry out for her to stop. "Are you better yet, Daddy-doo?" she asks me again, and kisses my stinging face.

"I would be if all you handmaidens would cease and desist immediately," I say.

"Maybe he'd just like to get into bed," says Cynthia.

"You got it," I say gratefully, but of course she cannot hear the gratitude, can only interpret as she wishes the half-smile at my lips. She and Kate escort me to my bed, drawing back the quilt, plumping up pillows, smoothing out sheets with an industriousness that amuses and also touches me. I have rarely seen Cynthia appear so capable, so eager to help get things exactly right; in my memory, she was always the one in bed, listlessly asking if I would mind turning down the radio, closing the blinds, tossing the newspaper her way—whatever it was she needed for her comfort. Watching her at this moment, I'm entirely certain of her love for the first time. I'm buoyant now and imagine myself flinging my arms around her, startling her with the news that I know her secrets. *Come on and admit it, you sly fox,* I want to tell her. *After all these years I finally have you where I want you!*

But she and Kate are ignoring me, the two of them sitting at the foot of the bed, Kate listening sympathetically as Cynthia spins out another one of her tales of woe. "I was trapped in that elevator for nearly half an hour," she tells Kate. "But it really did seem like a lifetime. And even though the super in my building talked me through it, very sweetly and indulgently through the intercom, I knew that I was going to die in there. When they finally got the elevator down and the door open, I collapsed in his arms. 'Oh, Santiago,' I kept saying, and soon the shoulders of his shirt were wet from my tears. Ironically, he doesn't even like me very much because I gave him a bottle of champagne for Christmas instead of money. I knew he didn't like me but I still thought of him as my saviour. Finally he had enough of me and just pulled away and—"

"Who the hell is this guy, anyway?" I interrupt.

"Her saviour," Kate says impatiently. "Now shh, I want to hear the rest of the story."

"I don't," I say, picturing all too easily the tearful sweaty embrace just over the elevator's threshold.

"Well I do," Kate answers. "Go on," she encourages Cynthia, and I clamp my teeth together in anger.

"I'm finished," Cynthia says. "The bottom line is that I lost my fear of elevators forever."

"Hallelujah," I say. "One giant step for mankind."

"He didn't like your story," Kate tells Cynthia. "I think it was Santiago's tear-stained shirt that—"

"Thanks a lot," I say. "I really appreciate that. What are you trying to do, make me look like some idiot consumed with jealousy over a—"

"Well you are, aren't you?" Kate says, narrowing her eyes at me. "How stupid do you think I am?"

"That's it," I say. "Out she goes. Usher her to the front door immediately. Offer to pay for her plane ticket if you have to. Don't think for a minute that I'm going to let her do this to us."

"Do what?" Kate says innocently. "I'm afraid you'll have to spell it out for me in black and white."

"I love you," I say. "Come over here and I'll tell you more. There are a couple of sweet nothings I want to whisper in your ear."

Kate shakes her head. "I prefer to keep my distance, if that's all right with you."

"It isn't."

"Tough break," she says.

All this time Cynthia has been at Kate's side, politely examining her nails, the hideous charm at her neck, the gold-faced watch that fits too loosely around her wrist and which she swivels now in slow motion. "Something tells me I'm at the very center of this," she says, looking first at me and then at Kate, for confirmation. "Anyone going to come to my rescue and fill me in?"

"Ah," I say as Kate raises her hand. "A volunteer from the audience."

"He's in love with you and wants to bear your child," Kate says evenly.

"Pardon?" Cynthia murmurs, but the bewildered expression on her face tells me she's heard every word perfectly.

"She's deranged," I tell Cynthia. "And also very angry at me. Don't listen to a word that comes out of her mouth."

Kate lets out an extravagant sigh. "I think I'll just leave it to the two of you to work things out on your own," she says, and rises from the bed. "I'll be in the kitchen washing the floor, if anyone needs me."

"No!" Cynthia cries. "Please."

"Funny thing," says Kate. "They said it was a no-wax floor when they installed it, but it never looks shiny the way it's supposed to." Poised in the doorway, she shrugs her shoulders.

"Get back in here and set the record straight," I say. "Tell her you were joking around, trying to embarrass me and make me feel guilty. Which you certainly have," I add. "If it makes you feel any better."

"Tell her yourself," Kate says, and strides down the hallway and out of view.

"Good one, Kate," I call after her furiously. I'm furious at myself, too, for being so transparent, so easy to read that Kate knew exactly how jealous I was as I sat listening to Cynthia's story. I can't remember the last time Kate and I argued like this; grief-stricken and miserable, I contemplate how to make amends. And then I imagine myself on my deathbed, surrounded by feuding wives, the air bristling with hostility and disappointment, the two of them urging me to stop lingering and make it quick, and put us all out of our misery.

"I must have been crazy to have written that letter," I tell Cynthia. "It was this fantasy I had of calling you back for one last encounter, maybe even something romantic, with dim lights and a little Gershwin in the background, and whispered declarations of undying affection. An hour or two was what I had in mind; you know, short and sweet, and then back you'd go on the plane, eyes shining with tears as you took off down the runway and then rose in the sky. Bet you never knew I was such a sentimental fool, did you?"

"Your wife," Cynthia says, as she tosses back a tiny white pill, "is not at all happy with me. But once she sees what a help I can be, she's going to be grateful for my presence. In fact, she's going to wonder how she ever managed without me."

I shake my head as vigorously as I can, but she doesn't get the message.

"It's going to be all right, Henry." She sits at the edge of the bed, right up close to me, and holds my hands. "I just can't bring myself to leave you."

"Well, you're going to have to force yourself," I say. "Because I have a wife who's going to be hell to live with unless you get a move on."

"Oh, and the icing on the cake is that I've become a wonderful cook," Cynthia announces. "Kate and I can alternate fixing meals, and you can be sure this household will be running a lot more smoothly in no time. What would you say to corn casserole for dinner? It's got a lovely Ritz cracker crust—you'll be very impressed."

Again, I shake my head. "The household's running beautifully as it is," I say. "We have Day for that and he's a wonder, a whiz at everything." It occurs to me that I haven't seen him since I got back, and for the first time in our friendship, I feel let down. I'm surprised that he wasn't stationed at the piano when I made my entrance, welcoming me home with my favorite music. Perhaps it's Cynthia who scared him away, letting him think she was taking over his job, the household, everything.

"Where is he?" I say out loud, and call his name in my strongest voice.

"I'm going to learn your language," Cynthia promises. "And then neither of us will have to feel so helpless."

"Day!" I shout, stretching out his name so that it sounds like a lament.

"Day?" says Cynthia excitedly. "Look at this, I'm learning already!" She rushes out and returns a few minutes later, triumphant as she leads him into the room.

"You've got to help me, buddy," I say, when Cynthia takes off again. "Time to get the typewriter out for another assignment. We've got another letter to write and it's serious business, let me tell you."

Day moves reluctantly toward me and gazes at me with a shyness I can't figure out. "How you doing, Henry," he says.

"Not even a hug," I say. "What a welcome!" He does not respond to this but jams his hands into the back pockets of his dungarees and turns away, staring out at the ocean. "Bad news from the front?" I say. "Don't tell me I've taken a turn for the worse and didn't even know it."

"I have to go get your mother-in-law at the airport."

"Mother-in-law?" I hoot. "Wouldn't you say at this stage of the game I'm a little too old to have to worry about mothers-in-law?"

Day smiles. "I don't think Kate wanted her to come, if that makes you any happier."

"I like the lady, actually; it's her husband I could live without. I just don't need another person snooping around here while I'm trying to get some rest. It's a funny thing, but this home of mine doesn't seem to be a restful place, all of a sudden." All I want is to close my eyes and disappear for a while, but even with my eyes shut there's too much going on here, too many voices to listen for, too many secrets being exchanged in whispers I cannot quite make out.

"Don't talk so much," Day says in a soothing voice. "Let me sit here for a while and watch you fall asleep." He settles himself into the chaise longue, parked so oddly in the middle of the room. He crosses his ankles, clamps his hands down over the arms of the chair. Shutting his eyes, he looks like a sunbather who has mistakenly wandered into a sickroom.

"Wake up!" I holler, and his shoulders twitch in alarm.

"Go to sleep, Henry."

"So what do you think of Cynthia?" I ask.

"I don't know."

"Sure you do."

"Actually, she strikes me as kind of weird," Day admits. "A little too formal for my taste, all those silk dresses and high heels she's always wearing. And she looks around a lot for things to do, offers to help out, and then loses interest halfway through and wanders away. She starts to clear the table after every meal, puts a few dishes in the sink, and the next thing I know she's reading the newspaper or one of those academic journals she must have loaded up on for the plane trip."

"That sounds about right," I say.

"Darlan's crazy about her."

"You're joking."

"No, really. Don't you think kids sense when people aren't much interested in them? And then it turns out these are the very people they're drawn to, and so of course they have to try their hardest to win them over. Darlan's gotten Cynthia to brush her teeth for her every night so far, to get her dressed in the morning, to fix her hair for her. . . . It's kind of a kick, actually, watching the two of them together, huddled over a game of Candy Land, discussing things so earnestly."

I try to envision this unlikeliest of friendships and find it awfully difficult. But after a while I see Cynthia clumsily gathering Darlan's wild hair into a loose untidy ponytail, hear her sigh of satisfaction and Darlan's familiar babyish chatter and at last I float toward an untroubled sleep.

When I awaken, my mother-in-law's in town and the joint is jumping.

CHAPTER NINETEEN

It's nearly three A.M. and for several hours now Kate and her mother have been at opposite ends of the kitchen table, drinking instant coffee and smoking cigarettes, talking in hushed voices that will not disturb the sleeping household. Kate is in an ankle-length long-sleeve nightshirt and thick pink socks, her mother in a velvety lavender robe. On the other side of the wall, in the den, Cynthia is in bed flipping through a magazine, and from time to time Kate finds herself wondering if Cynthia is at all interested in the murmuring sounds she can surely hear coming from the kitchen, and if she imagines that they have been talking about her through the night.

"I just had to see for myself that you were okay," Bunny is saying. She puffs on her cigarette amateurishly, exhaling a fat cloud of smoke that lingers above the table until, with a flutter of her hand, she waves it away. "You sound so good and strong on the phone all the time that I had to think you were holding back, that you couldn't possibly be as chipper as all that."

"I'm all right," Kate says.

"You're a young person," her mother says. "This wasn't meant to be."

"What wasn't meant to be?"

"All of this, every bit of it, going all the way back to day one, when you met him in that ridiculous class. You should have had better sense than to march yourself straight into the eye of disaster like that. Ordinary common sense is what I'm talking about."

"Common sense?" Kate cries. "What has any of this got to do with common sense?"

"Isn't it wonderful that we can be so honest with each other?" Bunny says as she puts her cigarette out. "It's love that lets us be so honest. For instance, if I didn't love you so much, I'd be sitting here pretending that you did the right thing, telling you that the couple of good years you had with him were well worth it, all the suffering, the difficult—"

"Six almost perfect years," says Kate, "from the day we met until he got sick. Don't you dare try to minimize that."

"Don't get so excited, *mamalah*," her mother says. "I wasn't trying to cheat you out of anything. It's just that it breaks my heart to think that you could just as easily have fallen for someone born in the right decade as—"

"Why am I listening to this?" Kate says. "It's three in the morning and I'm letting you lecture me as if I were some teenager who made the mistake of going to the senior prom with the wrong boy."

"You did go to the prom with the wrong boy, but never mind about that. Just listen to me: you have a daughter. Is this what you would wish for her? This?"

Slowly, reluctantly, Kate shakes her head. *Of course not.*

"Okay, then," Bunny says in a near-whisper. "Okay."

Kate tries hard to ignore the look of satisfaction that settles briefly across her mother's face. In her mother's presence, she is overcome with loneliness, with the knowledge that her life is her own, its burdens entirely hers. She thinks immediately, with excitement and also with a flash of shame, of Day, of his wonderfully vigorous body, the reassuring strength of his arms and legs wrapped so tightly around her in his narrow bed. She imagines—senselessly, she knows—that he will stay on after Henry's death, that she, and not Henry, is the reason he is here at all. Henry's death. Only recently, at odd moments, she has caught herself envisioning it, yearning for it, almost. She has seen herself closing his eyes for him, sitting at his bedside with her hand in his, waiting for it to grow cold. She is young and exceptionally selfish, she thinks, deeply in love with a man whose death she daydreams of. And when it finally comes, it will seem so familiar to her, not at all frightening, but simply the end of something that could no longer be. It is the loss of love she fears most, the loss of that certainty that is Henry's love. How will she survive without it? It anchors her to life; without it she will surely lose her way.

"Gimme shelter." It's Darlan, standing in the kitchen blinking up at her, an elfin figure with disheveled hair and flushed cheeks.

"Excuse me?" says Kate, knowing she cannot possibly have heard right. "What do you want, sweetie pie? What are you doing out of bed?"

"Gimme seltzer," says Darlan. "And ice."

Gathering her swiftly up from the floor, Kate breathes in her daughter's innocence, the absolute pureness of her love. "Who's the best girlie in the whole wide world?" Kate says gratefully. "Who?"

"Amanda."

"Who's Amanda?"

"Amanda at my play-school," Darlan says. She traces the arc of Kate's eyebrow, begins tweezing the hairs with her fingertips. *"She's* the best girl."

"Wrong," says Kate. "I meant *you.*"

"No," Darlan says firmly. "Amanda."

"If I say you're the best girl, then you are, goddamnit."

"Kate," her mother warns, but Darlan is already in noisy tears.

"It's all right, sweetie," Kate soothes her. "If you say you're not the best girl in the world who am I to contradict you?" She lets go of Darlan and watches as she pulls the refrigerator door open and grabs a bottle of seltzer down with both hands.

"I want to drink it the way Daddy does." Throwing her head back, Darlan brings the neck of the bottle to her lips. "This is broken," she says disgustedly.

"You have to take the cap off first," Kate says, and smiles. "And incidentally," she adds, as she unscrews the cap, "that's not the way we drink in this house."

"Daddy does. When I was a little girl he did."

"Daddy used to do a lot of things."

"That's right," Darlan says. "When I was a little girl he used to talk to me. He used to tell me stories that weren't true."

"And what else did he do?"

"I don't know," Darlan says. Seltzer dribbles along her pajama top but she ignores it and takes another slug from the bottle.

"He used to give you rides on his shoulders and let you touch the ceiling. And color with you in your coloring books. And tickle you. And powder you up when you got out of the bath."

"He did not."

"Sure he did," Kate says. She cannot bear it that Darlan will not remember the slightest thing about him. Years from now, her daughter will study an album full of photographs, shake her head in amazement at the smiling stranger upon whose shoulders she sits so happily. In whose arms she lies contentedly. An unimaginable loss; everything, every bit of time spent together utterly forgotten.

"Listen to me, Darlan," she says urgently. "You have to pay attention."

Handing Kate the seltzer bottle, Darlan says, "I want to go to sleep."

"You have to watch Daddy very carefully. Talk to him and watch his face. Hold his hand, climb in bed with him, do all the things you like to do."

"Now?" Darlan asks.

"Of course not. It's the middle of the night."

"You're so silly," Darlan says. Not quite three, still a baby, really, she is capable of many things—operating a VCR, setting the table for a meal, understanding the rules of a household. But so much of the world is still beyond her reach. Knowing this, knowing her own foolishness, Kate presses on, pretending the tiny sleepy figure at her side is someone else, already grown, already finished.

"You'll have nothing," she says. "Unless you pay attention now there'll be nothing for you afterward."

Darlan nods, then says, "I want Grandma to lie down on the floor next to my bed and count to ten in all the languages and then I want to go to sleep."

"Grandmas don't lie on the floor under any circumstance," says Bunny. "But what are the languages I have to know?"

"French, spinach, the ugly language, and English."

"What's the ugly language?"

"German," says Kate. "Do you think you could find it in your heart to go and lie down with her?"

"As a rule," says Bunny, "I don't lie on floors in the middle of the night or at any other time. However, in this case, I'm going to make an exception."

"Thank you, your highness. I'm really very grateful," Kate says.

"Are you angry at me?" Bunny asks. She lifts Darlan into her arms and presses the child's head against her shoulder. "Go to sleep, you."

"In the heat of the moment I was," Kate says. "But now . . ." She shrugs her shoulders. "You were hard on me and I didn't expect that. Not from you, anyway. You disappointed me. And you said a lot of remarkably dumb things." Her mother is staring at her, her gaze steady, unafraid. "This is my *life*," Kate says. "What do *you* know about it?"

"Not enough, apparently," Bunny says, and is silent. "I fantasize about coming here by helicopter," she soon says, "hovering above the house for a while, lowering one of those ropes and pulling you and Darlan to safety."

"And Henry?"

Bunny shakes her head.

"Say it!" Kate cries.

"He's what I'm rescuing you from," whispers Bunny. "He's—"

"Don't talk to me anymore."

"I'm your mother," Bunny says helplessly. "It's just the way a mother sees things. There's no other way."

"I know," Kate hears herself murmur, astonishing them both, she thinks. She waves her mother and Darlan away, out of the room, and watches their retreat, her mother's shoulders slumped in obvious sorrow. She pushes the coffee cups and ashtrays toward the center of the table and puts her head down, hoping for nothing more than solitude, and to savor the darkness behind her closed eyes. In a while, minutes or hours later—she has no idea which—someone tiptoes past, then stops, turns back, places an arm gently across her shoulders.

"Go to bed," Cynthia whispers close to her ear. There's a rustle of silk as she stands up and backs away slightly so Kate can see her face. "Or would you like me to make some tea?"

"What time is it?"

"4:04," Cynthia says cheerfully, as if she were delivering good news.

"Why is it that a little bit of sleep is so much worse than none at all?" Kate stares in amusement while Cynthia fills the teapot at the sink, opens and closes cabinet doors, takes down cups and saucers, slices a lemon, sets out napkins and placemats. She does every bit of this with great confidence, as if she were perfectly at ease in this house belonging to her ex-husband and his wife. It hardly seems likely, Kate thinks, and yet here is Cynthia parading around in the kitchen in a silk robe and bare feet, happy to be of use, happy to be just where she is. Kate studies the dark shining polish across Cynthia's toenails, her small, bony ankles and wrists, her pale eyes and face. She is lovely in a delicate way that Kate admires and perhaps would envy, if Cynthia were some thirty years younger. So this is the one Henry had stubbornly set his heart on so many years ago. An ordinary woman, clearly smarter and prettier than most, but not much of a presence. And still Henry grows cranky at the thought of her briefly embracing a man he's never met. Kate's heart begins to beat swift and loud at the thought, as if she were in real danger. In danger of what? Losing out at the last moment to this fragile-looking gray-haired woman who lives on Valium and has finally triumphed over her fear of elevators? How could she possibly be someone to be afraid of?

"Can't," Kate murmurs.

"What?" says Cynthia. An excellent hostess, she pours Kate her tea, offers her lemon, sugar, and milk.

"I don't know why you're here," Kate tells her. "I can guess why you came, but I don't know why you're here now."

Meticulously, Cynthia tips teaspoons of sugar into her teacup, then takes her time stirring it. "Will you let me stay?" she says finally.

"I have no idea what to do." About anything, Kate almost adds.

Cynthia smiles slightly at this. "I'd leave if only I could," she says. "But somehow I just can't."

"Deserting a sinking ship and all that?"

"Partly. And also it seems that I've never *done* anything for him before, never tended to him in a wifely way, the way other women seem to do so naturally. Like you," she says quietly, enviously, Kate thinks. "It was something that was always missing from our marriage, something that Henry must have missed terribly. And I wasn't even aware of it. And even if I had been, I doubt it would have been any different. What would I have done—forced myself to be attentive? Toward the end of our marriage, I used to watch friends of mine when they were out with their husbands, watch how one or the other of them would take her husband's hand and play with it, maybe bring it to her mouth for a kiss, absently, almost without thinking, and I would say to myself, What is this all about? Why is it I don't feel the urge to approach Henry like this? And you know what, it just seemed to be one more piece of evidence proving that I was a solitary creature, someone who didn't need to be so deeply entangled with another human being."

"So you want another chance, is that it?"

"I just want to watch over him, let him know I'm capable of that, at least."

"This is my husband you're talking about," Kate says. "What am I supposed to do, share him with you?"

"That really does sound laughable, doesn't it."

"Bizarre, anyway."

"Insane," Cynthia says.

"Demented," says Kate. She feels herself softening, loosening, dangerously close to laughter.

"Deranged."

"Loony," Kate says and gives in to the laughter that fills her eyes with tears and leaves her wheezing. Looking at her, listening to her, Cynthia loses all control and the two of them rise from their seats and stumble about the kitchen, as if they were walking off a drug-induced stupor. They bump into chairs, against the stove and refrigerator, and finally into each other. Casting her arms outward to steady herself, Kate closes them, lightly at first, around Cynthia, who staggers into her embrace, eyes startled and a little afraid. Feeling Cynthia's weight against her, and then her arms rising uncertainly, and falling across her back, Kate nods her head in gratitude, wishing Cynthia knew what *she* knows for certain; that this was inevitable, this oddly satisfying moment in her kitchen just before the sun rises soundlessly over their shoulders and above their heads and the household comes to full life.

CHAPTER TWENTY

I'm feeling a bit cloudy, I tell Day as he sponges me down in the bed that has become, these past few weeks, my little home away from home, as I call it. Too lazy and weak to leave it except to venture out to the bathroom, I stay here and let the world come to me.

"Cloudy?" says Day. He thinks he has misunderstood me and tries to read my lips as I reassure him he's got it right.

"Fuzzy," I say. For the first time in my life, at least as far as I can recall, I don't know what day of the week it is.

"Thursday," Day says helpfully. "Third week in February."

"Weather?"

"Icy, the kind of air that makes your face hurt, and your teeth, too, if you've got any cavities that need to be filled." Day slips my sweat pants down, washes my thighs and between my legs, dries me off, dusts me with baby powder. He's sweet and tender, almost like a lover as he handles me. I've grown used to his touch, grown unashamed. I love him for his friendship, for all the good he has done this household.

"Are you going to miss me, buddy?" I ask him. "When I'm gone from here, I mean."

"I try not to think about it too much." Wringing out the sponge into a plastic basin, he turns his back on me.

"What will you do? Where will you go? You've got to begin thinking about these things," I say. "I'm sure Kate will be happy to have you stay on for a while, but after a few weeks it's probably going to start feeling a little awkward for you. For both of you, don't you think?"

"She . . . ," he says, and turns to face me.

"She what?"

"Nothing," he says. And then he's all business, arranging an assortment of pillows behind my back, shaking out crumbs from the comforter, folding an extra blanket at my feet. There's a nervousness in his movements, a jumpiness about him that puts *me* on edge, too.

"You're holding back, buddy," I tease him. "What's going on? You been hanging around those bars in Portland, the ones you need a password to get into? Don't tell me you're in love."

"I'm not in love with anyone," he says.

"Too bad," I say. "You ought to be. It makes life a lot easier. And harder, too, of course. Especially in your case."

"I've been straight for a long while," he tells me. "Years. You know that."

"Well, you're not being straight with me now. I'm the one who can read your mind, baby, remember?"

His face blazes at this, but all he tells me is old news. "I'm not in love with anyone," he repeats.

"Suit yourself," I say. "If there are things you can't tell me, I have to respect that. I wish you well, buddy, that's all." Without warning, a wave of self-pity hits me full-force and I begin to weep, keeping it as quiet as I can. "I wish I could take all of you with me," I blubber noisily. "That's going to be the hardest part, leaving all of you behind to fend for yourselves." And then I have to laugh, thinking of Kate and Cynthia arguing over the arrangements for the memorial service, dividing up my ashes in two separate containers, one marked "Henry Part I," the other "Henry Part II." I tell this to Day, hoping to get a smile out of him, but he's not biting.

"Come on, buddy," I urge him. "Not even a bitter little smile?"

He wipes my eyes with a warm washcloth and shakes his head. Rubbing his palms along my cheeks, he says, "You're in desperate need of a shave. It's been a few days, at least." He heads for the bathroom and returns with a can of coconut-scented shaving cream and a silvery razor. "All set to go," he warns, "unless, of course, you're planning on growing a beard in your old age."

"Just watch it," I say. "Cut my throat and you'll never forgive yourself." He lathers me up gently and takes the razor to my face. "I want you to speak at the memorial service," I tell him. "I can't think of anyone I'd rather have."

"I couldn't," Day says. He looks at me fearfully, as if I'd suggested something dangerous to life and limb.

"Why the hell not?"

He tries to come up with a reasonable response and then at last says, "I'm not a public speaker. I'm too shy for that sort of thing."

"That's a lot of bullshit," I say. "You played the piano in public. In front of strangers in the food court, day in and day out." I give him the fiercest look I can manage. "I'm not buying this shy business," I say. "You're lying to me and I hate that. What is it with you, buddy?"

"It isn't anything," he murmurs. He finishes up the shave in silence and gives me a look at myself in a small round metal-framed mirror. What I see is a man with a dot of shaving cream on his nose, a man who's been betrayed. Of course. *Of course.*

"You shitty little bastard," I say quietly.

"What?" Taking the mirror away, he rinses out the razor in the basin of water with a surprisingly steady hand.

"What? You and Kate, that's what, lover boy. This is the way it starts: she can't sleep, you can't sleep. No one can sleep except Darlan, who, fortunately for those involved, sleeps through the whole thing without a whimper." With my foot, I strike out at Day, catching him sharply in the thigh so that he falters for a moment and then regains his balance. Not all that much of a kick, but it does wonders for my self-esteem. "I'm sorry," I say immediately afterward. "I had to do that, but I'm sorry anyway." I stare directly into his dark mournful eyes. "And you?" I say. It's easy enough to see him as Kate surely must—a tall well-built guy with all his parts in good working order, a piano-player, a juggler, a sweetheart of a guy who came to call in the dark. I can't say that I blame her. But still, I'm astonished. And somewhat humiliated. My own track record, of course, hardly speaks well of *my* loyalty; a lover of women, of tangling my body with theirs, I'm only too aware of the comforts and consolations of sex. *But still.*

"I'm sorry, too," Day says.

"You got off easy," I tell him. "At some other time in my life I would have enjoyed beating the shit out of you."

"Not you, Henry. Come off it."

He's right: not me. One swift kick to the offending party and I'm done with it. I'm not even going to confront

Kate with my disappointment, I decide; we have enough on our hands as it is. And I want to make my exit a peaceful one, with Kate standing by lovingly, the two of us generous with each other until that last moment when I fade out and am on my way. Coolly now, my excitement gone, I tell Day there's no reason for Kate to hear about any of this. "If she does, I'll break you in two," I say. "And that's no idle threat."

Day smiles. "I'll bet," he says.

"I'm still pissed off at you, buddy," I say. "So you better not go sneaking around in the dark anymore. I'm all ears from now on. I'll hire a sentry and post him outside your goddamn door if I have to. Get the picture?"

"Vividly," says Day.

"And tell your paramour the deal's off until further notice."

"There *is* no deal. I mean, there *was* no deal. It was strictly a one-night stand," Day confesses eagerly.

"Ah," I say, greatly relieved. "Ah ha." A one-night stand! A single moment of weakness, unexpected, unwanted, instantly regretted, perhaps. Lightened, rejoicing, almost, I shout "I forgive you, buddy! Case closed!" Day seems uncomfortable with this, and also perplexed. He gives me a look that suggests he thinks I've flipped completely.

"What?" I say. "What is it?"

"You should be angrier," he says. "This isn't what I expected."

"You feel cheated," I explain. "You wanted a little melodrama and all you got was your leg kicked. I'm sorry, buddy, it's the best I can do."

He shakes his head at me, and leaves in disappointment, feet dragging across the carpet, chin nearly touching his chest.

"Cheer up!" I call after him, but I can see that it's a lost cause.

CHAPTER TWENTY-ONE

Cynthia is the most contented she has ever been, and springs from the pull-out couch in the den every morning feeling purposeful and exhilarated. She no longer relies on her supply of Valium to steady her; all on her own, she is absolutely serene. She loves the chilliness of the house in early morning, the heat just beginning to rise underfoot from the kitchen floor at breakfast, the circle of drowsy heads surrounding her at the table, the muted talk, mostly about Henry, at the start of the day. She knows herself to be a part of this family and cannot imagine that things might ever be otherwise. She is fondest of Kate, whose strength, emotional and physical, she has come to admire. Invited to watch her play volleyball last night in the junior high gym, she planted herself at the very top of the bleachers and sat there envying Kate's spirited leaps, the hard thump of her sneakers against the varnished floor, her powerful serves that carried the ball so swiftly over the net. Her skin was luminous with sweat, and with happiness, Cynthia thought, and she realized suddenly that this was what Kate must have looked like in the aftermath of sex. With Henry, of course. She envisioned them on a broad white mattress with plenty of room for rolling and tumbling, an athletic kind of sex, inventive and noisy, lots of murmuring and panting and words repeated over and over again, softly at first and then rising in volume as they moved together toward perfect satisfaction. So unlike the quiet that accompanied *their* lovemaking, hers and Henry's, during the life of their marriage. Imagining this brought on a mild attack of guilt and nausea and she had to turn her head from the movement on the court and the endless flight of the ball back and forth. Afterward, she and Kate and some of the players had gone out for overcooked Italian food that no one except Cynthia seemed to mind. Seated between Kate and a despondent-looking woman named Nancy, Cynthia ate very little of the food that came her way and listened without much interest to the talk of real estate prices and all the little shopping centers that were going up everywhere and gossip about two teachers in the elementary school who had broken up their marriages for each other. Everyone at the table was friendly enough, but of course she was an outsider, Kate's husband's ex-wife, who'd come to say goodbye and was sticking around forever, it seemed. Later, when she and Kate drove home, she felt inexplicably shy and unsure of herself, and switched on the radio to fill up the silence between them. Kate ignored her, concentrating on the unlit roads, the dramatic turns here and there that she barely slowed down for. It came to Cynthia that to observers looking into the car, they might have been mother and daughter, and that seemed to her no more unlikely than the truth. She told this to Kate, who laughed pleasantly and began to sing along with the radio and all at once Cynthia felt utterly safe in her hands. Leaning toward her, she planted a kiss in

Kate's hair, a kiss she could not quite explain but did not regret. Kate went on with her singing, the slight turn of her head in Cynthia's direction the only acknowledgment she would offer.

At the breakfast table now, Cynthia welcomes Darlan into her lap and allows her to pick the dried apples and raisins from her cereal bowl and feed them to herself.

"You have your own food in your own bowl," Kate says sharply. "Leave Cynthia's alone."

"I love my Cynthia so so much," Darlan says, and goes on eating, sucking the bits of food from her fingertips energetically.

"Be that as it may, we still want to encourage good table manners around here. So shape up or ship out, sweetie."

"Leave her," Cynthia says. "It doesn't matter."

"It does matter. It just doesn't matter enough," says Kate. "At least not to me at this moment, after a lousy night's sleep on a chaise longue I wouldn't offer to my worst enemy."

"Take my bed from now on," Day suggests. "I'll sleep in your bedroom on the chaise. I'm terrific at getting Henry in and out of the bathroom in the middle of the night. It's one of my great strengths as a human being."

"I hate to do it," says Kate, her voice wavering. "First my bed, now my bedroom. It's like the end of all hope, the end of everything. I can't let Henry think I've given up on him, that there's nothing left of ordinary life for him, not even a wife who listens to him breathing at night."

"He'll forgive you," says Day. "I think he'll forgive anything at this point."

"I can't do it," Kate says, insistent. "I want to be able

224

to say, to know, that I did everything right." She nods at Day. "Or almost everything."

"You let me know. Even in the middle of the night we can change places. And when Nina comes tomorrow you may want to give her the chaise and move it into Darlan's room. Or else she could sleep on the living room couch, I guess."

"Musical beds," says Kate. "What a game."

"Nina?" Cynthia murmurs. She feels Darlan slipping from her lap and does not try to stop her. What she remembers of Nina is a little girl with whitish hair in a velvet coat and hat, a child who would not speak to her as they rode the ferry to the Statue of Liberty one winter afternoon, she and Henry and this child from his first marriage who held onto Henry's hand but barely had a word for him, either. The afternoon was nightmarish, she recalls—Henry talking enough for all three of them, his face flushed with the effort, Cynthia herself almost as quiet as Nina and just as miserable, she suspected. After the Statue of Liberty, Henry had insisted on a trip uptown to F.A.O. Schwarz, where he announced to Nina that she could choose anything she wanted. He and Cynthia had trailed behind her as she examined dolls in extravagant costumes, enormous stuffed animals, puzzles and magic sets and science kits. I want nothing, she said finally, and it is the stricken look on Henry's face that Cynthia now recalls most vividly of all. Recovering, he'd taken Nina by the arm and marched her straight ahead to a display of globes, from which he selected the very largest, one that lit up when you plugged it in, showing off the world spectacularly. He spun the globe for her and when it came to rest, placed it in her arms. This is what you want, he said, but Nina would not submit to him. She had Henry replace the globe on the shelf and then she chose a much smaller one, the smallest and most insubstantial, made of cheap metal and perhaps already dented in places. This one, she said, this is all I want. How grateful Cynthia had been when at last they'd climbed into a cab and taken Nina back to her mother. She had never done well with children, had never known what to say to them, and the afternoon spent with Nina had left her shaken and weak, as if she'd endured a great deal more than a handful of hours with an unhappy and utterly unapproachable little girl. She made Henry promise not to include her in his plans with Nina ever again; as it turned out, Nina disappeared from their lives soon afterward, unwilling or unable to acknowledge or return her father's affection.

So Nina is a grown woman now—in her mid-thirties, Cynthia calculates in amazement. Unimaginable! She doubts that Nina remembers her at all, except as the woman who stole her father from her mother, from her. Cynthia is prepared to set the record straight, to let her know that it was Henry who did the stealing, Henry who robbed *her,* a thief who took away her comfortable solitude, almost by force, it seemed, barging in on her life and shattering the stillness that she thrived upon. She had tried, at first, to send him on his way, back to his wife and child, where he surely belonged, but the man would simply not give up! Endless phone calls and concert tickets and extravagant homemade desserts, all of these mysteriously wore away at her resolve, opening one door and then another and another, letting him deeper and deeper into her life, until there was no going back, no way to reclaim the intimacy she had so unwisely allowed him. She had put off their wedding day for as long as she had been able to, until finally, weak with love and the confusion that love had brought her, she allowed Henry to get her into a cab and shoot her downtown to City

Hall. He didn't care about the ringing in her ears, her thudding heart, her moist palms. He laughed at the symptoms of her fear, *laughed at them,* as if they were merely silly and had no meaning at all. She had known better, certainly, had been proven right again and again through the roughly textured course of their marriage. And where had it all led to but the breakfast table in the kitchen of this rather modest house that looked out forever over the ocean; a kitchen, a house, in which she had, until a few moments ago, felt entirely at peace, at home. How funny, she thinks, and, like Henry in the face of her fear, she laughs and laughs.

Everyone at the table is regarding her curiously, wondering, no doubt, if she's gone absolutely crazy.

"Pardon me," she says, and covers her grinning mouth with her hand.

"Heard any good jokes lately?" Day says, smiling.

"Me!" Darlan says, waving her arm in the air. "Me!"

"Go ahead," says Kate. "What's your joke, sweetie?"

Darlan gazes around her, then says shyly, "Guess what?"

"What?"

"That's what!"

"I don't get it," Day teases.

"That's what!" Darlan says again. "That's my joke." She looks worried, then smiles, again shyly, as her audience begins to laugh.

"It's a wonderful joke," Kate tells her.

"I know," Darlan says.

Cynthia rises from her seat now and grabs hold of Henry's breakfast tray on the counter. "I've just appointed myself in charge of breakfast," she announces. "Any words of wisdom for me before I start out?"

"You know he hasn't had much of an appetite these

past couple of days," Kate says. "You can't let yourself take it personally."

Cynthia nods, and sails out of the kitchen in her new pink high-top sneakers that are identical to Kate's. When she reaches Henry, he's sitting up with a magazine open in his lap, but his eyes are closed, his reading glasses out of sight.

"This is your eight o'clock shift reporting for duty, sir," she says, and salutes him. "Need a page-turner? Don't forget: no request is too large or too small."

"Ah," Henry says, and smiles.

"Cinnamon toast?"

Another smile, another "ah."

Settling herself in a chair beside him, she cuts the toast methodically into eight small pieces, tucks a paper towel into his pajama top, and begins to feed him. "Good?" she says. His response is a paragraph of shapeless sounds, but she makes no attempt to follow them, having given up almost immediately the hopeless task of learning his language. She is embarrassed by her failure where Kate and Day have succeeded so splendidly, though she has noticed recently and with perverse satisfaction, that they have been reading his lips more and more, and can no longer rely on simply listening as he speaks. He is slipping away from them, from all of them, and from the world, and, unbearably, all they can do is keep watch.

He sips now at some tepid tea and lapses into silence. Cynthia plays lightly with the swollen fingers of his left hand, taps the narrow band of his wedding ring with her fingertip. "You know," she says, "when I heard Nina was coming, it all came back to me—that horrible day we took her to the Statue of Liberty—and there was just this image I had of her as a silent, hostile little girl in her velvet coat. Do you remember?" she says. "You talked enough for all three of us but it still wasn't enough. We didn't belong together, you and Nina and I; we were a deadly combination, nervous and unhappy and disappointed in each other, I think. Do you remember?''

Henry shakes his head vigorously: no no no!, saying no to the accuracy of her memory, to the sorrowful portrait of Nina as she has drawn her.

"Look, Henry," she says, "for all I know, she may have grown up beautifully, into a wonderful and lovely young woman, but that doesn't alter the past any. We couldn't wait to ship her back to her mother, *couldn't wait,* that's how badly things went. And then she was gone and I was so grateful. And you were too, Henry. You lost her and your life was that much easier. Not necessarily happier, but easier. You can't deny that, not to me." He is growling at her now, like an animal just before it strikes out at its prey. "Don't you dare talk to me like that!" she hollers.

His growling soon subsides, but he glares at her fiercely when she asks if he'd like another piece of toast.

"A simple 'no thank-you' will suffice," she says. He continues to glare at her and she turns away, shifting her gaze downward to her brand new sneakers, which are a lovely soft shade of pink but exceptionally clumsy-looking, she thinks. In the shoe store yesterday, Kate had pressed her to buy them, when what Cynthia had really wanted was another pair of black patent leather heels. But what she also wanted, she discovered with surprise, was to yield to Kate, to have her nod her head in approval at the choice they had made together. And so she had bought these ridiculous sneakers simply for the pleasure of gratifying Henry's wife. She does not know what to make of this; it seems at once both sweet and the slightest bit troubling, probably something that her therapist would

229

feast upon greedily. She has done well without Blossom this past month, not missing their sessions in the least, she realizes. She has the urge to call Blossom and tell her so, to hear the triumphant sound of her own voice.

"I've got to make one quick phone call," she tells Henry. "It's long-distance, but I'll charge it to my own phone, of course. Is that all right?"

"You," Henry seems to be saying to her. "You you." He narrows his eyes at her, purses his lips. And then he lets forth a flood of sounds, telling her a thing or two about life, family, love, happiness.

Cynthia listens to all of this patiently, at first stroking his hand, then holding up her fingers across his mouth, as if she could read the patterns his lips are making so gently against her skin.

"Everything you're saying is true," she whispers, and knows that she has been forgiven.

CHAPTER TWENTY-TWO

Sometime between midnight and dawn, Kate and Day meet by chance in the little patch of hallway opposite the bathroom. Day is leading Henry back to bed; Kate is simply loitering about in confusion and cannot say what she is doing there. Henry and Day pass by her without a word. She can hear Day settling her husband in his bed, the rustling sound of sheets and blankets being rearranged. And then Day returns to her and they are pressing themselves against each other, her spine hard against the wall. Through her nightgown she feels the soft bundle between his legs stiffening. She needs him, needs this, but already, astonishingly, Day is pulling back, whispering to her that they will simply have to wait. For what? she says. She's so hungry, so needy, but Day has vanished, a ghost in sweatpants and bare feet who can walk through walls in the blink of an eye. Wait for what? she asks again. She's dreaming, and knows it; it's the sound of her own insistent voice that awakens her. A trickle of saliva has leaked past the corner of her mouth. She wipes it away and opens her eyes to early-morning light. Across the room, in their bed, Henry is staring at her, reading her mind, perhaps. For only an instant, she fears him and his disappointment in her. She wants to apologize for her dream, for betraying him in enjoying that sweet moment just before Day turned hard against her. It is his softness that she found so appealing, so erotic. The memory of this heats her up again, makes her joyous. She climbs off the chaise longue and approaches Henry with a smile.

"Hey baby," he says, and winks at her. "Take a walk on the wild side."

She crawls over him and lies on her side, facing him. She kisses his smooth cheek, wishing she loved him less or not at all. She hears herself telling this to him and then his pleased reply.

"You're stuck with me, baby," he says. "I'm absolutely irresistible." What a struggle for him to get that last word out, what a struggle for her to read it right!

"Irresistible," she says, and they both admire the perfect smooth sound of it as it slips from her mouth like magic.

"Today," Henry soon says, "is the day I'm getting up and at 'em. And dressed. We have to go through my wardrobe and look around for my tuxedo and patent leather dancing pumps."

"Got a heavy date?"

"Yup. My daughter's coming to town. I can't let her see me like this, lying around in bed like a lazy bum, can I?"

"Oh, I wouldn't worry about it too much," Kate says. But she goes through his closet anyway, sweeping past shirt after shirt on their hangers, past herringbone sport jackets, cuffed pants, a wool suit or two, all the things he'd once worn close against his skin. Lifting a shirtsleeve to her face, she breathes in the light scent he's unknowingly left behind, a scent barely noticeable and so all the more precious to her. She can't go on, she can't *do* this, she thinks, pretending to look casually through his wardrobe when she is so shaken by this empty sleeve held across her face, a length of pale blue fabric so beloved at this moment that she cannot ever let go of it. This is a rehearsal, she knows, for the day in the not-at-all distant future when everything in this closet will have to be sorted through and arranged in heartbreaking piles, some for the Salvation Army, some for friends with just the right shoulders and waist line, and some for the pair of plastic trash cans that sit behind the house until pick-up time every week. She remembers a roommate in college returning to school after her father's funeral and saying that the worst of it all was the sight of her father's loafers under the coffee table, carelessly shoved there just before he went to bed the last night of his life, never to wake up again. A pair of shoes the worst of it all! She understands so well now what she had only dimly sensed all those years ago listening to her grieving friend.

She has an impulse to race around the house gathering treasures, Henry's toothbrush, his comb, his wristwatch, his favorite argyle socks, the pink-and-blue plaid flannel shirt from Brooks Brothers that he loves, his tennis shorts and hat—everything that will intensify her grief later on—and toss them into a trash bag and take them down to the dump.

"Where's my toothbrush?" Henry asks.

"Toothbrush?"

"You know, that little plastic thing with bristles that people use to brush their teeth?"

"I know what a toothbrush is, Henry."

"Great. So where is it?"

"I had to throw it in the trash."

"What?"

"Along with your favorite argyle socks and your Brooks Brothers shirt and a number of other things I won't be able to bear the sight of once you're gone forever from this earth."

"You're joking."

"I'm not. I'm coming apart, that's all. I can't concentrate on anyone's needs except my own."

"You're mumbling," Henry tells her. "Or at least that's the way it sounds to me."

"You've got to help me get through this, Henry." She moves away from the closet and comes around to his bedside so she can see the familiar rosiness of his cheeks, his thick, silvery hair, his pitch-dark eyes focussed upon her now with concern. "You," she says.

"Can't," says Henry. "I'm too busy lying here going backward through my life. It's such a long way back, and so tiring. I don't even know if I've got the energy for it, to be honest."

"What are you telling me?" she says, fearful, suddenly, that he's about to let go, to drift away miles above her and into the distance, leaving her behind without apology.

"I'm asking you to take a hike and leave me in peace for a while. It's too distracting, all these people in this house. How am I supposed to concentrate?"

"I'm just going to sit here very quietly," she says. "You won't even know I'm here."

"There are too many people in this house," Henry says. "And now Nina's about to descend upon us. What are we doing, running a hotel here?"

"It's just Cynthia, really. And oddly enough, I've grown accustomed to her face."

Hearing this, Henry smiles. *"Accustomed to the tune, she whistles night and noon . . ."*

"You're singing!" Kate cries, thrilled at the sound of it.

"Her joys, her woes, her highs, her lows . . . Am I right?" Henry says.

"Absolutely. I'm not about to throw her out, Henry."

"Keep her away from Nina, that's all. I don't want this place turning into a battlefield."

She pictures Nina and Cynthia in combat boots and fatigues, bayonets poised threateningly, the two of them fully prepared to do each other in at a moment's notice. She does not know their history, but cannot imagine their resentment lingering thirty years. What foolishness, she thinks, already knowing she has very little patience for any of it.

"*You* keep the peace between them," she says firmly. "And if there's any bloodshed, I'm holding you personally responsible, buster."

"Me?"

"That's what you get for running after an assortment of women and insisting on marrying them."

"I never ran after *you*," Henry says, smiling.

"Sure you did."

"Never. That was you, chasing me down into the subway, following me home, whipping off your clothes with abandon in the middle of my bedroom—"

"Hold it right there," Kate says, raising her arm in the air. " 'With abandon'? What kind of talk is that?"

"It's my kind of talk," Henry says. "And that was you yielding to your natural impulses, right there in broad daylight in my bedroom. You couldn't get enough of me, baby."

"True." She remembers them that very first time on

235

the mattress laid out on the floor of his bedroom, remembers the surprising sturdiness of his body, the strength of his limbs, the hard weight of him against her. He had seemed as powerful as a young man; the only softness was the smooth hairless surface of his limbs and chest. She'd understood then that in being with him she was giving up nothing, missing nothing; in all the world there was nothing better than what she had at that moment. Later, she had married him without hesitation, with the confidence of someone who knew that she was getting exactly what she wanted—a noisy generous man who talked up a storm and still had the energy left over for everything else. Living with him had been a simple joyous thing. Except for Cynthia, she had nothing to forgive him for. And wisely, and without a word, she had forgiven him. She needs to be forgiven too, she sees. To even up the score and to make things right in her own mind. And, possibly, to feel the thrill of confession. She had never made plans for this moment but still she knows precisely how to proceed.

"Henry," she says. Her heart is beating away like mad as she lifts him up against the headboard. "There's something we have to talk about. I never expected that we would, but suddenly it seems like a good idea, something I won't regret. Of course I could be entirely wrong, but I'm going to take my chances."

"Hold up your hands," Henry orders.

"Why?"

"Do as I say, that's all."

Obediently, her hands go up and both of them stare at the faint trembling that grows more distinct the longer she keeps them raised.

"Nope," says Henry as she hides her hands behind her back.

"What?"

"Nope nope nope. I ain't gonna listen to this. No way."

"Why not?"

"Because I have better things to do with my time."

"I'm going to tell you anyway," Kate says. "I *have* to tell you."

"It's a can of worms," says Henry. "Right? Now why would I want to listen to something like that? You want to confess something, go to a priest. Or a rabbi, as the case may be." He's smiling at her now, looking at her fondly, sweetly. "You just be on your best behavior for the next couple of years and let's leave it at that."

"You can't dismiss me like that," Kate says. She knows he is being generous with her, that she should accept this gift graciously. But she feels let down, cheated of the opportunity to unburden herself.

"Sure I can," Henry says. "At this point in my life, don't you think I ought to feel free to do as I damn please?"

"Without regard for anyone else? Not even me?"

"Bingo," Henry says. "When it comes to this particular subject, anyway."

She has to admire his self-assurance, his absolute determination to resist her. She imagines him standing before her, arms folded across his chest, foot tapping sharply, impatiently, as he waits for her to slink away in shame, thoroughly defeated.

"You're one tough cookie," she says respectfully.

"And smart, too. I never give in when I know I'm right."

"Well, you don't have to smirk about it," Kate complains.

"Just picturing myself in a tuxedo and dancing pumps,

taking over the dance floor, knocking them dead with my fancy footwork."

"Tell me more," Kate says, and leans over to kiss the top of his head.

"Too tired."

"Too tired to talk? Not you," she says as he turns his face away.

"I'm winding down," he says. "Every bit of me is moving in slow motion, but it's all right; it's as it should be."

"How do you know?" she says frantically, stupidly. "How do you know any of this?"

"Can't wiggle my toes anymore," Henry says into his pillow. She catches this, but misses the next string of misshapen words. Delicately she pushes Henry's face toward her on the pillow. "I'm closing up shop," she hears him say, but pretends to have misunderstood him.

"You want me to go shopping for *what*?" she asks.

For a long while he is silent. "Raspberries," he says at last. "And don't tell me they're out of season."

"Now where am I going to get raspberries this time of year?" She is combing his hair with her fingers, absently, and without purpose, except for the momentary comfort it brings her.

"Raspberries and cream in a silver bowl," Henry says dreamily. "I'm going to ask for them and you'll come running. You'll have it all laid out beautifully on a tray for me, with a linen napkin, and a bud vase with a rose in it."

She nods at him, having lost the power to speak. She can see her hand trembling as she lifts the first spoonful of raspberries to his lips, can hear the soundless fall of the berries down his chin and along the pure white napkin tucked neatly into his pajama top. She will fail him, of that she is certain. Shaky and unnerved, weak with the pain of fresh grief, she will fail him utterly.

In the girls' locker room in the junior high gym, Kate sits on a scarred wooden bench, her knees drawn up to her chin. She watches Tiki warming up, endlessly throwing a grayish volleyball against a metal locker a few feet from where she is standing.

"So you left a houseful of people right before dinner to play a few games of volleyball," Tiki is saying. "So what?"

"I've got to go home," Kate says. "Nina had barely put her suitcase down when I flew out the door. She stared at Cynthia and Cynthia stared back at her and I ran past them with a volleyball in my arms. What are they going to do all night, sit and chat about the good old days?"

"What are you, their social director?" says Tiki. "My suggestion is you ship them out to a motel and let them fend for themselves a while."

"They're family," Kate says.

"Really." Tiki shoots her a look of exasperation.

"Well, they're Henry's family."

"Fuck 'em," Tiki says mildly. "Now get your knee pads on and let's go."

"Actually, Cynthia and I have reached a certain level of understanding," Kate announces. "We're like old friends, in an odd kind of way. We wander around in nightgowns at two in the morning and somehow find ourselves having coffee together in the kitchen. There's no resentment, we've just kind of made room for each other, I think."

Without warning, Tiki sends the volleyball straight

toward her. "You're too accepting," she says. "The woman slept with your husband, for crying out loud."

"It's over," Kate says. "It was over long ago, in another lifetime. And it just doesn't matter anymore." She tosses the ball back to Tiki, and slips on her knee pads. "We're tied to each other now and neither one of us is about to let go. Not now, anyway."

Tiki is staring at her in disbelief. "It doesn't matter?" she says. "What *does* matter?"

Getting through this moment, this hour, this day, this week, Kate thinks. Easing Henry out of this life with her eyes wide-open, with perfect vision. And afterward, learning to live in the absence of a steady, reassuring love. She doesn't know if she is capable of any of it, of even the least of it. The truth is, she doesn't know anything at all.

She gazes up at Tiki, who's hugging the ball to her middle and resting her cheek against it, looking at Kate regretfully.

"Make my life easier," Kate says. "Don't challenge me so much; just tell me I'm doing a pretty fair job of impersonating a normal human being."

"You're doing beautifully," Tiki says. "Especially for someone who's not made of steel."

"I'm *not* made of steel?" Kate says. "You're kidding." She raps the knuckles of one hand against the side of her head. "Sounds like steel."

"That's just an illusion of grandeur," Tiki explains. "I'm sorry to tell you you're just like the rest of us."

Thinking of her early-morning dream, imagining again the feel of Day through her nightgown, Kate nods her head at Tiki, and says nothing.

Out on the court a few minutes later, she takes her place among her teammates and savors the slap of her palm against the ball and then the applause that rises up around her as her serve bounces at their opponents' feet. Soon she is sliding on her knee pads across the cold varnished floor as the ball spins above her and heads straight for the ceiling and right through the roof.

CHAPTER TWENTY-THREE

I have to admit it: I'm absolutely resplendent in royal blue satin pajamas brought to me by my daughter all the way from California. I'm holding court in my bedroom now, buoyed by the sight of her, and listening hard as she carries on unpleasantly about Cynthia.

"You'd damn well *better* believe it," Nina tells me. "If I'd known she was on the scene, I would have made other arrangements. What the hell is she doing here, anyway? I thought she lived in New York and was married to a sociology professor."

"*She's* the sociology professor," I say. "As for a husband, I'm pretty certain she doesn't have one."

"You look real spiffy in those pajamas," Nina offers. "Royal blue is definitely your color." Sitting cross-legged on my bed, she suddenly leans forward, grabs me by the lapels of my pajama top, and looks me right in the eye. She's a sweeter version of her old self, I notice, her hairstyle a bit fuller and softer than it was at her last visit; she no longer has that hard, punked-out look that I have such a difficult time appreciating.

"There's been a ghost hanging around outside our condo," she tells me matter-of-factly. "A little blonde girl with eyes the color of your pajamas. I saw her hovering above the skylight in our kitchen a few weeks ago, but as soon as she caught me looking at her, she disappeared, which is too bad, because needless to say, I had a number of important questions to ask her."

My response to this is to laugh out loud, but Nina's composure isn't the least bit disturbed. "Oh, I know what you're thinking," she says good-naturedly. "Here I am a woman of science, a toxicologist by profession, telling you something that utterly defies reason. But doesn't that make it all the more credible, knowing I'm not just some flake who doesn't know her ass from her elbow?"

"It's got to be California," I say. "Six months out there and even an exceptionally level-headed person like me probably starts going flaky."

"Here's the thing," Nina says. "I did some checking with the neighbors, and it turns out a little girl fitting the description lived in the condo some years ago. She drowned in the swimming pool, apparently. So it all makes sense, doesn't it?"

"Oh sure."

"You don't get it, do you? The point is, Henry, you may very well be hanging around here long after you're gone. There's clearly some kind of life after this one. Isn't it exciting to think about? If I were you, I'd be thrilled." She squeezes my shoulders enthusiastically. "I'm so happy for you, Henry," she says. "Just think of the possibilities!"

Think of the possibilities! I can see myself peering into the lighted windows of my home every night after sundown, overcome with longing as I watch the ordinary domestic scenes unfolding sweetly before me: Kate giving Darlan her bath, lifting her from the tub and wrapping her in an enormous towel, both of their faces flushed in the sultry air, the music of their playful chatter drifting toward me through the glass; Kate preparing for bed, stepping out of her clothes, standing naked for a moment or two before getting into her nightgown, tears in her eyes as she thinks of the sound of my voice, the touch of my flesh upon her. Another night, months later, I stare in horrified fascination as she and Day, or, perhaps, a man I've never seen before, make love in our bed, murmuring uninspired endearments, their arms and legs wound around each other fiercely. This is what I'm hanging around for, this heart-rending look into my own goddamn bedroom window? Forget it! I don't want any part of this life-after-death business. Just give me some of that eternal rest they're always yapping about at funerals.

"Forget that Peeping Tom stuff," I say out loud. "The idea just doesn't appeal to me. And you, sweetie pie, ought to get yourself straight to a shrink. Anyone seeing ghosts in their skylight has obviously got to be under a tremendous amount of stress."

"Something tells me you've rejected the possibility already. That's very depressing, Henry," my daughter says. "The least you can do is have an open mind."

"Will you stop calling me 'Henry.' "

"You seem awfully grouchy," Nina says. "Aren't you supposed to be at peace with yourself at a time like this?"

"I *am* at peace with myself," I grumble. "Or I was until you marched in here and started putting those dopey ideas into my head about my ghostly self peeping into all those windows."

Nina gets up and begins pacing the room. "The funny thing is, Henry, I feel real comfortable talking to you. I feel as if I can tell you anything at all, things I wouldn't dream of telling anyone else. The fact that I don't know what you're saying, that I can only sense what's on your mind, might have something to do with it. But that's not it entirely. I just see you as a sympathetic presence, someone who inspires affection and loyalty and all that. And that's why I feel compelled to tell you that your friend Day doesn't belong here. I have these very disturbing vibes about him. It's bad news, Henry, believe me. I don't have any real proof, of course . . . well actually, I do, but never mind about that, it was a long time ago. Let's just say I know whereof I speak. And that I want everything to be good, to be right, in this house."

I don't believe what I'm hearing: if one more person comes in here and tries to spill the beans, I'm going to put a sign on my door saying "The confessional is closed for the season—if you must unburden yourself, please see your friendly neighborhood priest!"

So Nina knows whereof she speaks. I wonder briefly what it is she saw—a furtive embrace, a soul-stirring kiss, a look of such longing that she had to turn her eyes from the sight of it. Whatever it is, it's old news, and I can surely live with it.

"Oh that," I say, in what I hear in my mind as the most casual of tones. "That was brought to my attention ages ago. Let's talk about something more interesting. Me, for instance. You haven't even asked me how I've been."

"Henry," Nina says, coming toward me in a hurry, tripping over the pink rubbery feet of Darlan's most extravagant doll, which is lying on the floor with its eyes closed now. "D-dad," she says. "You have to—"

D-dad? Oh what a moment of triumph! That I lived to see this day! "Say it again!" I cry.

Nina shakes her head at me, and backs away from the bed. "Here I am trying to help you get your life in order and you're not taking me seriously. You're not, are you?" She picks up the doll and hugs it to her, unwittingly activating its speaking powers. "Hug me!" the doll orders. Her lips move and she bats her eyes at Nina. "Love ya!" she chirps.

"Was that you?" I ask Nina. "Or was that that 99-dollar bundle of joy over there?"

"Love ya. Love ya," the doll insists, then runs out of steam and shuts down by itself. There's an embarrassed silence between Nina and me now: the doll's easy confession has made us both look bad. Reluctant to make any declarations of our own, the two of us study this miracle of technology that runs on eight batteries and can talk about love with an openness that has to be envied.

"You're my daughter," I say finally. "Without a doubt, I loved you when you were a little girl. And without a doubt, I love you now. I'm no fool," I explain. "I tell it like it is."

Abandoning the doll on the floor, Nina flies to me. "Start from the beginning," she says. "I'm going to read your lips."

Laboriously, I repeat every word, giving each one as much shape and definition as I can. But I can see that she's not getting any of it and when at last I fall silent, tears of frustration spring to my eyes. "Fuck it," I say. "Just use your imagination."

"You want to know what I remember?" my daughter says. "I remember watching television on the couch with my head in your lap. *Gunsmoke*," she says. "You used to eat tangerines and spit the pits into your hand while we sat there watching *Gunsmoke*. Sometimes, the next morning, I'd stick my hand between the cushions and find some of the pits there, hard and dry and bleached-looking. I collected them and kept them in the top drawer of my dresser, as if they were little pearls. I never even thought about why I was doing it," she says, and shrugs. "But one day, after you'd left us, I scooped them all out of the drawer and threw them away."

"You loved me," I say, and savor the image of that small figure bent over the couch cushions, searching for the little hard white jewels I'd carelessly left behind. "You loved me and then you hated me," I tell her. "And then you just stopped thinking about me. But here we are a lifetime later, and I'm so grateful."

"Got any tangerine pits for me now?" Nina asks softly.

I imagine her taking home a little box full of them and carefully hiding them away in her top drawer. And every now and then, I know, she will lay out these family jewels on a length of purple velvet and eye them with something like love.

For the past few days, since Nina's arrival, Darlan has refused to go to school, a three hour/three day a week program at the Methodist Church in town, where Kate recently enrolled her. At first Kate tried to insist that Darlan had no choice, that she absolutely had to go, but eventually she caved in and agreed with me that Darlan could stay at home with the rest of us, if that was what made her happiest.

"It's clear she just wants to be where the action is," Kate says now, lying on the chaise longue with her hands crossed behind her head. "I can't say that I blame her."

"If you're worried about her education," I tease, "we can educate her right here at home. I'll draw up a program: we'll start her off on a little Chaucer and work our way up through the ages to *Tom Sawyer*."

"Can you imagine it?" Kate says. "Darlan old enough to be reading Chaucer?"

The truth is, I can't. She's at the foot of my bed now, working out a cardboard puzzle that shows a scene straight from the pages of *The Cat in the Hat*. Her unruly-looking hair, a lovely reddish-brown these days, is held back from her face by a single plastic barrette. Her skin is winter-pale, the curve of her nostrils reddened by a lingering cold, but still she is beautiful. In two or three years her face will lengthen and grow narrow, no doubt; she will probably never look quite so beautiful as she does now. But I, of course, will never be disappointed by her, will never have that opportunity; perhaps in some small way, this is something to be grateful for, I think, as I watch my daughter put the final pieces of her puzzle in place.

I've not much farther to go; my body cannot keep up with the business of life anymore. Early this morning, when Day came to take me to the bathroom, my legs simply would not move, and I had a good cry as he went in search of the bedpan. He swept the tears from my eyes for me, then looked away as I peed into the plastic basin.

That's it for me; I have no wish to go on and so I will not. Outside my window, everything is unchanged and as it should be. This seems cruel and yet also comforting. I look out the window now and watch the ocean pitch toward me. The sun sits blindingly over the water, heating the side of my face through the window. In the distance, the lobster boats travel slowly and silently across the horizon. A solitary figure in a red down vest, hands in his pockets, hood up over his head, walks along the water's edge, growing smaller and smaller, until he is nothing more than a bright bit of color.

Opening my eyes, I see Kate standing over me, feel her lips sweeping gently across my forehead. "What time is it?" I ask.

"It's just about two-thirty."

"Have I had lunch yet?"

"Day made you one of his famous omelets, but you barely ate a mouthful. And then you dozed off for a while. You don't remember?"

"Sounds vaguely familiar, but I don't know. It's this fuzziness that comes and goes," I say with embarrassment.

"Are you hungry, sweetie?"

"I'll have those raspberries now, I think."

"You can't have any," Kate says in alarm. "I mean, they're out of season. And anyway, you don't want them, not really." She sits at the edge of the bed and rests her hands on my knees.

"Come on, honey," I say. "You've got to sit right here and listen up. I want those raspberries more than anything; I want to die with the taste of them on my lips. And that's exactly what I'm going to do." Hearing this, Kate stiffens. She withdraws her hands from me and scoots away, farther down along the bed.

"I'm not ready," she murmurs. "And I probably never will be. I'm just too much of a coward."

"First of all," I tell her, shaking my head, "you're no coward. And second of all, I'm packed up and ready to go. I'm ready, baby."

"Why?" she says in the tiniest of voices.

"I'm down to nothing," I say. "I've lost it all. And so I'm ready. That make any sense to you?"

She nods slightly, and I smile at her. "But what about *me*?" she soon says. "What's going to happen to *me*?"

"You're a lovely big strong girl," I say. "Everything in your life is going to be good." I watch as she travels toward me, moves all the way up along the bed until our thighs are touching. She flips one hand over, palm upward, and offers it to me. "What *now*?" I say. "You want me to read your fortune?"

"Tell me what's going to happen," she says.

Love, work, marriage, babies, lasting happiness; it's all there, of course, but I can't bring myself to admit any of it. Instead I announce, "There's a short trip in your future. A trip to that fancy little market in town. Wait, I see the name—Nature's Gifts, that's it. I see you there, clear as anything, forking over one hundred dollars for a half-pint of fresh raspberries. A stiff price, you say? Perhaps. But surely nothing's too extravagant for your husband's happiness."

"That's it?" Kate says, laughing. "A short trip to an expensive store?"

"Sorry. Your palm was resistant to giving away secrets today," I explain as she takes her hand back. "It happens sometimes in this business."

"A likely story," says Kate, and turns to look as Darlan appears in the doorway, brandishing a silver plastic sword nearly as tall as she is. She's a vision—in dangling pink plastic earrings, a pink plastic pearl necklace, and army-green rubber boots, the tips of which are a pair of frogs' smiling faces.

"Hoo hah!" Darlan says, and thrusts the tip of the sword at her mother's chest.

"I see you're dressed for the occasion," Kate says. "Where'd that sword come from?"

"My sister gave it to me."

"I see. Doesn't your sister know we don't allow weapons in this house?"

"It's the thought that counts," I say. "Always remember that."

"You always like to give people the benefit of the

doubt," Kate says, sounding as if she were accusing me of some minor sin.

"She's my daughter," I say. "My firstborn."

"She's a flake," Kate says.

"I can think of worse things a person could be."

"The first night she was here, at dinner, she told Cynthia that she'd always held *her* responsible for wrecking her childhood."

"Ouch," I say.

"Don't worry: Cynthia did fine. She said she was truly sorry Nina felt that way and that she hoped she would someday come to see things differently. So Nina looks right at her and says, 'Fat chance,' and then fortunately for almost all of us, Darlan fell off her chair. She wasn't hurt at all, but she cried so hard and so loud, no one could hear a word anyone else was saying."

Damn! If only I had been there, sitting at the table with the rest of them, I might have straightened out a few things, assigned guilt and innocence to the proper parties, letting Nina know that I was the one who had set things in motion, who had gone after Cynthia with all my energy and without an instant's hesitation, leaving Nina and her mother behind as if they were never there at all. But surely Nina knew this, had known this her whole life, had heard it from her mother a thousand times and more. When her mother died, about ten years ago, I'd written Nina a note, apologizing at last for the grief I had caused them both. As I expected, there was never any response. How could there have been? What was there to say after so many years? Contemplating these things now wearies me. And why should I have to be thinking of them, when all I want is to skip town peacefully and without a sound? Perhaps it's simply as Kate said, that this is what you get for running after an assortment of women and insisting on marrying them.

"I'm terribly tired," I tell her now. "I'm going to rest some more and then I'm going to have those raspberries for dinner. Okay?"

"We'll see," is all she says, and leaves me with a nearly silent kiss. Darlan tramps out after her in her frog boots, using her sword as a walking stick.

CHAPTER TWENTY-FOUR

J ust before dusk, Kate parks the car in a lot in town, and carries Darlan in her arms along a narrow, hilly street, past the Clam Shack, the Jewel Box, the Village Barbershop, two or three galleries, a row of guest houses, a store that sells hand-painted clothing. Through the perfectly clear window of a pizzeria, she watches as a teenaged girl inside wipes tears from her eyes, then throws her blonde head back in laughter.

"I'm going to make Daddy some snakes with Play-Doh," Darlan says. "Some big big snakes he can wear around his neck like a necklace. And Cynthia's going to help me, right?"

"Right," says Cynthia, and pulls lightly, playfully, at one of Darlan's pigtails.

"You hurt me," Darlan says. She wails insincerely into her mother's ear, then falls silent as Kate says, "Cool it, will you?"

"I think you're a phony baloney, Darlan, that's what I think," Cynthia says, and Kate smiles, realizing with surprise that after all the weeks she has spent with them,

253

Cynthia has begun to pick up bits and pieces of their vocabulary and to use them in just the right breezy, casual way that she and Henry always have. Looking at Cynthia now in her sweatsuit and high-tops and down vest, she is suddenly astonished at the sight of her. It is as if Cynthia has shed her skin and fit herself with something entirely new, a new self, supple and generous. Cynthia is, she thinks, very much at ease with the world, and oh how she envies her! It is *she* who is stricken with sorrow and dread, she who is soon to lose her way. How will she have the heart to awaken in the morning, to put one foot in front of the other and simply move forward? Perhaps she will live the rest of her life in a trance, absorbed in her sorrow. When Day approaches her, as she is sure he will, she will let him know she is lost, that she has forgotten the comforting rhythms of everyday life, that she no longer remembers the hum and buzz of ordinary happiness. Perhaps he will stay patiently by her side, guiding her step by tiny step out of herself and into the world. She sees him walking with Henry along the water's edge, months and months ago, light-years ago, Henry leaning his weight against Day's hard shoulder, utterly dependent on him for balance. She imagines what that must have felt like, to have had that faith in someone else to keep you on your feet, that knowledge that without the bone and flesh of someone else's shoulder, you would fall headlong and helplessly into the coarse and gravelly sand. And now she can see herself with Day beside her, crossing the beach on shaky legs that might give way at any moment. Hold me up, she cries as she begins to slip, but the voice is Henry's, the words slurred almost beyond recognition.

"Here we go," Cynthia is saying, swinging open the glass door and leading them inside Nature's Gifts. Immediately Darlan scrambles away to examine a small hill of red-skinned potatoes, baskets of bright white mushrooms, a green slope of shining Granny Smith apples.

"I want this and this and this and this!" she yells joyfully.

"We're not going shopping, sweetie," Kate says. "We're just here to get one thing for Daddy and that's it. That's all we have time for." But Darlan is busy loading up a wire basket with waxed, gleaming peppers in an assortment of colors—red and green, a dark orange, a deep, surprising yellow.

"Give me some money from your wallet, okay?" Darlan says. "I need all of these," she insists, gesturing toward her collection of peppers.

"What for?"

"I need them, Mom. I like them and I need them, okay? I'm going to keep them in my room next to my bird's nest and watch them grow."

"They're not going to do any more growing," Kate says, smiling. "They're all grown up." A half-pint of raspberries is between her hands, and she dips her head forward to smell their faint fragrance. Her hands are perspiring, she realizes, her heartbeat swift.

"My treat," a voice says sweetly, and then Cynthia is taking the green paper carton from her and handing the cashier a five-dollar bill.

"You can't," Kate says. "I mean, thanks, but I can't let you do that."

"He used to buy these," says Cynthia, "whenever he was feeling exceptionally good about something, I think. A project at work he'd just finished, a raise, the start of a vacation . . ." Her voice trails off to a murmur. "You're right, *you* have to buy them."

The cashier is a teenaged boy in a black smock. On

the back of his hand, a small peace sign is drawn neatly in ballpoint pen. "How are you all doing?" he says.

"These are my peppers," Darlan says, gathering them in her arms. "But I have to go to the cash machine for some money."

The cashier leans over the counter and reaches for them. "They're beautiful, aren't they?"

"We don't have time for them," Darlan says gravely. "We're just here to get one thing for my daddy and that's it."

"It's all right," Kate says. "I'm going to get them for you because you're such a terrific kid." She puts the raspberries on the counter and listens to the wild beating of her own heart. "It's all right," she says again.

"I *am* a terrific kid," says Darlan. "I don't kick or hit anyone at my school and I don't say 'shit.' "

"Darlan."

"Well, I *don't*. I'm always nice and I always say 'shoot' when I'm mad."

"This is for you," the cashier says, dropping a tiny red-and-yellow apple into Darlan's hand. "This is called a lady apple and it's for you because you never say 'shit.' "

"Well, I do sometimes," Darlan admits. "Can I still have the apple?"

"Sure you can." The cashier smiles at Kate. "Cute kid," he says. "But I have to tell you the raspberries are a little on the sour side. We've gotten a couple of complaints about them, actually. You still want them?"

Darlan nods. "We *need* them," she says. "For my daddy."

"Well, don't say I didn't warn you, cutie," the cashier says.

*　　*　　*

"He was having a little trouble breathing while you were out," Day reports. "I gave him a hit of oxygen and he seemed better. He's sleeping now."

"I know," Kate says. "I checked on him a minute ago." She is at the kitchen sink, washing each raspberry one by one under a gentle flow of cold water, then laying it out on a paper towel. Her fingertips are icy, and she shivers in the warm kitchen. Out of the corner of one eye, she sees Day select three berries for himself and then pitch them into his mouth. She turns away from the sink and slaps him on the underside of his wrist, harder than she'd meant to. "Those are Henry's," she says. "Hands off, buster."

Day makes a show of rubbing his wrist for a while, then points out the pinkish mark left by her slap. "You know I detest violence of any sort," he says. "Especially when it's inflicted on my person."

"Take your person and scram," Kate says. "I want to be alone with Henry's raspberries, okay?"

"They're as sour as can be. I'm going to make some whipped cream for them." Getting no response, Day takes out a stainless steel mixing bowl, pours a half-pint of heavy cream into it, and a large amount of sugar. He turns on the electric mixer and bends his head over his work, and Kate studies the tiny pale circle of his bald spot until she is nearly overcome by the urge to cover it with a kiss. The mixer buzzes on, and into its insistent whirring she finds herself whispering a secret or two. And then, suddenly, the room is shockingly silent and Day is staring at her.

"What is it?" he says.

"What?"

"Don't look so surprised. Didn't you know I could read your mind?"

"As a matter of fact, I didn't."

"Actually, your lips were moving just as I happened to look up."

"And what were they saying?"

Day shrugs. "Damned if I know." He dips a fingertip into the bowl of cream, then glides it into Kate's mouth. "Too sweet?"

Shaking her head, she says, "Perfect."

"Good. Now you're all set for Henry when he wakes up."

Day's sweetened fingertip slipping noiselessly into her mouth. Wanting to ask for more, she somehow cannot. Instead she sighs, and drapes her hair across her face.

"What is it?" Day says again.

"He's dying, and I'm having erotic dreams."

Understanding instantly, perfectly, Day says in a near-whisper, "You and I have got all the time in the world."

"But I feel like I'm dying!" she cries. She is surprised to hear herself say this and yet knows that it is the truth; like Henry, she feels she is close to the end of her life.

"You're frightened," Day says. "Who wouldn't be?"

"I know it's Henry, but I feel as if it's me, too, as if I've come all the way to the very end of things."

"You've come to the end of *something*," Day says gently. "But not everything." He picks up her hand and warms it, then lets it go. "It's his time," he says, "but not yours. Henry's not shy; ask him and he'll tell you. Let him tell you himself."

"He told me."

"Maybe you need to hear it again."

"No," Kate says.

"Go sit with him. Watch him. Hold onto his hand."

Lowering her head, Kate says, "I don't have the heart for it anymore."

"It's been so long," says Day. "And you've held up beautifully through all of it."

"Look at me," she says, and slowly raises her eyes to meet his. "I'm a hundred years old."

CHAPTER TWENTY-FIVE

There's a light, hesitant knock at my open door and then Kate's voice calls out brightly, "Room service!"

"What have we here?" I say.

"One bowl of raspberries and cream, elegantly served on a silver tray, one bud vase with a single rose, one linen napkin."

"Just charge it to my account."

"No no," Kate says, and eases me into a sitting position. "Compliments of the house."

"Wow, I'm impressed. Do you treat all your guests this well?"

"Only the big spenders," Kate says. She arranges the napkin around my neck and feeds me a spoonful of sour berries and sweet cream. "Is it everything you hoped it would be?" she asks.

"If you mean did I see fireworks, absolutely," I tell her.

"The raspberries," she says, smiling at me. "You're supposed to be concentrating on the raspberries."

"Embrace me, my sweet embraceable you," I sing

out as best as I can. *"Embrace me, you irreplaceable you."* I've got the tune perfectly, at least. "We're out there on the dance floor," I say, closing my eyes. "Just you and me, cheek to cheek. I'm in my tuxedo and you're in your sexy black dress and there's romance in the air like you wouldn't believe, baby. Old George Gershwin himself is at the Steinway, his tails hanging over the back of the piano bench. He made the trip just for us, how do you like that?" I open my eyes to the smile of longing that plays so sweetly at Kate's lips.

"Are you with me, baby?" I ask.

"I'm right there where you want me," she says dreamily, "safe as can be."

"Call the two of them in here," I hear myself say. It's the middle of the night, and I've got important business to attend to. Kate is sitting next to me on the bed, looking at me in utter confusion.

"Who?" she says.

"Nina and Cynthia, who else. I don't care *what* time it is, I've got to set the two of them straight."

"Let's wait a few minutes, all right? They're eating their dinner now."

"In the middle of the night?"

"It's dinnertime, Henry."

"Are you sure?" I say. Now I'm the one who's confused, and also a little embarrassed. "Well, anyway, it feels like the middle of the night."

"Do you want the rest of your raspberries? You left nearly the entire bowl."

"Nope," I say. "Just get the two of them in here, please. And listen, you've got to stick around for a while, okay? I need you to translate for me."

"No long lectures," Kate says. "Promise me."

"Promise," I say, and send her off with a wink.

In fact, I'm as unnerved as if I were about to deliver a speech before an auditorium full of people, every one of whom is eager to trip me up, to find fault with the manner in which I've lived my long life.

"Listen, ladies," I begin shortly. Cynthia and Nina have seated themselves as far apart from each other as they can on the chaise, and are looking at me apprehensively. "Relax," I say, and nod toward Kate, who says absolutely nothing. "Pretend you're an interpreter at the UN," I say. "Every word counts. Every word!"

"Relax," Kate says impassively.

"Not like that! With inflection!" I order. "If you're going to do this thing, do it right, for crying out loud."

"Ree-lax!" she calls out with false enthusiasm, then turns to me for approval. "How'm I doing?"

"So far, so good," I say, and begin again. "Listen, ladies," I say, "I'm as lucid as I'm ever going to be, so please pay close attention. Pretty soon that awful fuzziness is going to overtake me again and I'm going to drift right out of here to a place where I'm going to be unapproachable. So this is it, our final chance to settle things between us."

"What do you mean?" Cynthia says as Kate finishes up her translation. "Why is this necessarily *it*?"

"He was waiting for *me*," Nina says, a trifle smugly. "He saw me and now he's ready to move on. And I think I ought to let all of you know that death is not the end of a person, or at least it doesn't have to be. If Henry chooses, he could be looking straight into any one of our lives, say three, four, or even ten years from now."

"What!" Kate hisses. "What do you think, you're talking to a roomful of three-year-olds?"

"That kind of sarcasm is very painful to me," Nina

says. "Can't we all just put our arms around each other and hang together here?"

"What did you have in mind?"

"Just what I said. Did you ever see that very last *Mary Tyler Moore*, the one where they all learn they're fired and they kind of clump together in their sorrow, Mary and Lou and Murray and Ted, all of them come together in kind of a group hug? And then the telephone rings or something and they all move sideways in a group to answer it. Do you know what I'm talking about?"

"This isn't the *Mary Tyler Moore* show," Kate says, sounding gloomy. "This is us."

"Well, did you see it?" Nina asks.

"I saw it."

"What about you, Cynthia?"

"I've never really watched much TV," Cynthia says apologetically. "Only *Nightline* and a few things on PBS now and then. I'm sorry."

"Figures," says Nina.

"You don't have to sound so disgusted," says Cynthia. "Really."

"To be honest," Nina announces, "you're not one of my favorite people on this earth."

"I'm sorry for that, too," says Cynthia. "But you have this mistaken notion of who I am and what I may have done to you. Ask your father, he'll tell you."

"She's right," I tell Nina. "If anyone should have had a lasting place on your shit list, it was me, not her. The truth is, I went after Cynthia so relentlessly it was almost unbelievable. I just wouldn't give up. She didn't much want me but she got me anyway. And that's it, in a nutshell. But look, I don't want to talk about this anymore. I just want you to promise me you'll stop thinking of her the way you always have. I'm the bad guy in this picture; she was just the bad guy's wife."

"Finished?" says Kate, who's kept pace with me all the way through. "I've got to take a breather, okay?"

"Finished," I say. "And thank you."

"I don't know," Nina says after a while. "No matter what, she's still not ever going to be one of my favorite people."

"I don't *want* to be one of your favorite people!" says Cynthia impatiently.

"You don't?" says Nina. "I can't tell you how relieved I am to hear that."

Cynthia smiles at her. "Good," she says. "I'm delighted."

"Hallelujah!" I say. It occurs to me that no one's asked me if *I'd* seen that last *Mary Tyler Moore* show, which I did, probably more than once. And the image of Kate and Darlan, Cynthia, Nina, and Day, all with their arms wrapped around each other, is a pleasing one to me. All of them in my house, my bedroom, a constellation of mourners standing over me and weeping until at last they slowly and reluctantly come apart, each of them, except for Kate and Darlan, heading for her own corner of the world. And it pleases me, too, to think that I'm what holds them together, that without me, the bonds between them would be tenuous as the filaments of a silken spider web. And yet, maybe not; maybe it's just sheer egotism, my own exaggerated sense of who I am, that shapes my vision. I don't know why, but the thought of these unlikely relationships flourishing without me is hard to take. All these months, in my mind, at least, I've been the bright sun around which the members of my family have been spinning. This is what has sustained me for so long—to have been sure of my place at the very center of things.

"I'm the sun," I murmur, testing the sound of it out loud, making it absolutely true.

"You're what?" Kate says, and she leans toward me, trying to read my lips.

"This is one lucky son-of-a-bitch you're looking at!" I announce. There is silence after Kate translates this, her voice trembly and as soft as can be. And then comes the choked sound of quiet weeping, and Nina's and Cynthia's swift flight from across the room. They gather Kate to them, sweep her into their midst with generous, wide-open arms. And I see that I'm not there, that it's only the three of them, rocking now from side to side, swaying gently in their grief.

I'm no longer the sun; I'm already gone.